When Em

My Haunted Garden Book 1

Michael Weems

Copyright 2021

For Bella, Baylor, and Joy

Chapter 1

The Incident

It was the flowers that killed the farmer's wife. I dreamed about it after getting shot in the head.

I was thirteen when *The Incident* happened. Anyone who has lived in town more than a few years could tell you all about it. They probably wouldn't, though. Not at first. If you were to come here and ask them about it, you'd be politely informed, "*The Incident?* Oh, we don't talk about *The Incident.* That was years ago, anyhow."

But everyone still talks about it, often and with ever more embellishment. They just talk amongst themselves. Outsiders would have to do some cajoling to get someone going about it. Once they get started though, there's no shutting them up. Their voices go down to a hush, their eyes look around to make sure nobody's listening in, and then they tell the story I'm about to tell you. Except, I'll give you the accurate account. Lord only knows what someone else would probably add if they told you the tale. I've heard the strangest things.

Mom made some mistakes, no doubt, but these days folks in town have elevated her to something near *Blair Witch* status, which is really just hurtful. And let me preface this by saying I loved my mother. She was a good person who made some bad decisions. And as Lemony Snicket might say, what followed was a series of unfortunate events.

Pops, as I have called my father since I was about seven, used to be a truck driver before he gave it up on my account to become the groundskeeper of our fine local cemetery. That's more or less a part-time job, though. It allows us to live in the caretaker's cottage for free, but the income is nominal. He supplements it by fixing motoring things and occasionally buying a hooptie or two and fixing them up to flip.

Foxglove, Texas has a public cemetery and they built a new metal building for the grounds' mowers and tools a few years back, so Pops gets to use the old barn that's still standing for fixing up the cars. He just loves cars. And motorcycles. And mowers, even. Pretty much anything with an engine. Pops is most happy when he's got oil under his fingernails and is cranking a wrench to make something broken work again. I think he's a hero for it. Everyone should hear the immensely satisfying sound of an engine that hasn't run in ages firing up and growling once again. The soot shoots out the back in a cloud of gray smoke and something that has been sleeping for years is suddenly alive and awake again. It's a good reminder that just because something looks like it's tired, worn, beaten down and done for, that doesn't mean it is. Good hands, with elbow grease and pressure, can bring back broken things. It ain't always so with people, but we hope and hopefully try, and that's all we can do sometimes.

Anyway, back when Pops was driving the trucks he was gone for long stretches. Mom was pretty in a way I can only aspire to, although I think that ship has sailed. She looked ten years younger than she was and had more pretty than good sense, I'm afraid. People confused her for my older sister on a couple of occasions. She couldn't stop for gas without someone making a pass at her and after a while of Pops' long runs, I guess that kind of attention helped placate her growing loneliness and restlessness.

I'm not making excuses. Wrong is wrong. But it was a recipe for disaster and a grand disaster it did make. Mom liked attention. There is no two ways about it. And she occasionally was a pretty bad judge of character. She lucked out with Pops but came up short with Dale.

Dale Roberts was an old high school boyfriend she got to flirting with on occasion when Pops was away. His name still tastes like vomit in my mouth whenever I speak it. I still remember the awkward conversations they'd occasionally have around me. He'd smile and try to make nice with me. "Hey, Ruthie, you doin' good?" Ruthie, he called me. Like he was somebody to call me by a nickname. He'd heard Mom call me Ruthie and assumed, quite incorrectly, that I'd be just fine and dandy with him calling me Ruthie.

I wasn't. "It's just Ruth," I'd remind him. "I'm fine."

"Well, I bet you're having to beat those boys off with a stick, aren't ya? You look more and more like your mama every day." I know he meant it as a compliment and all, but from him it was just creepy. I instantly disliked Dale Roberts and thought there was something off about him. Mom, however, thought he was funny. Hence, her tendency to be a poor judge of character.

I was right about him. Intuition is our life experience whispering to us an answer to a question we never asked out loud. I should have listened closer. We had talked about it, Mom and I, but I didn't delve deep enough. The truth is sometimes buried down in the mud, where we don't like to look. And if you're not willing to get some dirt on your hands, you may never find it.

"Why don't you like Dale?" Mom asked me one day as we drove off from the store where he just happened to need to stop in for a few things after he saw our car there.

"Because he's always hitting on you," I told her flatly.

"Ruthie, why would you say a thing like that? He's just trying to be nice."

"Nobody who's genuinely nice has to try that hard to be nice," I informed her. "He's hitting on you. And if Pops saw it, he'd punch him in the face."

"Ruth," she gasped, "now, don't go saying things like that. And don't be telling your father that you think Dale's hitting on me. He's an old friend from high school is all and he's only trying to be friendly. And your father doesn't need to be hearing stories that'll give him the wrong kind of worries while he's working. You know, you're just a pessimist, sometimes. You always assume the worst in people. I don't know where you get that from. I truly do not."

Her words stung me, enough so that I backed off the subject. At the time, I thought she was just being oblivious. But in hindsight, I realized a harder truth. I was the one being oblivious. Mom knew he was hitting on her. She knew it and she liked it. I just didn't want to see it in her at the time.

Before long, she just happened to be bumping in to him all over the place. He'd happen to be wherever she happened to be going. Both of them feigned coincidence, but they were both coordinating even if they didn't outright plan it each time. She went to obvious places to be found. He went looking at obvious places. And lo and behold, they'd just happen to run into each other.

I suppose we all know what came next. It wasn't long before they had themselves a steamy affair going. Or a sickening, gross as all get out affair, if you ask me. The appropriate adjective is in the eye of the beholder. I guess Mom thought it was exciting and romantic, though. At least, at first.

She tried to hide it from us, of course. Pops, God bless him, had always been a little oblivious to anything that wasn't under a hood, even more so if it related to a fault with Mom. But it didn't take long before I could tell something was going on. Whenever Pops was on the road, she'd find the strangest reasons to leave the house. "I'm just going to run down to the store right quick," she'd tell me, "won't be but a few minutes. You'll be all right?"

What could I say? "I'll be fine," was all that came to mind.

"Okay, lock the door behind me. I'll be back soon."

And off she'd go. A few minutes always meant about an hour, sometimes two. She always came back with something from the store, but sometimes it was ridiculous things that didn't even make sense. Bread and toilet paper, okay. But when she came home one night with mustard and some chips from the gas station, it was like she wasn't even really trying anymore. "I had a craving," she feebly explained.

And it takes a damn hour to go the gas station and back? I thought. But I didn't say anything. I tried debating with myself, w*ell, maybe she's not sleeping with him. Maybe she's off doing something else.* Part of me knew I was lying to myself, though. That's the worst kind of lies . . . the ones we tell ourselves. I wanted to say something to her. I wanted to confront her right then and there. *You're sleeping with him, aren't you! You're cheating on Pops and breaking his heart and mine!*

But I said nothing, because she was my mom and I loved her. And I didn't even want to think about the look on Pops' face if he ever found out. We both put mustard on those potato chips that night and ate them like they were good and tasty things instead of bitter and cruel. And that night I cried in bed.

Benny, our little mixed mutt we had at the time, sensed something was wrong and curled up next to me with a whimper. I pet him for at least an hour, and it was like I was petting myself, trying to make myself feel better. Dogs are like that, little living mirrors. What you give to them you get right back in return. As long as you treat them right, they don't care about the rest of it. All they know is how you treat them. Do it right and they'll fight bears, cougars, demons . . . whatever's coming at ya. They'll be loyal to you until their last breath. Ole Benny was as loyal and loving as God ever did make a dog.

Soon, Mom took up jogging. I guess trips to the store could only account for so many late-night errands. One night she was in her usual short-shorts and t-shirt. I hated how pretty she looked in her running get-up. It was an affront. "I'm going to take a little jog. Be back in a bit."

"Right now?" I asked. "It's nine o'clock at night."

"Yeah, it's much quieter, less traffic on the roads. I'll be just around the neighborhood and back in a few."

You know that inner voice we all hear? That inner voice that is our brain interpreting the world around us that we come to know as our conscious . . . well, mine was pissed. *I call bullshit!* it screamed in my head. *Tell her this is bullshit! Hell, get out of my way and I'll tell her,* my little voice raged. I could feel it clawing in my thoughts struggling to come out and give Mom a good tongue lashing.

That little voice and I had called bullshit a long time ago, actually, but we made a compromise that night that I'd at least muster the courage up to confirm our suspicions once and for all. Ignoring a problem only works out if it's temporary and disappears rather quickly with no ill after-effects, which is to say not very damn often. Otherwise, it festers under the skin. Irritated skin gets awfully itchy and I needed to scratch something bad that night, so I followed her.

She went running, alright. Right down to the middle school soccer field where Dale's truck was waiting for her. I'd never been so disappointed in my mother. Even though I'd already known by that point, seeing her jump in that truck with that big smile on her face just made my heart sink.

I told you, my little voice scorned in satisfaction.

Shut up, was all I could retort.

Like I said, I loved my mom. But I won't forget that image 'til the day I die. It's sharp glass shattered underfoot when a child loses respect for a parent she loves. I didn't say anything, though, when she returned a while later pretending to be flushed from running. "Whew! That took it out of me," she said, breathing hard and heading for her room, "I'm going to go shower up."

I bit my tongue so hard it almost bled. Had she bothered to look my way she would have seen daggers in my eyes. But she was lost in her adventure and darted down the hall to her bedroom without noticing.

Why didn't I tell her I saw her or call her out on her lies? I don't know. Lots of reasons, none of them all that great or persuasive, really. Unconditional love is a two-way street and admittedly I was scared if the affair ever got out in the open it'd mean divorce. I didn't want that. And I was sure that was exactly what Dale wanted. He had divorced his ex-wife less than a year before and in retrospect I'm sure he was plotting to see Mom go the same way. I don't think he even loved Mom truth be told. In fact, I know he didn't. He had just wanted her in high school and instead she turned him down and ended up marrying Pops. It was the getting he wanted, not the keeping. And I didn't want him to get the satisfaction of breaking up Mom and Pops just to fulfill his stupid high school conquest.

The thought of the devastation it would do to Pops kept me awake in fear some nights. I kept waiting for the day she announced she was leaving him . . . leaving us. But that day never came. One much worse than I had ever imagined came in its place.

A few weeks later I walked into the living room and saw Mom crying quietly to herself. "Mom, what's wrong?"

She smiled and wiped the tears away quickly. "Oh, nothing. I just miss your dad is all."

"Pops will be home the day after tomorrow," I reminded her.

She nodded, "I know. I'm going to make us some of that lasagna he likes so much." She was staring off into space at the empty screen of the television which wasn't even turned on. It wasn't real hard to figure out what might be going through her mind.

We once had that mother, daughter talk about drugs and she'd been surprisingly insightful. *After the high comes the guilt and the crash,* she'd said. *It's never worth it, then. Never. Remember that, Ruth. Don't you go trying those things. They'll bring you nothing but pain and regret.* I knew she knew from experience in some form or another, but I didn't ask. I should have. I would have liked to have known my mom a bit more. I guess I just assumed there would always be time. I figured we would have grown up conversations when I was grown up.

Looking at her then on that couch, her words echoed in my mind and I realized that was where she was. Dale's attention and courting, the excitement of it all, that was the high. But this was the low – knowing she was hurting Pops, a good man who loved her, and me. The smile that'd pained me so when she got in that truck was now replaced with tears she fought to keep hidden from me. Guilt was slicing and chewing her up from the inside and it was starting to show. She had that hollow look of someone losing themselves piece by piece to it.

I sat down next to her. "He always misses you, you know."

She put forth her best smile, "Oh, what makes you say that?"

"He told me. Pops and I talk sometimes. He told me how much he hates leaving but loves coming home. He said he's seen some of the prettiest parts of the country out on the highways, but nothing is prettier than Foxglove because this is where we are. And Pops thinks you're the most beautiful woman in the world," I told her.

"He said that?" she asked.

"He did." And there was no lie on my tongue. He'd said it more than once. "He loves us a lot."

Another tear rolled down her cheek but was swiftly thumbed away. "He's a good guy, your dad. I just wish he was home more."

"I know." There was an awkward pause between us. "You're good, too, Mom. You just get lonely sometimes. But I'm here." She couldn't say anything in that moment, she just looked at me with eyes full of regret and tears. "It's not so bad, right, you and me?" I asked.

She was really holding them back now. And she reached over and hugged me hard. "No, of course not, baby girl. You're my sweet girl and I love you," she said.

As we held each other tight, I asked quietly, "So, no jogging tonight?"

She pulled back a bit and looked away, guiltily. But after a quick moment she said, "No, not tonight. I don't feel like running."

Another pause. "And you don't need anything from the store, huh?"

A moment passed between us where we said a thousand words without speaking a one. She looked worried now, realizing maybe she hadn't been so clever in her deceit after all. She looked into my eyes and after a moment she flinched. What had she seen there? Maybe a mother's eyes just saw a child's heart at that moment . . . full of love, disappointment, anger . . . I'm not really sure, but she saw something there. Then she took a deep breath and said, "No, no shopping, either. I've got everything I need right here," she told me, reaching over again and giving me another hug, a little tighter this time. And after a few seconds, I squeezed back.

And that was that. She knew I knew she'd been up to some kind of no good, but we'd had our talk. I'd forgiven her without saying as much and she'd promised to give it up, also without saying as much. We had an accord, silent though it was. And I couldn't have been happier. In that moment, I felt like someone had lifted a hundred pounds off my shoulders that I'd been carrying around for weeks without even realizing it. I felt light as a feather. *Things are going to be okay,* I thought.

Mom loved Pops. I know that much and have never doubted it. Good people don't always make good choices. It's the human condition. Sometimes you need the consequences of bad choices as a reminder to appreciate and understand the rewards of the good ones. But sometimes the lesson costs more than the benefit.

Mom ended the affair that night. She tried to, at least. It started with a fight over the phone. There were a few phone calls that night. Ole Dale was a persistent bastard. At first, Mom kept disappearing out to her car. She even took a drive at one point, but apparently Dale wasn't done. Just after ten o'clock she was in her room still trying to end it. "There's nothing left to talk about," she rasped, trying to hide the heated conversation from my prying ears. I was squeezed up against her door listening in, though, as a dutiful daughter does. "Don't try to threaten me, Dale. We already talked about this. I may have to tell him anyway. And I think Ruth already knows something's been going on. . . . It doesn't matter! No matter what happens from here, you and I are done. I mean it, Dale. This was a huge mistake and it's done. . . . I'm sorry you're upset but you knew I was married. We should have never done this. I should have never done this. . . . I know. I know! Well, what do you want me to say, then? I know you're right. I never said you weren't. It is my fault. It is, but it's done. We just keep going round and round about the same things, Dale. Done is done. I can't say it any clearer. Don't call again. I won't answer. I've let you have your say . . . more than. It's done. Goodbye!" I heard the bed springs on her bed as she sat down. "Jesus," she whispered to herself, "what have I done?"

I wanted to go to her. I wanted to open the door and tell her I knew it all and hug her and tell her this was good and right that she was breaking it off and to be strong. But I didn't. I sat hidden in the hallway listening to her silently chastise herself. The hurt me found approval in it. We're all human.

She sat there for a while, probably just waiting for him to call again so she would have to decide to answer or not or maybe just turn the phone off for good. But much to my surprise, and probably Mom's, too, he didn't call again.

She did it, I thought. *She finally got rid of him.* She probably thought so, too. We were both being naive. Dale had felt rejected by Mom in high school. He'd been hell-bent on getting her to leave Pops for him. But now he felt rejected all over again. And, well, people like Dale don't handle such things well.

An hour or so later there came a knock on the door. An unexpected knock at the door late at night is seldom a good thing for anyone, I suppose. But it was more than that. Something in my gut told me it was him and I remember the fear lurching in my chest as I opened my bedroom door and saw Mom already standing in the hallway, looking towards the front door like a death row inmate who had just finished her last meal and now heard the echo of footfalls coming for her. "Stay here," she said.

I didn't. I quietly followed behind her. My intuition was screaming at me and I should have listened and told her not to open that door. I should have twisted the deadbolt and yelled that I was calling the police. I should have gone to the bedroom and got Pops' old shotgun out of the closet. I should have screamed. I should have screamed bloody murder so loud the neighbors heard and all the lights on the street came on, signifying everyone was watching. Maybe that would have stopped what came.

I should have done so many things. But I didn't. I ignorantly was restrained by the belief that even though I was shaking and everything in my gut told me something horrible was about to happen, that somehow things like that just couldn't happen. Not to us. Things like that always happened to other people, strangers on the news. Things like that were always someone else's problems, distant and detached from my life. It wouldn't happen to us.

And then it did. With a deafening kaboom, fire, and smoke, it did.

Mom opened the door and there was Dale. I think we both knew it would be him. But Mom was probably thinking like I was . . . that there'd be an argument, he'd cuss, she'd cuss back and threaten to call the cops, we might wake the neighbors and have an embarrassing scene we'd all be embarrassed about later, but he'd leave. Folks would gossip on Sunday. Mom might have to avoid the grocery store for a week or two. Then it would blow over and things would be all normal again. But none of that happened.

The sound was so loud. My ears were ringing, and I smelled the gunpowder in the air. It reminded me of a dwindling fire from the prior summer when we had gone camping. We'd made s'mores and ate fresh bass we'd caught out of the lake. It'd been a perfect night, that night around the campfire eating fat, greasy bass covered in salt and pepper. The s'more had melted, and the chocolate mixed with the greasy oil from the fish that was still on my fingertips. It sounds gross but for me, sitting around that fire with both my parents, I thought it might have been the best thing I ever ate.

"Now it's done," Dale said in slurred speech with alcohol on his breath.

Mom stumbled a few feet backwards, reached her hand out towards me, and then collapsed. Her eyes were wide and stunned. "Ruthie," she said, "run." And, then she was quiet. Her eyes were still looking at me, but there was nothing behind them. She was gone. Here then gone, just like that. It shouldn't be so quick or easy for someone to die. It doesn't seem natural.

I was too much in shock to run. I couldn't even scream. I heard this scream, somewhere down deep in my soul. It was loud . . . so loud it might rip the fabric of reality right before my eyes. But it never made it to the surface. It just screamed silently in my mind, terrifying me yet affecting nothing in the world around me. It begged to be released, but still I stood silently.

It all happened so fast. Benny was barking like crazy, but I barely heard him over the pinging in my ears. I was shaking and didn't know what to do – run back to my room, run to Mom. My mind was full of horrid noise, like a train whistle had just blasted in my ears. Benny was running towards something. My little, brown fur-ball was moving in a way I'd never seen him go before. I looked up and saw Dale looking at me.

He was pointing the gun at me. His eyes . . . I didn't see anybody in those eyes. Just a thing. Just a dumb thing moving around on its own, like a shark on Discovery Channel with dead black eyes. They kill and chomp with sharp teeth, but all the while their eyes denote nothing intelligent or empathetic to the other poor thing they're destroying. To them, whatever is in their teeth is just food. That was Dale in that moment, just a stupid thing. "You're just like her," said the thing.

Benny leapt into the air with a ferocity that, had you told me he was capable of it before that day, I would have laughed at you. He was the sweetest dog. He'd growled at strangers before, but he had never attacked anyone before that night. He would damn near pee himself if any of us yelled at him. But at that moment, he was all love and protection, a pack animal whose pack was under attack. He lunged for Dale and all I saw was fur and sparks. And, that was the last thing I remembered about it. I couldn't even tell you if getting shot hurt at the time. It was *Pow!* Light's out. And if it hadn't been for that sweet, brave, dumb dog of mine, the lights would have never come on again.

Chapter 2

The Division of Corpus Callosum

Now you have the accurate account of *The Incident* right from the source. My survival and subsequent recovery was all very technical. I was never one for geometry, but apparently it had a lot to do with angles and degrees.

Our old house which Pops and Mom and been renting for years had been on a pier and beam foundation with two steps at the front door. Benny's rush had managed to keep Dale from entering the house, so he had one foot on the first step. The bullet traveled at a slight upward angle, blazing through my Frontal Lobe right about where it meets the Temporal Lobe, severing part of the Corpus Callosum portion of my brain, which is basically the bundle of nerves that connects one side of the brain to the other, before finally embedding itself in the Parietal Lobe, which a kindly neurosurgeon later explained to me processes many of our senses.

Had the bullet gone straight, I'd have most likely died instantly. But instead, it kind of sped through this little alleyway. Numerous bridges of my brain were either damaged or wholly disconnected, but instant death was not a result. I called that a win.

The bullet still did a ton of damage, though. It took out part of my internal bridge of the hemispheres, which needless to say ain't good. I became somewhat of an academic horse race to brain specialists. Some of the doctors were betting I'd be unable to ever read or do math again, while others thought I might have depth perception issues and trouble determining the size and shape of objects, and probably have terrible coordination and zero balance.

Basically, my future career as a juggling ballerina accountant was out the window. Bummer. I had high hopes for it. Every doctor seemed to have a different opinion about how things would shake out. But there was one consensus. I was going to be messed up. They all agreed on that on. A suggestion of g*o ahead and pre-order that disability parking permit, because you're going to need it,* was about the only thing that would have reached unanimous approval.

And one or two said chances were good I'd have all of those problems and then some. "Poor kid. She'll be lucky if she can dress and feed herself," one doctor opined as he stood over my bed while I was still in the ICU. He doesn't know I heard him because supposedly I was in a coma at the time. But I heard him. I even tried to open my eyes and glare at him to let him know I heard him, but instead I just drooled a bit more menacingly. "Well, we'll see how bad it is soon enough," he told the watch nurse, and he shook his head like I was a lost cause as he turned and strolled out of the room.

I'm pretty sure I dreamed about hearing and seeing the doctor that day, particularly since my eyes were closed and I was loaded on meds in a deep sleep, but I'm also pretty sure it actually happened and somehow or another I just viewed it as a dream. That was something of a preview to the weirdness yet to follow, I suppose.

I kept that doctor's words in the back of my mind, along with the bullet, the entire time I was going through therapy and rehab after the shooting. I was determined to prove him wrong. If Pops had heard him say it, he would have socked the guy, but good.

At the time of *The Incident,* Pops had been a good eighteen hours away delivering pre-fabricated lab cabinets to Ball State University up in Muncie, Indiana, the birth place of Garfield. The cat, not the president.

Although, it's worth noting President Garfield got shot, too . . . July 2, 1881 at the Baltimore and Potomac Railroad Station in Washington D.C. at 9:30 a.m. He was on his way to a vacation, which has to be just about the worst time to get assassinated, really. The guy who shot him, Charles J Guiteau, bought an ivory handled gun for the deed because he thought it'd look neat on display in later years when folks talked about his murdering the President. He also tried to tour the jail where he thought he'd be incarcerated before he shot Garfield to check out where he'd be staying. Guiteau was crazy, as you may have surmised. His family tried to have him committed in 1875, but he escaped, much to the misfortune of President Garfield. Garfield managed to hang on for 79 days after being shot, dying September 19, 1881 from blood poisoning and a heart attack.

The irony is that had his doctors left the bullet alone, he probably would have survived just fine. Instead, doctors kept probing the wound with dirty fingers and unsterilized tools, and one doctor accidentally punctured Garfield's liver with his finger. That all led to an infection which led to sepsis which then led to death. They had even tried using a new metal detector made by Alexander Graham Bell to locate the bullet in the body, but the bed springs kept screwing up the reading. Hence, the finger prodding and liver puncture.

They tried Guiteau, who testified in poem and sang *John Brown's Body* during the trial. He cussed out witnesses in court, the lawyers, even the judge. He quite correctly argued in his defense, however, "The doctors killed Garfield, I just shot him." He really thought he was going to be acquitted and even began planning a tour of lectures for his release. The jury, however, had other plans and convicted him. To which Guiteau responded in Guiteau fashion by cussing them all out.

Upon conviction, he danced up the stairs to the gallows, shook hands with his executioner, and then recited yet another poem. And once he was done he was then promptly hanged. Like I said, he was crazy. He was right about the gun, though. It was put on display in the Smithsonian, just like he'd hoped. Well, until someone stole it as a souvenir, if you can believe it. So much for best laid plans and all. But hey, because he was so crazy, they saved part of Guiteau's brain and put it in a jar on display at the Mutter Museum in Philadelphia where future physicians still ogle it to this day. So, the pretty gun he picked out is gone, but his brain is still on display. Silver medal?

Ugh. Shut up, Eddie. Eddie is this dead guy obsessed with American Presidents whose leftover memories often pop unbidden into my thoughts. I probably got an A in history class my junior year thanks to him, but he's also a royal pain in the ass as his crazy nonsense invades my mind on occasion with little to no warning and often with information wholly unhelpful when not taking a history exam. Eddie liked weird facts in history, especially about former Presidents. We can talk about all that later.

Back to my personal bullet. Pops returned the next day to find his entire world upended. They got a hold of him as he was already driving back, but they didn't want to tell him Mom was dead and I'd been shot in the head. Instead, they just told him there'd been *an incident* and that we were both at the hospital. Thus, the moniker *The Incident* was born. How the rest of the town latched on to it so quickly, I never knew. The hospital told Pops it was an emergency and he needed to get back home as quickly but safely as possible.

Pops filled up his three-hundred-gallon diesel tanks and drove sixteen hours straight over a thousand miles without stopping. I didn't even know trucks could do that. He later told me he spent that entire time cursing our old water heater and his failure to buy a carbon monoxide alarm. He thought for sure Mom and I were dying of carbon monoxide poisoning from that rusty tin can of a water heater. He wasn't at all prepared for what had really happened. "I never would have suspected it in a million years," he told me later. "I guess it was pretty stupid of me, but never once did I worry about your mom cheating on me."

When he finally got to the hospital, they broke the news to him. "She'll have a long road to recovery," a doctor told Pops as I lay there with tubes sticking out all over me, "but we think she's going to pull through." Mom wasn't so lucky, of course. Nor Benny. And to add further insult to injury Dale had left me another permanent souvenir. "It's not worth the risk to try to remove the bullet."

Pops was understandably confused by that one. He'd obviously not heard about what happened to Garfield. "You're leaving it in there? You mean she has to live with that thing inside of her? Can she even live with a bullet in her head like that?"

"Yes. It's somewhat rare but there's been many people who have lived full and complete lives with a bullet present that was too risky to be removed. The brain is a delicate thing. We can re-examine at a later date, but for now, we are recommending not attempting removal. With the swelling, it's far too risky to attempt that kind of surgery right now."

Somebody should have told Garfield's doctors, I guess. He might have had an outcome more like President Teddy Roosevelt, another fascinating President who apparently drew the ire of a fanatic. Teddy got shot, too. Several former Presidents did. It's been a pretty hazardous occupation over the course of history. Teddy left the bullet alone and managed to live several relatively healthy years with a bullet in his chest. He was on his way to a speech in Milwaukee, of all places, when he got shot with a relatively small caliber pistol by some disagreeable fellow. This was after he was President the first time but was running for President again on the Progressive Ticket. He apparently should have quit while he was ahead.

The aides with him wanted to rush him to the hospital but Roosevelt insisted on being taken to the auditorium to deliver his speech before doing so. He coughed into his hand and then held it up to show his aides there was no blood on it. "Look there," he said, "didn't even puncture the lung. Now, on with it. I have a speech to give and supporters awaiting." Or something along those lines. So, they went to the auditorium . . . Roosevelt still bleeding from the bullet freshly punctured into his flesh. That must have been an interesting car ride.

With his aides looking on in horror and disbelief Roosevelt stood on stage and prepared to deliver his speech. When he pulled the fifty-page speech from his breast pocket, it was covered in blood with a bullet hole clean through. It likely saved his life as it had stopped the bullet from hitting his heart. Then Roosevelt, still bleeding, stood on that stage and delivered his speech for ninety minutes . . . ninety freaking minutes. He even started it off by telling the crowd he'd just been shot, opened his coat to show them, and made lemonade out of lemons by exclaiming "It takes more than that to kill a bull moose!" which was the theme for his political party, a bull moose. When he finished, he finally went to the hospital where the doctors decided it was safer to leave the bullet where it was, much like my condition.

See, I had a point. It just took me a while to get to it. And that point is, it's not that weird I have a bullet in my head. I'm just saying. Teddy had one. Nobody made fun of him for it. If anything, it made him a more interesting historical figure, right? Hell, Andrew Jackson had two bullets in him from two different incidents. One he acquired in his chest right next to his heart. A man named Charles Dickinson accused Jackson of welching on a horse bet and, to throw a little more shade on him, accused Jackson's wife of having an affair. That turned out to be a bad idea because what old Chuck apparently didn't know was that our future seventh President Mr. Jackson was an avid gun duelist, participating in over one hundred gun duels over his life, which is more bananas than a banana split.

So old Chuck got a nasty surprise when he hit Jackson square in the chest and probably thought he won the duel, only to see Jackson keep standing there, aim carefully, and Pow! He shot poor Chuck dead. Then Jackson walked off the dueling field and carried that bullet in his chest for the next forty years. And that wasn't the only one. He had another bullet in his arm that was never removed. The man had so much lead in him it's believed he finally died of lead poisoning at the age of seventy-eight. So there, it's settled. I am not that weird for getting shot and walking around with a bullet in me. It happens, okay?

Okay, enough of the odd history. That's not my fault, really. It's Eddie. Eddie and his weird ass obsession and all his old books he left in the house. When Pops and I inherited the groundskeeper's cottage, which I'll explain about in a bit, it came with a steamer trunk filled to the brim with very old and dusty books. And sure, I could have found all the information in those old books on the internet, but there's just something about holding a book in your hands, thumbing through the pages with that nice pfft, pfft, sound as they turn.

I've read most all of them, partially just from boredom. Several of the books were biographies of American Presidents. I didn't even really want to read them. But for reasons I'll have to gently explain as we go along, I couldn't help myself. Sometimes I find I know things I've never even read. That's more of Eddie and this house. Well, it's sort of both of them. I'm getting ahead of myself. We'll come back to it.

There I lay in the hospital with a bullet in my brain while the doctors wagered on just how screwed up Ruth Gonzales would be when the dust settled. They'd put me in a medical coma to lower the swelling in my brain and I was on vacation from the world for a good three weeks. They also tried something kind of new called hypothermic therapy, taking my body temperature way down while I healed then slowly bringing it back up. I was basically a popsicle for a little while, my metabolism, heartbeat, all that barely operating at all. I don't know if that had anything to do with how I would later turn out, but something went sideways, I can attest to that much.

They'd already arrested Dale and had his confession by the time I woke up. One of our neighbors had seen him tearing off after hearing gunshots. She called 911 and with the couple of digits of his license plate and a good description of his truck, he wasn't hard to find. Cops in town knew right away who had a truck like that, small town and all.

The police found him barricaded in his little house threatening to shoot anyone who came in after him. He was stupid drunk. They popped a few cans of tear gas in there, which I'm sure they were thrilled to finally get a chance to use, because it was the first time anyone in town could recall the police ever using tear gas, and out crawled Dale coughing up a lung.

One of the cops in town, Billy Crutcher, had been friends with Mom her whole life. I'm told he beat the tar out of Dale when they arrested him. "Stop resisting!" he yelled at Dale, who was sprawled out on the ground while Billy kept smacking the hell out of him with his baton.

"I ain't resisting!" he pleaded, trying his best to surrender.

"Stop resisting!" yelled Billy some more, still beating the fooey out of him.

Dale's old neighbor, Ms. Floyd, who could have been in her sixties or eighties at the time, nobody could really tell, told me all about it. "Ooh, they worked him over good, Ruth. That Mr. Crutcher was hittin' him something fierce. I know it ain't much salve to the kind of wound he done, but they beat him black, blue, green, and yellow."

"Green and yellow?" I asked.

"Oh, yes, dear. You know them greenish, yellow bruises are the worst, now, don't ya? Them the ones when you know someone really got a whoopin'. Shoot, I even found me one of his teeth out there the next morning."

"You found his tooth?" I asked, both a bit disgusted and curious. "What'd you do with it?"

"Oh, I just threw in the trash," she said with a hearty laugh. "He won't be needing it anymore. I don't reckon they serve much steak where they're sending him."

They went ahead and added a slew more charges on him like resisting arrest, attempted murder, animal cruelty . . . I don't even know all the charges he got, honestly. But there were a lot of 'em. It's a small detail on the part of our small-town police officers and county district attorney's office, but don't think I didn't appreciate it, because I sure did.

Mr. Crutcher came by some month or two after I got out of the hospital and visited with me to let me know he was glad I survived and how sorry he was Mom didn't. Poor guy ended up crying when he saw me. He was trying to play it off, but I could tell. My hair was growing back after being shaved but I had a nasty scar going on my forehead and couldn't hardly walk right. I knew I looked a mess but seeing that big ole grown man trying to choke back the tears like that really sent it home for me just how bad I must look. I know he didn't mean to do it, but he really kind of sparked off a long road of me being self-conscious about how I looked after *The Incident.*

"I wish he would have pulled a gun on us so we could have ended him right there," he told me. "I'm not supposed to say things like that. But after what he did to you and your mom, he deserves it. But I have to do my job right, you know? I can't do something like that even if I want." I wasn't sure if Mr. Crutcher was trying to convince me or himself at that point. His glossy red eyes suggested he was about to lose his composure.

"No, you did right," I told him. "It's better he lives with it."

Now admittedly, that was not entirely how I felt about it. Between you and me, I'd have preferred to see things go down a slightly different way, but I suppose wishing him dead is both normal but not very helpful. It would've been a little easier if he'd have been shot dead in the arrest, but a solid butt whooping and life in prison would give him lots to think about and a lot of time to do it. Let him sit a few decades and think about what he did. Maybe he'd feel guilty. Maybe not. But regardless, he'd be stuck in a cage for years and years. He'd hate that, ole Dale would. No more hunting. No more fishing. No more pretty ladies. No more beer. I didn't know Dale all that well, but I knew he wouldn't get to do any of the things he loved to do anymore. I won't say the thought brought a smile to my face because I'd lost too much for that, but maybe a satisfactory smirk now and again as I thought on it.

And he'll never get out. Never ever. He signed a deal saying as much pretty quickly in the case. He didn't really have much choice. I lived, so of course could identify him. And our neighbor had been spot-on accurate with the truck description. Dale was pretty stupid, but his lawyer wasn't. His counsel advised it wouldn't be a prudent course to face a Texas jury after shooting a young mother in front of her daughter and then, just to prove what a true SOB he was, shooting the daughter, too. I mean come on, he even killed poor Benny. Do you know how many people love their dogs practically like children? Well, Dale's lawyer did.

Pops and I got the low-down from the district attorney's office at the time. Part of me was glad there would be no trial, but another part of me had wanted to see him torched. Dale had some malarkey story about how he was overcome with despair over the affair ending and how he had gotten blind drunk and didn't remember anything. It looked for a brief moment like he might try a temporary insanity defense and blame it on the booze, but his lawyer had the foresight to inform him nobody really gave a crap about his lame excuses and it was the deal or the needle, nothing between. So, he took the deal. And there he sits, off in prison growing old. He's none too popular in there, I hear. Good riddance.

And there were some silver linings. I ended up coming out of it better than most of the doctors thought I would. My brain did some rewiring. Some wires got crossed here and there, but I suppose that's to be expected. While some of my senses, such as smell and taste, were altered in odd ways (avocados inexplicably taste like bananas to me now and bananas taste like kale . . . which has totally ruined banana splits for me), there were other pretty weird things going on, too, that to this day I can't even begin to try to understand or properly explain.

Chapter 3

The Groundskeeper's Cottage

It is a well-known fact that the quickest thing you will find in any given small town is a rumor. As you might suspect, Pops and I became reluctant celebrities in town. Mom's murder and my shooting quickly and widely became known as *The Incident.* But you knew that already.

People were talking and by the time I was able to leave the hospital everyone knew exactly what had happened at the Gonzales' house. They knew every sordid detail with several additional ones tossed in I won't even dignify by mentioning of Mom's affair and its Armageddon of an ending.

I wanted to get away. Pops did, too. Guam might have been far enough. I saw a travel show on it, once, and the beaches looked awfully nice, but they apparently have almost no birds left due to a nasty tree snake problem. I thought it still seemed like a pretty viable option as opposed to hanging out in town and being the subject of most every whispering conversation happening around that time.

Pops' lease on the house was coming up soon and he decided that whether we moved far away or not, we weren't staying in that house. Not after what had happened there. I think the landlord was nervous about trying to re-lease the now infamous little house. Either that, or he just felt real sorry for us, because he offered Pops a huge discount on the rent, but Pops wouldn't have it. "I just can't stay here," he told me one night over dinner.

"Me, either," I told him. Not a day went by that my eyes didn't get fixated on that spot where Mom died.

We contemplated moving to lots of places . . . Hawaii, Colorado, maybe even moving to Mexico, although I didn't know any Spanish. Pops still did, but I had never really learned. "Maybe we can get back to our roots," he suggested. Pops' family had come from Monclova, Mexico, the steel capital established in 1577. But they'd moved to Texas when he was a kid. Pops was about as Mexican as I was at this point. And a Texan in Mexico or anywhere else in the world is invariably still Texan. Some things just don't wash off.

We did start to get a bit serious on the idea of Siesta Key, Florida, near Sarasota. Pops had been there a few times on some runs. "Oh, it's beautiful down there," he told me. "It's not like our Texas beaches. They have white, sandy beaches, Ruth, with bluish green water like a big ole swimming pool. You can actually see what's swimming around with ya." Pops even started looking for a job down there and checking out the rental market. "We can just get us a nice apartment to start, somewhere with a good school for you. I'll get a regular job during the day, so I'll be home early. And we'll go to the beach all the time, Ruth. We'll get out and do stuff every weekend."

I started to get excited about the idea and Googled the place probably five hundred times, clicking through pictures of beautiful beach scenery and happy people in flip-flops and shorts walking along the white powdery sand. It looked like the kind of place you would go to on vacation. I couldn't imagine people actually living there year-round. I thought, *Is this real? Can we really move to this place and live there?* But if there was one thing *The Incident* had taught me it was that yes, it absolutely was possible Pops and I could move there. Why? Because anything was possible. If *The Incident* could happen to us, so could pretty much anything. Good or bad, I no longer believed impossible things only happened to other people. Anything could happen to anyone, I had learned.

Siesta Key was a nice idea and maybe it would have worked out. But things ended up working out a different way when another opportunity came along that, given Dad was a single parent now and money was as ever short, was just too good to pass up.

Pops had buried Mom while I was still in the hospital. "I was going to do cremation," he told me, "but I wanted a place where you could come visit her when you're older." We went out to the cemetery at least once a week and almost immediately Pops became fixated and angered by the state of the place. The grass was always overgrown. Weeds were everywhere. There were about a thousand ant piles so you couldn't hardly sit at Mom's grave without bringing a folding chair or something else to stay up off the ground. Pops couldn't abide by it. How could he leave Mom in a place so run down? Why couldn't they at least make an effort to properly take care of the place? So, one day, we stopped off at the funeral home so Pops could complain in person after being told one too many times over the phone that Mr. Baker was always busy. "There's no way he's that busy," Pops told me on the ride over. "There just aren't that many people dying around here."

Pops was right. Mr. Baker had been avoiding him when he realized Pops was calling because he was upset by the condition of the cemetery. Turned out, though, it was the city. "I know it," he explained apologetically. "The old caretaker, Eddie, died last year and the city can't afford to pay anyone full time." I was surprised to learn the city owned the cemetery. I guess I just assumed the funeral home did. "Eddie had his social security and was content with just living in the caretaker's cottage rent free with a small stipend," continued Mr. Baker, "but nobody wants to live there now. We tried to rent it, but nobody was willing to pay even the small six hundred a month the city was hoping to get. Superstitious folks say it's haunted, what with it being so close to the cemetery and looking a little spooky, I guess. The cemetery is just getting worse and worse. I wish we could do better, believe me. I mean, it's bad for business, you know? The city's trying to hire someone, but funds are low and not many folks are interested in this kind of work. We pay a yard company and they come out and mow, but that's about all they do. It's a waste, really. There's a good house out there just falling to ruin along with everything else. It needs a little work and all, but it's a good place. It's the oldest house in town, actually."

Pops knew his trucking days were over, at least for a while, so a different idea sprung up rather spontaneously. "How bad is it?" he asked.

Mr. Baker looked like a man fishing who just spotted potential dinner swimming near his hook. "Oh, not that bad at all, really. It's just old. Why do you ask?"

"Well," said Pops. "I'm just thinking maybe I could fix it up," he told Mr. Baker. "The house and the cemetery, I mean."

"Could you, now?" asked Mr. Baker with a gleam in his eye. "Well, I'd be happy to show you the place if you'd like."

Don't judge us too harshly. It's hard leaving what you know. Better the devil you know, as they say. And there were lots of good folks in town. There'd been a GoFundMe set up that paid for Mom's funeral and we even had a few thousand left over Pops put into a savings account for me. We had casseroles and pies for weeks even after I got out of the hospital and we were a regular subject of Sunday prayers both in and out of the church. Most meant it. And that's something. We were the subject of Saturday gossip, to be sure, but Sunday prayers none the less. Foxglove was our home, we decided. We just could use a little distance from everything was all. "We need a nice quiet place so you can heal up," he told me. "It'll just be for a little while. Florida isn't going anywhere if we change our minds."

It didn't exactly provide the fresh start I might have been seeking, but at least it was quiet. The caretaker's cottage, as Mr. Baker insisted on referring to it, was an old farmhouse that, for as long as I could remember, had been rumored to be haunted. Pops and I weren't scared of such things, though. Neither of us remotely believed in nor feared something as absurd as ghosts.

I was fresh out of the hospital and hadn't started having the dreams yet at that time. Come to find out later, it turned out people were right after all. The place was haunted. In a way. It sounds just as strange to say this as it must be to hear it, but one of my best friends in this world is a dead woman named Lilith. Well . . . maybe strike that. It might be a bunch of flowers that ate a dead woman named Lilith. Or maybe it's Lilith. I don't know. She can't talk to me or anything, but I feel like I know her from all the dreams I've had about her memories. Either she or the garden or both gave me a hell of a gift one time. I'll try to explain it but even I don't fully understand what the deal is with Lilith and the garden. I think it's a seriously dysfunctional relationship.

It was hell trying to walk in those first weeks. My body seemed to have a mind of its own. I had to limp my leg along and my left hand was perpetually curled up in a ball. It felt like it was trapped in a vice grip. No matter how hard I tried to relax it, my left hand just stayed clamped shut. I truly hated it, but my limbs wouldn't listen to me. I was lucky to even be walking at all, but still, it was really frustrating.

I joined Pops as we met up with Mr. Baker to check out the "cottage". I did my best to walk around and look at everything despite my infirmity.

"It's been vacant a year or so," explained Mr. Baker, "since Eddie passed on. It had a total remodel in the seventies and a bit more in the nineties. It has lots of potential, though." *The seventies,* I thought. *Good grief.* "It has really good bones. These old houses are made of the good stuff. The city covers the taxes and insurance, so you don't have to worry about that, just the utilities and the upkeep. The town is on a pretty tight budget, as you can imagine. We've still got several roads and sewer lines that need work, but I could probably get them to give you a thousand or two to get the place back in habitable condition if you were willing to do the work. It'd be a lot cheaper than hiring a company or a contractor, which I can tell you right now the city council ain't going to approve.

You don't see little farmhouses like this much anymore. It's all cookie-cutter these days. And you've got a solid three acres of land. Not to mention the barn over there," he said, pointing to a small barn adjacent to the home.

Pops was all about the barn. "Can I use that for my own things, maybe fix up some cars and the like?"

"Oh, sure," said Bill. "We ain't using it anymore since the new building was put up. As long as you don't clutter the place up too much. We might need to store something in there once in a while, but on the whole you could pretty much do what you like with it."

I could see Pops' mind working as soon as we walked in to check it out. He was already imagining where he'd put his tools and the work bench he'd make along the wall. I could tell he loved it, or at least the idea of it that was quickly forming in his head. Pops wanted a distraction after Mom's death. Even back then I could see how this would go. He was going to bury himself in work. If not the cemetery, then out here with his projects. And I understood that. It was what he needed. He'd always been a natural mechanic and a hurting heart is sometimes eased by busy hands. I could already see him out here, late into the evenings, working on carburetors and wiring harnesses. He'd drink a few beers and work until his mind was numb. That would be a lot better than drinking until he was numb, which candidly I was getting worried might end up happening.

He needed to stay busy. Then he wouldn't see her face every minute of the day and constantly be thinking about what was gone or what he could have done so things wouldn't have happened the way they did. He needed to get on with a big distraction before he got ate up by depression, and this place was offering that. It needed a lot of work. So did Pops.

"What do you think, Baby Ruth?" he asked. How could I say no?

And allow me to digress yet again here a moment and explain that nobody else is allowed to call me Baby Ruth. Pops gets a free pass since he's been calling me that since I literally was a baby. Which is why when I was seven, I decided I needed a nickname for him and switched from calling him Dad to Pops. He laughed the first time I called him that so whenever he'd call me Baby Ruth, I'd call him Pops. He'd say, *how was school, Baby Ruth*? And I'd say, *just fine, Pops. How was Memphis*? Or how was Houston or Detroit, or wherever he'd been. It was just a gag at first but after a while he was just Pops to me. So please don't think I give license or invitation for anyone else to call me Baby Ruth. Anyone doing so, does so at their own peril. After Dale, it frankly bothers me a bit if strangers start trying to call me by anything other than Ruth. Okay, I feel better now that we have that out of the way. It's Ruth, if you please. I'm not a freaking candy bar.

"It's got a rustic charm to it, I'll say that much," I told him. Although, the nails sticking out around the barn looked more rusty than rustic. I tried to remember when I had my last tetanus shot.

I'd tried to hide my actual feelings about the place, but I supposed something in my expression hinted at my underlying trepidation because Mr. Baker seemed to pick up on it. "Hey, there's something you might like in the back," he told me, "come check out this garden."

"The old caretaker had a garden, huh?" asked Pops, "surprised it's not all weeds by now."

"Well, kind of a kicker of a story, there. Eddie once told me it wasn't his garden. There are these flowers back here, huge things, that just grow like mad. Eddie swore up and down he had nothing to do with them, said they just grew on their own back here. I guess they're wild but it's still pretty nice and it looks like a proper flower garden if you ask me. And you gotta see how tall these things are."

He walked us out behind the little farmhouse and there, sure enough, was what could easily pass for a gorgeous flower garden. It almost looked like something out of magazine, only wilder. It was part jungle, with weeds and vines everywhere, but there, interspersed throughout, were beautiful blooms. And Mr. Baker hadn't been exaggerating . . . they were tall, some only a foot or two, but others as tall as me, some sticking straight up, others looming over a small walking path with stalks full of color. I'd never seen such tall flowers.

"What are those?" I asked.

"Foxgloves," said Mr. Baker. "Just like the town. Folks say the town was named after 'em. Like I said, this old place is the oldest house in town, maybe even the county. You're standing right where Foxglove, Texas was born. Good bit of history to this place."

"Huh," said Pops, clearly not overly impressed with the history lesson. But I thought it was pretty interesting.

The flowers weren't just growing in the garden, they were defiant. I could see the weeds trying to eat up the ground and take out the flowers, but they had this presence about them like they were soldiers determined to hold their hill and beat back the enemy. I stepped along the narrow pathway and found the scene entirely fascinating the more I studied it. The tall ones had this sense about them . . . almost like they were sentries looking at me. And I felt something, too. I immediately felt just peaceful, like I could sit there for hours and hardly move, totally serene. Even the Vicodin they had given me recently (which I quit taking because I disliked the sensation it gave me of my head floating around on my body) hadn't made me feel as calm since *The Incident.* Somewhere nearby I heard the chirp, chirp of a bird and I looked up to see a cardinal sitting on the roof of the house looking down into the garden. It seemed rather interested in it and me standing there.

"This is so nice," I said, "like a fairy tale." I felt something brush up against my hand, but when I looked down, it was just a flower fluttering around a bit. I didn't think twice about it at the time. Had I, I may have realized there wasn't any breeze.

"Yeah, I thought you'd like it. It needs a good trimming, of course, and maybe even mow you a bigger path through here and a place to set up a table or something . . ." The wind seem to stir. That nice, calm feeling I had seemed to have the moment I walked in the garden was replaced with a chill. I felt a bit of fear . . . and anger . . . "but there must be some real hearty soil back here as Eddie said he didn't even fertilize or do anything to maintain it," continued Mr. Baker.

He laughed a bit, "Actually, he told me he tried to mow over it all once, weeds, flowers, the whole thing, but it all sprang right back. I asked him why he didn't just pull everything out or toss some weed killer on it all if he didn't like it and he told me the darnedest thing. He said the flowers got mad at him the last time he messed around with them, so he just left them be. He started getting a little loopy in those last few years, though, and honestly Eddie was always a little bit of an odd bird to begin with. He could tell you anything you wanted to know about old history but didn't know a thing about current events. He knew everything about old Presidents but had no clue who the current Vice President was. He was just an odd guy. Anyway, I imagine if you planted some vegetables back here or something they'd probably do right well. Although, you should probably watch out for snakes until it's cleared out a bit. We've seen some copperheads out by the barn now and then, probably after mice. A few coral snakes, too."

He trailed off to show Pops something else and as he did so, I felt calm and relaxed again. *Odd,* I thought. *Not sure what was bothering me, there.*

I was on board regardless because this was probably the only way Pops could afford to quit trucking and still keep a roof over our head. So, it all just kind of was working out this way. But the garden was a nice bonus. The house was ugly as sin, albeit in its own charming way, which made the flowers all the more beautiful by contrast. And Pops had the barn. So, he took the job and we moved in. And after we moved in, that's when I started having the dreams . . . like, really, really weird dreams.

Chapter 4

Thomas Jefferson and Shakespeare's Chair

After *The Incident* things were hard. But like so many hardships, love and friendship were the best medicine. Mom was gone, but I had a dad who I knew would do anything for me and who doted on me like a hummingbird seeking nectar and I was the last flower in the world. It was annoying how he was always hovering around me asking if I needed anything. But I also very much appreciated it. I knew Mom's passing was also really hard on him, so it was nice we could lean on each other like we did. And it was so great being able to finally spend so much time with him. Before, it had always been mainly me and Mom while Pops was working, but now, he was working right in the backyard every day. No more long trips of being days or even weeks away, only to turn around as soon as he got home to do it again. I had my Pops with me every day.

And I also had two good friends I could still rely on. Deja Lucas had been my bestie since kindergarten. She never minced words and basically told everything just how she saw it with no sugar coating, which I had always found both refreshing and admirably confident of her. And Alexi Bundt was another good friend. We called her Lexi. She was a goofball whose laugh was infectious and annoying at the same time. But it was always nice to be around someone so persistently optimistic and humorous.

Some of the other so-so "friends" fell by the wayside after *The Incident*. I guess maybe they didn't want to be seen with the freak, Ruth Gonzales. Or maybe I just made them too uncomfortable. But Deja and Lexi never wavered. They were the only people from school to visit me in the hospital. Well, them and Mrs. Jenkins, one of my eighth grade teachers. And leave it to Deja to dispel any tension upon seeing me all messed up for the first time after the shooting. "Ooh, girl, check you out," she said, prodding the bandage on my forehead, "You going to have a scar on your forehead just like Harry Potter." I smiled for the first time in days and tried to sit up to give her and Lexi a hug. But I wasn't doing very well.

And as I struggled to sit up, Lexi started waving her hand around and reciting "Wingardium Leviosa, Wingardium Leviosa . . ."

"Lexi, what are you doing?" asked Deja.

She laughed her funny little laugh, "I'm trying to help her sit up. It's a Harry Potter spell."

Deja gave her one of her infamous *girl, you stupid* looks. I'd seen that look a hundred times since we were five and it never got old. Except when she used it on me.

They visited a number of times while I was in the hospital and Lexi brought me some good novels to read. "Have you read this *Mistborn* series from Brandon Sanderson yet?" she asked me.

"No."

"Girl, you in for a treat. It's lit. It's got this badass girl who, when she pops little pieces of metal in her mouth, gets like temporary superpowers."

"Well, don't ruin it for me," I told her.

"I'm just giving you the preview. Oh, and there's this thing that eats people and uses their bones to shapeshift into them."

"Deja, I just said don't tell me."

"Alright, alright. Just read it, okay, and then tell me what you think." Even when she was thirteen, Deja was a voracious reader with a colorful vocabulary. She and I also shared similar reading tastes going way back. Forget *Twilight*, we liked us some *Wheel of Time* type of reads, long stories full of sweeping adventures and magic powers.

It was a blessing I could still read. I found it very therapeutic. After we moved into the farmhouse, I'd found a treasure trove in the attic one day. We'd been cleaning for weeks and I'd been helping Pops patch up the roof when I found it. I was in the attic and he was on top, banging away on some shingles, when I noticed an odd bulge in the recess of a nook where the roof sloped down.

At first, I thought maybe some wood had been piled there from years ago, but closer inspection revealed it was an old, horribly beaten up, steamer trunk. It was sitting on its side and I pushed it over. It made such a huge thud I really thought for a second it might go straight through the floor.

The hammering on the roof stopped. "What was that!?" I heard Pops' voice drift in through the vent. "You okay!?"

"Nothing! Yeah, I'm fine. Sorry about that, just found this old trunk in here and it tipped over."

"Well, be careful. Whatever that was shook the whole house, I think. What's in it?"

Good question, I thought. I confess I had this momentary vision of gold and jewels. The trunk did look the part of an old pirate's chest or something. But what I found instead later turned out to be a good consolation prize. Lots of old books. And in surprisingly decent shape. That old trunk did its job well. And I found more boxes of books stashed around the attic.

We unloaded them and later relocated our bounty to my room where I went through my new library. There was *Pride and Prejudice, Jane Eyre, The Count of Monte Cristo* (love it!), *Wuthering Heights, Great Expectations* (also love), just to name a few, and at the very bottom of the trunk had been one massive book which turned out to be the complete works of William Shakespeare.

I wasn't into Shakespeare before *The Incident,* but given my life's turn of events, I suddenly found a new appreciation. I used to read that book in the tub. That's when I learned from one of Eddie's odd errant thoughts that Thomas Jefferson once stole a piece of Shakespeare's chair. He and John Adams (before they had a falling out) visited Shakespeare's home in Stratford-upon-Avon in 1786. While there, Jefferson proceeded to cut a chip of wood from Shakespeare's chair as a souvenir for his daughter. What a little vandal. Adams and Jefferson died the same day, July 4, 1826. I can distinctly remember sitting in the tub once years ago when that memory suddenly popped into my head and I had this *wait a minute,* moment of *did I actually ever know that before? How do I know that?* Even if I had read that on my own at some point and was suddenly just remembering it, it still seemed really odd how precisely I was recalling the whole thing. It felt weird "remembering" something that I couldn't ever remember learning in the first place. And that was one of my first introductions to Eddie's memories which had saturated the house over many, many years.

I had always enjoyed reading a bit before *The Incident,* but it soon became a full-time passion. It was a way to escape, I guess. And for some reason, I ended up getting better at it. I was able to read a lot faster than I had before.

I had to see a specialist on and off back then and when I told her about all the reading I'd been doing she was thrilled. "That's amazing considering the injury you had."

"Yeah, and I think I can remember things maybe better, now. Except, the other day I remembered this weird fact about John Adams and Thomas Jefferson, but the only thing is, I don't remember when or how I learned it."

"Well, don't let that bother you, Ruth," she explained to me. "You've suffered severe trauma to your brain and it's only natural that you can't remember specific times or events in your life. For instance, do you remember when you first learned to tie your shoes?"

"I do, actually. My mom taught me with little bunny ears on my laces."

"Oh, that's good," she said, but was clearly a little annoyed I blew out her candle. "Well, there may be lots of things you can still do now even if you don't remember learning it in the first place. You may find you have lots of gaps, but that's okay. As more time goes on, those gaps may fill in, or they may not, but you're doing fantastic, Ruth. I can't tell you how proud of you I am and how happy I am to hear these kinds of updates. It's very positive news."

So, at first, I just chalked up my inability to remember how I knew odd little things I knew as a byproduct of my brain damage. I mean, what else could it have been, right?

And as far as the doctors were concerned, it wasn't a problem for them, either. Not given so many didn't think I'd even be able to read. And I found I had quite an aptitude for it. Words were practically leaping off the page at me like a story unfolding in a movie, only it was me that was creating all the visual effects. My thoughts would create characters as fast as I could read about them. I could see every face, what they were wearing, hear every word, even smells seemed to come to life, all like I was right there. Books became movies in which I had complete control – every scene, every actress and actor, down to every detail. Whatever the author wrote, I envisioned in IMAX splendor, just how I wanted it to be.

Even with that strangeness, though, science seemed to have answers. I later learned that odd things happened to lots of people after traumatic brain injuries. I read about a guy named Derek Amato who, after diving headfirst in a shallow pool, resulting in a concussion, suddenly found an inexplicable urge and talent for playing the piano. Another man named Alonzo Clemens suffered a childhood injury which left him mentally disabled but awoke with an extraordinary ability to sculpt animals. He since became a quite famous sculptor.

And then there was Kim Peek. Don't let the name fool you. He was a guy. He was born without the corpus callosum part of his brain which meant each hemisphere wasn't talking to the other, kind of like my condition only way worse. I still had my corpus callosum, it'd just received an unwanted haircut. Kim had no corpus. But guess what happened? Where the brain didn't have telephone lines so one side could talk to the other, it went tunneling instead for new routes. It was like his brain made this huge basement, which increased his memory capacity to extraordinary levels. And it sounds like something right out of science fiction when I read all the things he could do.

They called him the living Google. He memorized over twelve thousand books. And when I say memorized, I mean you could pick one of those books at random off of a shelf and ask him what was on page 234, paragraph five, and he'd tell it to you as though he were reading it straight from the book. You could tell him your birthday and he'd not only tell what day of the week it was on, but he'd also tell you what was in the newspapers that day.

I couldn't do any of those kinds of things, of course. But I seemed to occasionally know things I just didn't realize I knew until they popped in my head and the reading imagery was really pretty cool, so I just figured *hey, I lost some things over here, but gained some things over there.* It didn't seem all that crazy at first. I could at least rationalize it myself. But then things got weirder. The dreams started. That's when I started to realize something screwy was really going on. Like the odd thoughts popping in my head and the imagery conjured when reading the written word, my dreams suddenly were filled with vivid events that, simply put, did not belong to me. At first, I thought, *okay, my imagination is just super hyped up now for some reason. No biggie. Just go with it. It could be fun.* But then I dreamed about Eddie and something just sort of clicked that o*h . . . this is real. This actually happened.*

I had been reading in my room but taking occasional trips downstairs to the kitchen for snacks and tea when I noticed that for some reason, I kept swooping around this one particular part of the living room. But there was no reason for the swooping. We had a couch pushed back against the wall and a little coffee table, but where I kept subconsciously walking around, nothing was there. I must have done it a dozen time since we moved in before I even realized I was doing it. And when I realized it, I stopped and just kind of stared at the spot. *Where's my chair?* I thought. But then I thought, *wait, what? What chair? We don't have a chair here.* I shook my head and stared at the spot. The old oak floors definitely looked lighter here than other areas. I stepped into the spot and it felt just wrong. But why? "There's no chair here," I said aloud.

I didn't realize Pops had come in and was in the kitchen. He'd quietly watched me stop and ponder the empty place where a chair may or may not have once lived. But when I spoke aloud, he said "You okay there, Baby Ruth?" I looked up to see him with a slightly concerned expression on his face.

"Umm, what do you think about maybe putting a chair here," I suggested.

"In the middle of the living room?" he asked.

"Well, I'm just looking at the floor here and it seems like there may have been a chair here once or something."

Pops shoulder-rolled me. "Well, sure, if you want a chair there, we can put a chair there. Won't bother me."

"Nah," I said, waiving my hand dismissively, "just a thought. We'll see."

"Okay," said Pops, still eyeballing me as he sipped his own tea.

That whole thing had seemed odd enough, but that night, I had a dream I was an old man sitting a disgusting old chair right in that same spot with an ashtray full of burnt cigarettes on a lamp stand. I felt like the old man. I had a cigarette hanging out of my mouth and was deep into a biography about Ronald Reagan. Reagan used to smoke a pipe and switched to eating jelly beans to try to quit. His favorite flavor was licorice. "I ain't eating no jelly beans," I said, taking a drag on my cigarette. I knew I should quit smoking but screw it. I was too old to care anymore. And I didn't even like jelly beans.

Except I do like jelly beans. It was Eddie who didn't. That was when I also realized all this new odd history stuff I was remembering at odd moments weren't my thoughts at all, they were his. I think the quirky guy lived so long in this house and was so obsessed with the subject, it's like some kind of stain on the house that has managed to soak into my psyche. It's just like the brown stains on the walls from his cigarettes. Before we cleaned and painted the walls, there were these little squares around the house from where pictures were removed, evidencing those places the smoke didn't get to. It's like that with some of Eddie's old thoughts and memories. He's gone, but they're still here. And if you think that's weird, I haven't even told you all about Lilith and the flowers.

Chapter 5

The Dead Woman in the Garden

Weeks became months. I had many dreams, but there was one that kept happening more and more often. Well, it wasn't really the same dream, but rather the same person showing up in a series of dreams, like watching someone through glimpses in time. And it wasn't Eddie. Eddie's memories showed up now and then, but not so much him. Although, I did have a rather unsightly dream about him sitting in the bath tub wearing nothing but an old ballcap and still smoking away with a book in the other hand. It has nearly ruined bath time for me. Thank God he liked bubble baths, apparently. I wouldn't have thought it, but I'm so glad there were bubbles. I've seen more than enough of Eddie in my dreams, thank you very much.

Eddie's leftovers, as it were, mainly consisted of just the odd facts he read about, and I guess took particular note of. He even kept a notebook of them, but that was probably in a nightstand which ended up donated to Goodwill or something, because except for the things in the attic, all his old stuff was gone by the time we moved in.

Apparently, he never watched television. He just read. But he read with purpose. And his purpose was to find those dispersed odd facts to string them together into even odder conspiracy theories. He was really kind of brilliant and crazy at the same time, I think. And what really kind of scared me a little was that I was starting to find myself agreeing with him on occasion.

Einstein once said coincidence was God's way of remaining anonymous. I always liked that quote and I hoped he was right. I think Eddie's interest in the Presidents was definitely over the top and he undoubtedly held some weird theories about them. But some things I have to say he might not have been entirely off about. At minimum, I guess I could understand how someone who was kind of off the beaten path like Eddie was could look at the history of Presidents in a sort of beautiful mind style and come out thinking there were just too many strange coincidences for it all to be entirely random. The more I gathered from his old memories the more I looked up, both in the books and online.

Take JFK and Lincoln, for example, both great men who moved civil rights forward by leaps and bounds. They were elected to Congress one hundred years apart, 1846 and 1946. They were then elected as President one hundred years apart, 1860 and 1960. Both were succeeded by Presidents named Johnson, who were born one hundred years apart - Andrew Johnson in 1808 and Lyndon Johnson in 1908. Their assassins were also born 100 years apart, 1839 and 1939. They were both shot on a Friday and both were sitting next to their wife when shot. In fact, on the day Lincoln was assassinated, he told members of his cabinet that he had a dream in which he was sailing across an unknown body of water at great speed, something he said he had dreamed before just prior to major events unfolding in the war. And if that wasn't eerie enough . . . on the day he was assassinated, he had signed into effect the bill that created the secret service.

It's not mind-altering stuff, mind you, but it's still food for thought. Is that really all just coincidence? I guess so. Eddie, on the other hand, thought it was all some kind of plan slowly working its way through time. I never did understand from the dreams exactly who he thought was behind the plan, though. God? Aliens? Fate in general? Nothing would have surprised me with Eddie. I gather he was kind of anti-social and like Mr. Baker had said, most folks found him an odd bird. But if I wasn't adhering to *The Rule* and decided to blab to everyone about all the weird crap I had seen in my dreams and heard in my head sometimes, they'd think I was nuts, too. I'd probably be labeled schizophrenic or something.

But as I said, it wasn't Eddie I started having dreams about. I kept seeing a young woman named Lilith. After I finally gleamed her name in a dream I went walking through the graveyard and found her tombstone. It was the first tombstone ever put out there, although it's no longer in its original spot. It now rests on the edge of the cemetery that is closest to the house. But once upon a time, it was in the garden. Because that's where she was buried.

She was buried there over a hundred years ago, but one day, as I was sitting at the little table outside in the garden sipping on my glass of tea, I saw this odd shimmer and, without even thinking about it, I suddenly knew Lilith was there. I just knew it. The realization hit me the same way Eddie's thoughts had, like having some old song lyric on the tip of your tongue for months, not fully remembered, and then wham! Suddenly you remember it and you wonder how you ever forgot it in the first place.

I saw that shimmer and all of a sudden it just clicked . . . that woman lived here and she's buried right there, under those flowers. At least, this was what my screwed-up head was trying to convince my logical self, who of course countered with *getting shot has turned me into a crazy person. Shut up, Ruth. Just pretend you don't see it and finish up your tea.*

But that little voice in my head wouldn't shut up. And what's more, once I hit upon that conclusion, the dreams got a lot stronger. It was like gaining that fact opened windows and doors to who she was and how she got there. In some ways, I felt like a time traveler because I started having all these strange glimpses of the past. And I mean the way past. They were weeks, sometimes even months removed, but when I had those dreams, I knew they were very different than any other normal dreams I'd been used to having before *The Incident.*

I was salvaging old memories from the deep, left there by some other ship that had passed and left long ago. And it was a history that was as much about the town as it was the woman and the farmhouse. It was years before I really understood it all, but over time it all coalesced and I just knew. The story came together, and I understood the history of our little small town like probably no one else. And it was a story not without its own share of odd coincidences.

A little over a century ago the good people of Foxglove, Texas unwittingly named the town after a murderer, albeit a rather unconventional one. A lot of people in town, particularly the older ones who are interested in history, think they know the story of the town's origins, but they're missing one or two dirty little secrets.

I could have told them the rest, but besides the tricky task of explaining how I came by such information, which was the constant Catch-22 of *The Incident,* I didn't think they would really want to know. Their story was so much nicer than mine. I doubted they would have thanked me for ruining it.

But sometimes when I was out in the garden reading or watching the sunset, I looked at the flowers and just kind of chuckled to myself. Those sneaky, tricky flowers. If only everyone knew what they did. The farmer tried to tell them there at the end, but nobody knew what his last words really meant.

I knew, though. And so did the flowers. They didn't do it on purpose, mind you. It's like the story of the scorpion and frog crossing the river. The flowers were just being what they were. In fact, I don't think there was any sort of consciousness about them until Lilith was buried with them. And where the line of her leftovers ends and the garden begins, I couldn't venture to guess. It's part them and part her, I think. Or some mix of the two. Who knows if her own conscious mind is still working in some way, but my theory is no and that instead, something else has sort of evolved out there. Maybe the garden took the leftover memories and, like nutrients from the soil, soaked it all up and somehow kind of woke up. Hell, I have no idea. The whole thing is beyond strange.

Eddie had said the flowers had gotten mad at him when he mowed them over. And he was absolutely right. They didn't like that at all. This is their place, now. The rest of us are just passing through. I suppose if you took a bulldozer to the place you might actually get rid of them once and for all, but I sure wouldn't try it.

It all started back in 1884 when Lilith Greenley and her farmer husband purchased and settled upon land where the town now sits. The town's beginning came on the heels of Lilith's ending. They were settlers, young and adventurous with a desire to find and tame the wild lands.

There were a lot of folks like them around these parts back then and they purchased and settled on a hundred acres of land and began the arduous task of clearing the brush for crops. This was roughly fifty years after the Texas Declaration of Independence. Santa Anna signed the Treaties of Velasco with the Republic of Texas on May 14, 1836. The first Texas Congress met in October 1836 and during the very first session Stephen F. Austin died. All that work for independence, and then when he finally gets it, he up and dies first session. Bummer, right?

Anyway, skip ahead a couple decades to the civil war. Emancipation resulted in huge discounts of land as plantations folded with no more free labor. Plantations got divided into farms and uncultivated land got a whole lot cheaper. As conditions worsened, a lot of people moved to Mexico. I always found that part a little ironic.

Now we're up to 1884 and here comes Lilith and her hubby out trying to make their hundred acres into a life. It was during the clearing that Lilith first spied the beautiful flowers which grew wild on the land. She'd not seen the like before, what with some standing taller than she with beautiful blossoms that cascaded down like a flowery waterfall. Enamored with the flowers, she saved them when they came upon them by digging them up and transplanting them back to the new farmhouse they'd built, into her new flower garden.

Lilith found there were a few different types of the flowers growing in the area and gathered them up for the house. By the front steps she grew purple Foxgloves, their beautiful bell-shaped blossoms with red and white speckled spots inside the bell. Down in the garden she had Grecians with blossoms like seashells, white on the outside and yellow-patterned markings inside. All about the farm the flowers grew and blossomed in magnificent colors. Lilith eventually made a little sign post out by the wagon trail to their home which read *Foxglove Farm*, and so it became known to any visitors and passersby. They grew strong and tall, her flowers. How she loved them. How little she suspected.

As time went on, she began to fall ill. She felt light-headed and began seeing blurry images of strange colors. She thought it was the heat, the endless work, and the wilds of the land itself.

But then she began to have trouble keeping her meals down and lost weight. After a few years she was down to just a stick of a body but persevered. Her fingertips often felt numb and her legs were heavy. The colors around her seemed more ablaze than ever she remembered, particularly the flowers. How so very pretty they seemed in those last few months.

Then came the days when she felt she couldn't even leave the bed. But her husband, the farmer, seeing her weak and distressed, would remind her how the fresh air could work wonders and how if she didn't at least tend the garden the weeds would soon take over. So, she would muster the strength and see to the flowers she adored so much, right up until the day they finally killed her.

Lilith didn't know Foxgloves were poisonous. Just a single blossom or even a leaf can be fatal. But with Lilith it was a slow and steady death, the prolonged exposure to her skin day after day that did her in. She was constantly weeding and pruning the flowers. She often picked several of them and made pretty arrangements on the kitchen table which sat so colorful and cheery as she cooked and ate the family meals.

It would have taken years for the poison to kill someone in such a way. Little by little, day by day, the poison soaked in through her fingertips and palms, perhaps just the slightest of doses here and there in the garden, a bit more when she licked her fingers over the stove and at the dinner table. Lilith killed herself one loving caress at a time.

Her husband buried her in the garden. Normally it wouldn't be so close to the house but of course he had only thoughts of how much she'd loved her flowers when he did so. It wasn't until many years later that he learned the awful truth of it.

Now a known widower in the small community that had emerged around him, he hosted a picnic for the church gathering some years later. He never remarried. He'd taken up the tending of the flower garden, but he didn't run his hands through the blossoms like his wife had, for it was for her memory he kept the flowers not for love of the flowers themselves. He rarely touched them, usually just keeping the weeds at bay. It didn't require much effort on his part as the flowers seemed to be self-sufficient. They had found Lilith's body agreeable sustenance.

But that day as the farmer sat smoking his pipe, now a gray-haired old man with no grandchildren of his own and thus left to watch other people's children and grandchildren run and play around the farm, he was surprised by a woman's voice calling out to the children in alarm, "You girls stay away from them flowers," she scolded, "they're poisonous!"

"Poisonous?" he asked, a bit incredulous.

"Oh, yes, sir. Those Foxgloves are right pretty, but they're poisonous. Didn't you know? We called them Dead Man's Bells growing up. Others call 'em Witch's Gloves. We lose a bit of livestock round these parts to poisoning. Folks with cattle got to watch the fields and pull them flowers up whenever they pop up or they'll lose some, especially the calves. Bigger ones learn not to mess with them or just usually get sick if they accidentally eat some, but even some of them will keel over and die if they get to munching on a good mouthful."

The color drained from the farmer, his thoughts slowly churning back to the years past of his wife growing sicker and sicker before his eyes. "Get out in the garden and get some fresh air," he had told her. It all came back to him that day after that woman told him the truth about those pretty little blossoms. He felt sick. His wife had always been petite . . . not a very large woman at all and even less so as she fell ill. And, like a calf, her lack of body mass meant the toxin had that much more effect on her.

A few days later in a fit of rage he got rid of them. He pulled and tugged them up, every last one, and burned them in a pile. Then he spat upon the ashes.

But a few weeks later, they were growing again. Now the farmer thought that strange, but he would have really been puzzled if he knew foxgloves were biennial. They usually only bloomed from around June to September, but not out at Foxglove farm. As soon as the freezing spells ended, those flowers would start opening up as early as March and go right along to November. It was never natural the way they were constantly in bloom in that garden after Lilith died. Nor the way they grew back so quickly even after the farmer had yanked them out of the ground.

He pulled those, too. Burned them again. But a few months later, they were back. He tilled the ground, trying to get up all the roots, but they were deep and threaded like a tough spider web. They grew back. He tried poisoning them, but that didn't work, either. He even got so sick of them he salted them, but not even that stopped them. No matter what he did over the next year, eventually they just kept coming back.

They began to drive him insane. "Murderers," he whispered. "You killed her." He imagined he thought he saw some of the flowers turn, then. Like they were looking at him, snakes all covered in leaves and pretty petals.

He thought they were mocking him. It was the devil mocking him, he became convinced, for killing his young bride through his ignorance. The devil must have cursed the flowers to stay alive to torture him, or so he came to believe. He grew fearful of the flowers. He no longer pulled them up and burned them. He wouldn't even go out of the back door in those last couple of years. But the old walking path his young bride had made out the back door remained, even when nobody walked upon it. It was as though the garden held an open invitation via the walkway for the farmer or whomever else might come along to bask in the surrounding beauty of the flowers.

As time passed and more people came to live in the area, they became their own municipality and needed an official town name. And when someone who thought they were doing a kindness to the old farmer reminded everyone that it all began with the farmer and his wife and their Foxglove Farm, so shouldn't they call the town Foxglove? The old farmer didn't say a word. People thought he kept the flowers going in honor of his wife. Little did they know how he hated them, how they taunted him each and every day by persisting in their existence. And the truth remained a secret right up past the day the farmer lay on his death bed crying to the preacher, "I didn't know. God forgive me, I didn't know."

"What is it? What is it you didn't know?" asked the preacher.

The farmer's last words on this earth were, "It was the flowers . . . the flowers."

After the farmer died the new owners of Foxglove Farm figured it wouldn't hurt too much to just move the headstone a couple hundred yards out towards the pasture. They weren't moving the body, after all. They even partitioned off a little section of land out there just for the tombstone. And soon more headstones were in the pasture as people began paying a bit to put their loved ones to rest out at Foxglove Farm, where the pretty flowers grew.

Over the years, most people didn't pay much attention to the flowers out at the cemetery and their importance to the town's origins. But there they remained up until the day we moved into the little house.

Chapter 6

Gift of the Garden

After *The Incident,* the doctors had projected at least a year before I'd be back in school but I was able to return after six months. Things weren't quite the same, though. Friends at school seemed to drift away, except for Deja and Lexi. I didn't know it if was *The Incident* or maybe just the way I came out of it. I concede I was a different person afterwards in more ways than one. Losing Mom was hard. Trivial things and teenage angst and drama were more or less lost on me. Not to mention my interests were now out of whack with everyone else's.

I liked reading about other people's life goals, especially unusual ones like Ernest Vincent Wright, a little-known author who self-published a 50,110 word novel entitled Gadsby which omitted the letter "e" throughout.

"Why would anybody write a book without using the letter 'e'?" asked Julie Schmidt when I brought it up in English class one day. "I mean, that's just stupid."

"No, it's brilliant!" I objected. "Think of how hard that must have been. He literally had to tie down the e-bar on his typewriter to keep from accidentally using it. I'd have a hard time writing just a single cohesive sentence without the letter 'e'. Can you imagine writing an entire book that way? It's genius."

"What's genius about it? It just seems stupid to me."

"Well, I wouldn't say stupid," added Lexi, trying to come to my defense. "Maybe just a little bit odd."

There was no convincing them of why such a feat was not only interesting but relevant and worthy of acclaim, an admirable goal to pursue let alone achieve. It didn't matter that there was no great end game to it. The goal was to see if he could do it and he did it. I loved that. What better reason was there?

I suppose I didn't blame my old friends. Besides my odd fascinations which no longer ran parallel to theirs, I was an instant mood killer for the longest time because whenever I walked into a room everyone would clam up. People didn't know how to act around me. And for the first few months back everybody talked to me like I was five again. "Hi, Ruthie," they'd say real slow, "How are you feeling?"

"I'm fine, thanks," I'd say, brushing my fingers through my hair. I had a new hairstyle with bangs I used to hide the scar on my forehead, which made me a little self-conscious. I found myself constantly fiddling with it like it was my safety blanket.

The teachers were the worst. They would stop by my desk and whisper things like, "Now, if you don't feel up to tonight's homework assignment you don't have to do it. Just do however much you feel comfortable with, okay?" It was the doctors all over again. Everyone was convinced I was an idiot or handicapped or something. Granted, I walked with a limp and my hand looked like a claw, but I wasn't an imbecile.

There were a lot of tears in that first year and I spent quite a bit of time in the garden where the world seemed a little slower and more relaxed. That was how I started to notice the strange things happening out there. The pretty red cardinal I had seen on that first day came to our house often and would occasionally flutter down to snatch up a beetle or a caterpillar. I named it Ruby. Ruby didn't like it when I was sitting in the garden because it obviously was skittish of me, but eventually she (I just decided she must have been a she) got comfortable enough that she would still quickly flitter down and then back away.

As I would sit outside and watch Ruby grab her snacks, I noticed something peculiar. Whenever a leaf eating insect or caterpillar made the unfortunate decision of climbing on to one of the foxglove plants, it seemed to momentarily disappear . . . then drop dead. Ruby seemed to know this. She would watch from the roof, almost like a vulture waiting for its dinner to die. The moment the bug would fall to the ground, she would flutter down, snatch it up, and either fly away or return back to the roof to wait for her next free meal.

At first, I thought I must be seeing things. Maybe they were freezing when they saw Ruby and it only looked like they were dead. But why would they fall to the ground? One day, a fat green caterpillar started crawling up one of the plants while I was outside.

"Oh, here we go," I said with delight, and I crept over and watched it carefully. As it crawled over one particular leaf, the leaf began to close like a taco. I'd seen plants do this before. We have mimosa pudica all over the place and I remembered as a little girl my friends and I in second grade would go out at recess and poke them with our fingers and watch then snap shut, which was always immensely fun and satisfying. But . . . foxglove? I didn't think it was supposed to do that. Not that I was any kind of expert on plants, mind you.

I watched as the caterpillar pushed and wriggled trying to free itself, but the leaf acted as though it were a muscle or a python, and literally squeezed the larval thing to death. Then the leaf seemed to relax and open up, and the caterpillar fell to the ground.

"Cool," I whispered in fascination.

Overhead, I could hear the disgruntled chirps of Ruby. *Get out of the way!* She seemed to be chirping in offense. I poked the caterpillar with my finger. It writhed a little, but it seemed more of a nerve reaction. The thing was indeed dead. Ruby, apparently ticked off I'd dare touch her snack, flew off in a huff.

The more time I spent in the garden, the more dreams of Lilith I had. After realizing she was in the garden, I oddly spent more time out there. One would think my natural inclination would be to be freaked out and stay away as the farmer had done, but it was just the opposite. I felt closer to both her and the garden than I did a lot of people. It was an alien relationship, which also made it all the more interesting. There was no flow of communication at first other than I felt it knew when I was there and I could feel something like it having its own presence, like standing in a room with someone who speaks another language. You can't talk to each other, but you are both aware of each other. When I was lonely, it was somewhat comforting. From that first moment I had stepped into it and felt that serene calmness, I knew this was a place I could go and just be myself. As long as I didn't do anything to threaten it, the garden was okay with me, even welcoming. I suppose in some way it held the opinion that what was the point of being comprised of beautiful flowers if there was nobody around to see them.

I spent many sad moments out there, glad to feel accepted somewhere since I felt like an outcast most everywhere else. Plus, its unique nature made me feel less of a freak. Here was a place where the standard rules of nature seemed to be perpetually bent if not outright broken. It was weird. I was weird. Maybe that's why we seemed to get along just fine. That's when we started having our chats, for lack of a better word. Which eventually led to the *Gift*, as I sometimes think of it.

The *Gift* occurred my sophomore year after a particularly rough day at school. I happened to be using the bathroom when a group of girls came in giggling and cackling. I'd known them all my life, of course . . . Miranda Bennett, Emily Tolliver, and Amy Choi. In middle school I'd even been pretty good friends with Emily. But she'd joined this little clique in ninth grade, and they'd been inseparable since.

She was more the omega of the group, I suppose . . . the last in line to the hierarchy. But Emily seemed content just to be part of the group. She was a pretty girl with strawberry blond hair that, like the rest of her, was just a bit too thin. She looked frail in a way. She reminded me of Lilith, actually. I remember the boys teased her when we were younger and called her chicken legs because she'd been too skinny. But she'd grown out a bit since then. During our freshman year, she had still been friendly with me as long as the other two weren't around. But that seemed to wane going into sophomore year. And when they were all together, she latched on to whatever the other two were saying and doing. If they were being snooty or just downright bullying other people, she'd join right on in. It was pretty disappointing.

The evolution of Emily from a nice girl I used to like a lot to a cliché mean girl was a perfect analogy for one of the major downsides to high school, I thought. Everybody was jockeying for some place in the social hierarchy and too many people became willing to throw other people's feelings right under the bus to gain a rung. This particular day became a prime example. The first voice I heard belonged to Amy. She was of Korean descent but born and raised in Foxglove just like myself. Her dad was a dentist and her mom worked at the pharmacy at Walgreens in a town about an hour away. They divorced our eighth-grade year and that's when Amy went from a shy, quiet girl to a party monster. She had a younger brother, Kai, who was just as shy and quiet as Amy used to be.

Next was Miranda, who seemed to lead the other two around. I never really liked Miranda, but I had to admit she was she was not only pretty, but really intelligent. But she also knew it and just wasn't very nice about it. She liked to cut people to the quick and had the brains to do it, which seemed a poor use of such talents from where I was standing. The only girl I knew who probably had a sharper tongue and mind to accompany it was Deja. And the only way you could get Miranda to like you was to perpetually kiss her ass, which I wasn't willing to do. Hence, she regulated me to the unworthy pile back in middle school.

They were on the tail end of whatever they'd been talking about when they entered the bathroom. Without going into the sordid details, it involved Amy discussing a make out session she'd had over the weekend with a popular boy in school. There were references to his over-eager disposition, with Miranda adding "He'd hook up with anyone, I think, even Quasimodo." It didn't dawn on me at first who they were talking about when they mentioned Quasimodo, until Emily laughingly replied, "Oh, come on. It's not her fault she walks like that. I mean seriously, she did get shot in the head."

Oh. Yeah, that stung. Until that moment, I had no idea some of the other kids in school had been calling me Quasimodo behind my back.

I was tempted to hide in the stall until they left, maybe cry softly to myself. But then I thought*, no. Screw it.* I flushed the toilet and stepped out of the stall.

I don't think anybody actually said, "Oh, crap", but the expression on each of their faces said it for them. Emily looked even more pale than usual. I didn't bother looking at them while I washed my hands, claw and all. I did say something, though. I'm not sure why except that the silence was just too damn awkward. "You ever read that book, The Hunchback of Notre Dame?" I asked. Being rhetorical, I continued, "Quasimodo was a good man treated horribly by others for no other reason than he was born deformed," I said quietly. Then I held up my clenched hand. "I can't control this. And what happened to me was not my fault." I felt like crying. I really did. But I refused. *Not on my watch!* Defiantly yelled that little voice in my head. *We're not going down like that!*

Emily spoke. "Ruth, we didn't mean anything . . ."

I cut her off. "Yes, you did," I told her. I didn't scream or yell, but I forced my voice not to quiver or crack. "You did, Emily. You may feel a little bad I overheard you, but it doesn't change the fact that you said it and have probably been saying a lot worse for a long time." Amy rolled her eyes. I looked at each one of them. "You're making fun of me because of injuries I survived after an evil asshole murdered my mom in front of me and then tried to murder me." Then I stared back at Emily. "In what world do you live where you think that's okay?"

"We didn't know you were in the bathroom, okay," said Amy.

"Yeah, no shit," I responded. "That's why it's called talking behind people's back."

"Well, maybe you shouldn't eavesdrop on other people's conversations," said Amy. I couldn't believe she had the gall to say it, but I guess I shouldn't have been too surprised. But what really got me was when I looked at Emily, instead of correcting Amy or trying to apologize for her, she instead said, "I mean, that's kind of true."

I was flabbergasted. I just looked at her. Where had the Emily Tolliver I had known throughout elementary and middle school gone? Who was this person? "Wow. Just . . . wow. You're becoming a real bitch, Emily." I looked at the other two, then back at her. "I guess you finally fit in with your new friends."

Miranda just stared at me as though she found the entire exchange amusing, which was infuriating. Amy just snickered. Emily at least had the decency to look chastened. I think she might have even been trying to decide if she was going to apologize after all, but I was about as eager to hear it as she was to mutter it in front of her two little friends, so I spared us both the embarrassment by drying off my hands and leaving.

"Whoopsie," I heard Amy say as the door closed to the sound of her muffled laughter.

It really didn't bother me all that much Miranda and Amy were acting like that. I kind of expected them to act that way. But knowing Emily was in on it genuinely hurt my feelings. I won't lie and say I was holding my head high, but I was holding it at least level. I told them what I had to say. They could do with it what they will. And for the rest of the day, that was good enough for me. But that night, after Pops went to bed, I went down to the garden and sobbed like a baby. And I mean I sobbed. Hearing that everyone was probably calling me Quasimodo hurt. And hearing someone like Emily, who used to be my friend, say it was like having the knife twisted.

As I sat there bawling my eyes out, I felt a wave of . . . something. I didn't know what it was. Calm, I guess? Comfort. Yeah, that's probably a better description. I started to feel better, just content and suddenly filled with the thought that everything was all right in the world. The garden had that effect on me sometimes, but this time it was more. It was like a heavy dose of something being pumped through my veins.

I looked around at the beautiful flowers under the moonlight and they seemed to be swaying ever so gracefully. *It's so pretty,* I thought. For a brief moment I wanted to be one with the garden. I wanted to lie down and go to sleep and never wake up again. But no . . . I didn't want that. That was death.

Death is peaceful.

What was that? It did seem peaceful in that moment. *No, quit with the negativity, Ruth,* I tried to tell myself. I was sad, true, but I certainly didn't want to die. *Do I? No. Of course not.* Then I thought, maybe I'm just tired. Wanting to sleep is certainly not the same thing as wanting to die.

You can sleep here. Sleep in the dirt with us. It's peaceful here. There is no better sleep than here. You can rest while we'll watch over you.

I shook my head. *Huh? What?* These weren't my thoughts. These weren't Eddie's thoughts, either. But then whose were they? Something wasn't right. That wasn't me. What was happening? Nobody said it, but I felt it. Something was happening . . . an invitation was being extended to join the garden. And yes, I was sure I didn't want it. The garden was a beautiful place. It was my friend, strange as that may be, but I didn't want to just lay down and die and become fertilizer. Was the garden trying to convince me to kill myself? *Does it want me to die like Lilith so it can eat me or something?*

Uh, oh. I suddenly had the sense I may have offended, like the flowers knew what I was thinking. They seemed to be standing taller against the backdrop of the moon and there was an eerie pause in the night. The silhouette of the flower petals suddenly looked less like hundreds of flowers and more like eyes all staring at me.

I wasn't sure what to do. Should I say something? I just wasn't ready to die. I mean come on . . . I was upset, but not suicidal. Suicide is giving up, giving in to momentary despair when you can't imagine a better day will come. But I knew they were out there, somewhere, those better days. Even if I couldn't see them. That's the trick true depression can play on people . . . hide the better days from view so people can't see them, can't even imagine they're still there. But I knew they were out there. This, too, would pass.

All rest in the end.

I'm not at the end, my little voice replied. *It's not my time. I want to do things, see things.*

You tell 'em, little voice.

There was an eerie quiet. No rustling of leaves on a breeze. No sounds of cicadas in the trees. Just dead quiet.

Come and see came a thought after a few moments.

I still felt like I was in a daze when I saw that familiar shimmer appear over Lilith's final resting place. One of the short foxgloves there seemed to be enveloped by it. I walked, as if sleepwalking, over to it and looked down to see a new blossom blooming on the stalk. It looked different. This one was enormous, white with red splotches. And as I stared in wonderment, within the typically empty pouch of such a flower, I saw something round and white, like a quail's egg or a giant pearl. I leaned over, lost in a dream. I reached out with my good hand, but the flower seemed to pull back and close up on itself.

I withdrew and then tentatively tried my other bad hand, and the flower seemed to lean forward and open. In I reached.

Hello, pretty flower . . . you're a big fella.

Slowly, the flower closed around my hand. And inside, I felt the pearl-like egg melt like jam, leaving what felt like a spike in the middle. I was feeling almost intoxicated by the wave of calm in the garden, but suddenly I was jolted as the spike lanced my hand.

"Ow!" My senses coming back to me, I tried to pull my hand away, but with almost a whip-like slap, the bloom clamped down around my hand. And I felt something being injected into my hand, like getting a flu shot at the doctor. I could actually feel some kind of liquid or gel getting pumped right into my vein like a drug.

I pulled away hard, but much to my surprise the flower didn't pull apart. Instead, it pulled even harder and snapped back towards the ground, yanking me down to my knees. For a second, I seriously thought it was trying to drag me down into Lilith's grave. I thought it was trying to kill me. *It does want me dead. It's going to eat me like it ate Lilith!*

I was about to scream bloody murder when I felt it release its grip. I pulled again and rolled on my rear as my hand was pretty much belched up by the flower. Then the new bloom died, wilting dramatically and quickly as it withered away and fell to the ground.

I was breathing heavily by this point and that sense of calm I'd felt before washed over me again like a huge wave. It then became exhaustion. I was suddenly so sleepy. I had already been tired but now I could hardly keep my eyes open. I stared at my hand and it had a puncture mark on the top right by my vein that was throbbing in pain.

"What the hell?" I said, as much to the garden as to myself. I was going to get up and go back in the house to wash my hand and check it out, maybe even get Pops up in case I'd been poisoned or something, but none of that happened. "What'd you do that for?" I managed to croak as I conked over. "I thought we were friends." The last thing I remembered was one particular stalk of flowers looming over me as I fell asleep.

Chapter 7

Sleeping with the Flowers

"Ruth . . . Ruth!"

I woke up to the sound of Pops yelling my name and shaking me vigorously. "I'm up, I'm up," I said. "Alexa, stop." For a minute I imagined I was in my bed but late for school. My Alexa alarm must have been going off and I slept through it. Now Pops was shaking me awake.

"Alexa? Ruth, wake up!" he said forcefully. "What in the world are you doing out here?"

I opened my eyes and saw my surroundings. *Oh, crap.* It was morning and I was sprawled out in the garden. "Ummm . . .," I started to explain, "I guess I fell asleep."

Pops was staring at me, concerned. "Fell asleep . . . outside?"

"Yeah, I guess so. I came out here last night for some fresh air and I guess I just sort of fell asleep."

"Ruth, that's not normal. What were you doing out here?"

"Nothing." He didn't look like he was buying it. "Seriously Pops, I wasn't doing anything."

"Were you smoking some weed or something? You know you can tell me. It's me. I'm not going to freak out on you or anything. Did you take something? Do I need to get you to the hospital?"

I nearly laughed except my body was aching so much. "No! I woke up late last night and just came out here to watch the stars. I just fell asleep is all. I wasn't smoking weed or doing anything else like that, I swear." But I was staring at the flowers around me like they were a hundred little snakes. *You sneaky little bastards,* I thought to myself. *What did you do to me?*

He helped me stand up. "Are you sure you're okay? Did you get ant bit or anything?" he asked, turning me around and looking me over. "Oh, shoot, Ruth, look at your hand!" My bad hand was indeed not looking too great. Where the spike had got me it was bruised, swollen, and quite purplish. "Something got ya. Come on, let's get some medicine on that. Let's hope to hell that ain't a brown recluse or black widow spider bite what got you. Damn, Ruth, there could be snakes out here, too. Are you trying to give your old man a heart attack or something? You know we got copperheads around here."

I had to reassure Pops repeatedly I didn't need to go to the doctor. "I'm fine, Pops, I swear. I feel great." And actually, I did. I felt relaxed . . . like too many Vicodins kind of relaxed. And as Pops was washing my hand and prying my fingers open to check out my palm, the fingers, which normally clamped right up again, actually stayed open a bit. Pops didn't seem to notice, but I did.

"You have to take care of yourself, Ruth," he told me as he worked. And then he gave me a big, burly hug. "I can't lose you. You're all I got in this world. You have to take care of yourself."

I felt real guilty, then. "I know, Pops. I'm sorry. But I'm fine, I really am." After assuring him a few more times I was okay and that I would tell him if my hand started hurting or got worse, I went to my room and sat on my bed, examining it further. It looked bad, but I still felt pretty good. I tried moving my fingers, which hadn't worked well at all since *The Incident,* and to my shock they stiffly moved a little. *Whoa.* I did it again, and again they flexed ever so slightly, then went back like they were being held in place by lots of rubber bands. But rubber bands were a lot better than the metal vice sensation I usually had.

Stretching them even a little may not seem like much, but to me it was a big deal. I hadn't had hardly any control of my fingers on this hand for over a year at this point, so I was pretty stoked. I couldn't remember the last time I'd been able to make them move the way they were.

I stuck a Band-Aid on the puncture mark and went to school, but throughout the day I kept trying to move my fingers. They didn't improve much. But over the next few days the bruising and swelling went away and each day it felt like my hand was just a slight bit more flexible than it had been the day before. It was almost like the invisible rubber bands were getting stretched out and had less resistance.

But I noticed something else, too. After about two weeks, just as the hand looked pretty much healed up, some little whitish ringlets started appearing on the inside palm of the hand. I had to hold my fingers out of the way to get a closer look, but darned if they didn't look a lot like the little white circle things inside of a foxglove blossom. *What is that?* I pondered.

They didn't hurt or anything when I touched them, but they looked like something that had swam up from beneath my skin. I wasn't quite sure what to make of it, but as long as my hand was working better, I didn't care. And there was something else I was noticing, too. As impossible as it seemed, my limp seemed to be getting better. I still wasn't walking normal, of course, but it was noticeably better.

Pops saw me stretching out my fingers at breakfast the next morning. "What's going on there?" he asked. "Your hand okay?"

"Yeah," I told him. "Actually, I think that spider bite or whatever may actually be helping. Maybe it did something to the nerves. I've been stretching my fingers practically non-stop. Check it out!" And I did a flex of my fingers for him.

"Hey, look at that! Wow, I haven't seen you do that since before."

"I know, right?" I told him. "And check this out!" I got up and walked around. I was still limping, but not quite as bad as before.

"Wow!" he said again, and his eyes lit up. "Hey, you're really looking better. I'm not just saying it. I can tell you're walking different. But how?"

I shrugged. "I don't know. Maybe the spider bite, you think?" I had heard of venom immunotherapy. Bee venom was sometimes used to treat Lyme disease and even Parkinson's disease, so it seemed a plausible enough explanation, at least to give to Pops. I knew it was the flowers, of course, but I couldn't exactly try to explain that to him. "I've also been doing yoga at night," I said. "I guess it's been helping." This was the truth. I'd been doing yoga for a long time, but never had results like the ones I was getting recently. "I've been doing it for a while, but I've been super motivated lately with my fingers moving and stuff. So, I've been really working. Maybe it's actually working?"

"Yoga?"

"Yeah, you know, stretching and what not. It's on YouTube. I just practice along with it."

"Well, I'll be damned," he said. "Whatever you're doing, keep it up. It's working. That's amazing, Baby Ruth!" And he got up and gave me a big ole bear hug. "Look at you, girl! I'm so proud of you! See, those doctors don't know everything. They want everyone to think they do, but they don't. Everything they said you wouldn't be able to do, you're already doing it and getting better every day. You just keep trying and doing and proving them wrong."

"I will, Pops," I said, "I will."

"Yoga," he said again. "I may have to try that stuff out myself. What do you think?" he asked, stepping back to display his dad bod in all its glory. "I could pull off some yoga pants, right?" He did a few poses and nearly fell over.

I laughed. "You'd look awesome, Pops. You should totally do it. Hot pink!"

"I was thinking camo," he said. "Do they make camo yoga pants?"

"I'm sure we can find you some."

Chapter 8

The Rule

Now you might be thinking "Ruth, this all sounds like a wonderful fairy tale. Yes, you lost your mother, but the garden healed you up and now all's right with the world forever and ever." Meh . . . not exactly. My deal is probably more like one of the old versions of fairy tales, before Disney put its bubbly, family oriented, animated spin on things. The original versions of many of our beloved fairy tales were often a little twisted.

In *The Little Mermaid*, for instance, Ariel wasn't just mute, she'd had her tongue cut out. Her human legs gave her nothing but pain with each step and her beloved prince married another woman, after which Ariel toyed with the idea of murdering him but instead committed suicide. If Sebastian, the Jamaican little crab that was her Jiminy Cricket, was in the original tale, I'm pretty sure someone would have eaten him with a nice butter sauce and a chianti, a la all Hannibal Lecter style.

In the Grimm Brothers' 1812 version of *Cinderella* the step-sisters are so desperate to fit their feet into the glass slipper that one sister hacks off her toe to fit in the shoe, the other her heel. The prince sees the blood in the shoe when each wears it in turn and knows they are false. And when he marries Cinderella two pretty little doves flutter down to her shoulders on their wedding day just like the cartoon, except in the original tale they then proceed to pluck out the eyes of the two sisters when they come near. I actually kind of wish they had left that part in the movie.

You can probably guess what really happened to Goldilocks. Think blond hair in a pile of bear scat. And don't even get me started about Sleeping Beauty who went to sleep a virgin but then woke up to find she'd birthed twins during her slumber. There's a word for that which starts with the letter "R", but it isn't romance. And what happened to the evil king who took advantage of her as she lay incapacitated? She married him anyway. After he murdered his wife so he could be with her, of course. Bleck. Are you kidding me? Keep your fairy tales to yourself, thank you very much. Don't hope for a fairy tale life. They're horrid.

No, what followed for me was more mundane. Okay, maybe mundane isn't exactly the right word. I got a lot better from where I was just after *The Incident*, but not all the way healed up like before *The Incident*. My hand worked better, but it was still hard for me to type and sometimes cramped up when I was trying to hold things with it, but it was worlds improved. I never appreciated the convenience of a good hand until I lost significant function of one.

The kids at school eventually (mostly) quit calling me Quasimodo. At least, so I'm told. I wouldn't really know if they still did it behind my back. But Deja and Lexi told me people quit calling me that finally.

No boyfriends, unfortunately. Nothing kills a social life quite like a bullet to the head. There was one guy I really liked sophomore year, Logan Wallis. He was funny and nice. I had talked with him a lot in science class and we seemed to have similar interests. He had long black, curly hair I thought was pretty. One Friday night when Deja talked me into going to a football game, he kissed me under the bleachers, and we sat together during the game. He even held my hand. That was probably where I screwed up. I was on his right, so when he snuck his hand over and grasped the ole claw, I let him.

Something kind of odd happened while he was holding my hand. My head went a little cloudy while we were watching the game and I got a bit of double vision. I saw the game normal through my eyes, but some odd backup image of it formed in my thoughts like a little movie . . . kind of like what happened when I was reading books. It was a bit disorienting.

After a minute or two, my hand also cramped up some, so I pulled it away. Once I did, the double vision also faded. Logan looked at me curiously. People were also looking at us kind of funny, too. I thought he was okay with it, though. He acted like he was. I gave him my phone number when we left that night and I remember thinking, *wow, it's nice to just feel like a normal teenage girl.* I had the typical thoughts . . . would he call? Would we go out on a date? What would I wear and where would we go? I was enjoying the unanswered questions of it all.

But he didn't call. And that Monday, he acted like nothing had happened. And he kind of avoided me afterward. I don't know for sure or anything, but I think the looks and probably some gossip got to him. His friends probably made fun of him about me or something. It was the only logical explanation I came up with. So, I just left it alone.

I kind of withdrew a bit after that. I didn't go to anymore football games or dances and I didn't go to the parties and stuff like that. I didn't like the looks and the whispers. And I could only imagine what people would say had they known about me hearing thoughts that weren't my own or dreaming about dead people. That's when I decided to make and strictly adhere to *The Rule*.

The Rule of the Dead is a simple one – don't talk about it. After much thought and consideration, I determined that to tell someone about all these odds things would likely end up with me seeing a whole bunch of doctors again, or therapists, or getting outright committed to a mental institution or something. Even I think it's pretty crazy. And then there are the occasional shimmers . . . if I started telling people about those I might really end up on a funny farm.

The Rule has been tested a few times since *The Incident* and it's been a constant struggle not to just blurt something out accidentally.

Hell, just last summer little Adam Lancaster was pulling on my heart strings, but I stayed the course. I still remember his sad little eyes when first I approached him in the cemetery. I'd seen him at his dad's funeral, of course, but I usually stayed back on those helping out with traffic and parking. But I remembered him. He came back a few times with his mom. Then he started riding his bike to come down on his own. So finally, I decided to go say hi to him.

I walked on over to him, still with a hint of a limp, but nothing like what I had back just after *The Incident*. He watched me coming over, probably trying to decide if he should hang around or not. When I finally got there, he opened with a direct "Who are you?"

"I'm the groundskeeper."

He was naturally skeptical, but I was wearing overalls which is kind of the universal get-up for a groundskeeper, so he wasn't so sure. "You don't look like a groundskeeper."

"Oh? And what do you suppose a groundskeeper is supposed to look like?"

He shoulder-rolled me. "I don't know. An old man, I guess. I ain't never seen a girl groundskeeper before."

"And you know a lot of groundskeepers, do you?"

He seemed stumped there. "No, I guess not."

"Well, there you go. Anyone can be a groundskeeper. Anyone can be anyone. It's one of the perks to being anyone."

He thought I was weird. I know this because he told me. "You're kind of weird."

"Kid, you have no idea. But okay, you got me. I'm just the assistant groundskeeper. My dad's the official one."

"I knew it," he said proudly. "You're too young."

"Says you."

He pointed to the gravestone in front of him. It read, James Allison Lancaster with accompanying dates of time here on earth . . . *Loved Husband and Father.* There was a bicycle propped up against it with a baseball glove hanging from one of the handlebars. "That's my dad," he said. "He was in a car accident."

"I know. I'm sorry that happened." People used to tell me *sorry you lost your mom* and I never really liked the way it sounded. I knew what they meant of course, but it always sounded clunky to me, like I had misplaced her somewhere.

"Did you know him?"

In a small town like Foxglove, I supposed all the kids assumed folks older than they were probably knew each other. "No, but I heard he was really nice." There was a big turnout for the funeral, I remembered. Mr. Baker, still going strong as the funeral director these three plus years after Mom's death, apparently knew him pretty well and shed a few tears. "Good guy, that Jim," he had said, wiping his eye quickly, "has a boy at home. Poor guy." And he had shuffled away quickly.

"Yeah, he was. I really miss him," he said. "He worked a lot, but he was a good dad. We used to go fishing and play catch on the weekends."

Ouch. Right in the feels. I tried not to let it show.

An awkward pause ensued so I had to act fast. "Who's Allison?" I asked him.

"What?"

I pointed to the headstone. "Allison . . . his middle name. He must have been named for someone. Do you know who?"

He laughed a little. "Oh, yeah. My great aunt, or something. I think she died a long time ago. I didn't know her. I don't think he liked having her name as his middle name, but I heard my Nana insisted. My mom says Nana pestered her and my dad the whole time she was pregnant with me to name me Allison if I was a girl, but out I come a boy, so they named me Adam. Dad told me once he was real happy about it because he wasn't sure he wanted to be saying that name Allison all the time. He never liked it." He was smiling so hard now, his face was turning red.

"I think it's a pretty name."

"Yeah, but not for a boy," he countered.

"Yeah, I guess you're right. Adam's a much better name for you, I think. Well, hi, Adam. I'm Ruth. It's nice to meet you."

He shook my good hand. "I'm not supposed to talk to strangers," he apparently suddenly remembered.

"Nope, you're sure not. That's why your mom sent me over here to test you. I'm afraid you failed. I think she's going to be pretty upset about it when I have to go back and tell her."

His smile faded away. "What?"

I let it linger for a moment before smiling. "Nah, I'm just messing with you, man," I told him with a laugh.

"Oh," he said, now smiling again.

"But you're right. You shouldn't be talking to strangers."

He seemed to size me up, "Well, I think I could take you if I had to."

"Oh, really?" I laughed.

"Yep. And I'm real fast. I could just run away. I don't think you could catch me," he added. And then I think he realized that he might have hurt my feelings with that one as his expression changed again to one of concern. "I mean . . . you know, because I'm so fast and all."

I just smiled. "I bet you're pretty quick. But can you throw?"

He eyed me curiously as I reached into a tool belt around my waist. In it I had a spade, some small clippers, a pair of work gloves, and a baseball I had put there that morning. It was Saturday. He must have played baseball on Saturdays and then rode down afterwards as he always seemed to have his glove and hat. I took out the baseball and took his glove off the handlebar, slipping it on my own hand. Thanks to the *The Gift,* I could now flex ole lefty enough to get the glove on. Squeezing to hold the ball might be iffy, but I figured I could manage given the glove was a pretty tight fit anyway.

"You have a baseball?" he asked.

"Yep, I do. So, what do you say?" I tossed the ball up and down in my hand.

We spent the next fifteen minutes or so tossing the ball before it was time for him to go. "Well, I must say you do have an excellent fast ball," I told him, flexing my hand which was genuinely a bit red from all the hard smacks of the ball.

"He taught me," he said, pointing to his dad's gravestone. "He played in high school. I'm going to play in high school, too, when I get there."

"I think you'll do great. You're already really good."

"Thanks. Well, I should probably go before my mom comes looking for me. Will you be here next week? I'll be back Saturday again." And he seemed to say this last part to both me and his father.

"Okay, but you don't have to, you know. Your dad can watch you from anywhere. That's one of the perks they get. And I think he'd rather see you out playing with your friends instead of hanging out here."

He smiled and got on his bike. "I like visiting him. It's like he's not really all the way gone, you know?"

That was a little ironic, I thought. "Okay. Well, I'll be here, too." And I watched him peddle away.

"He's pretty good," I told the shimmer. It was a barely there shimmer, the kind I sometimes wondered if it was really there at all. "I'm sorry y'all can't play together anymore, but I think he's doing okay. He'll be alright."

I don't know if he did or didn't understand me. Sometimes I can pick up faint emotions from shimmers, but this time it just faded away and I was left to wonder if it was really Mr. Lancaster or just a trick of my mind. But I'd come far enough along in believing in unbelievable things that I thought it probably was.

I dreamed about Mr. Lancaster the day we buried him. After Lilith, I started dreaming about other people. That's usually how it happens, if it happens. It's one of the reasons I don't get too close to the deceased people when we have services in the cemetery. Something about that final farewell seemed to amp up my sensitivity. If I got within fifty yards of a dead person then there was a good chance I'd have some dreams about them. Like Mr. Lancaster and how he died. He always took the same country road to and from work. In the dream, I thankfully wasn't him, as sometimes happens. Instead, I was in the passenger seat, just along for the ride, headed to work.

Mr. Lancaster was wearing his seatbelt and wasn't speeding. He had done everything right. It was early, but the sun was coming up, the day looking to have clear skies. Mr. Lancaster seemed like he was in good mood. He was listening to *God's Country* by Blake Shelton and singing along. He had a good voice. He was a bit of a country boy, with his boots on and *Texans* ball cap. He sipped his coffee and turned up the radio.

As we rounded a curve, another truck came from the opposite side. And just as the two vehicles were about to pass, an old Nissan Sentra shot out from behind the other truck. I heard his name was Dustin Fields. Dustin was nineteen, in a hurry to his new job. He apparently didn't want be late his first week. So, when the truck in front of him was going too slow, he gunned his car on the curve and tried to slingshot around it. And he and Mr. Lancaster both paid the ultimate price for that moment of recklessness. It all happened in a violent blink of crashing metal and screeching tires.

I wanted to tell Adam his dad was there watching him throw that ball and that he wasn't all the way gone just as Adam had hoped. But I can't. I have my rule. Plus, I don't know what it is I'm really seeing when I think I see things in the real world, not the dreams. The shimmers look like nothing more than just sunlight glinting through glass . . . except there is no glass. And they move funny . . . like a person would move. So, after all the weird stuff started to happen after *The Incident,* I just made up *The Rule.* And it worked well for those three years or so afterwards. I started getting used to all the oddness. As much as someone can, I suppose. We all get used to the things we can't change.

Yes, all in all, things were going along pretty well given everything that had happened. Until I broke *The Rule.*

Chapter 9

Fireworks

The Fourth of July fell on a Saturday. Being the recluse that I was, Deja and Lexi had come over earlier in the day. Deja's dad, Floyd, had come over, too, trailering his '68 Ford Mustang he was slowly fixing up one part at a time. He needed Pops' help on a couple things.

Pops had barbecued and the girls and I hung out in the house while Pops and Floyd hung out in the barn drinking beer and working on Floyd's car. Pops didn't mind helping him. He loved '68 Mustangs. Although he wanted a Pontiac GTO for himself.

"Doesn't it get creepy living out here in this old house?" asked Lexi.

"No, I like it," I said.

"But you're surrounded by dead people," she noted.

"They don't bother you if you don't bother them," I said with a grin.

"You ever see anything freaky out here?" asked Deja.

"Nope." It wasn't really a lie because I didn't consider the garden freaky. By this point, I was used to it. "It's pretty boring, actually. But I kind of like it that way. I've had enough excitement to hold me over until I'm an old lady."

We ate and laughed until the afternoon snuck up on us and it was time for Lexi and Deja to head out. "We're going to go to the county fireworks show," said Lexi. "You want to come?"

I hadn't been since *The Incident,* but I had fond memories of the county Fourth of July celebration. Mom had always insisted we go back when she was alive. They had live music, a chili cookoff, games, contests, and of course the big fireworks show at the end.

But the girls knew what my answer was going to be. The same as it always was since Mom had passed. "Nah, but thanks. I'm going to just hang out and read."

Deja pursed her lips. "Come on, girl. You need to get out some. It's summer. Next year is our senior year. Don't you want to go live a little?"

"No, I'm good," said with a bit of a forced smile.

Deja knew me well and she didn't want to force the subject, but she ventured a bit anyway. "Nobody's going to make fun of you," she said. "You can't even tell anymore. Not by looking at you."

I blushed a bit. "It's true," added Lexi. "We're not just saying it, Ruth. You're the only one who thinks you look different than everyone else. If I didn't know you, I'd never guess anything more than maybe you had a sprained ankle you were healing up from or something."

"And this?" I asked, lifting my bangs out of the way and pointing to the scar on my forehead.

"You can't even see it with your hair," said Deja. "Besides, it's really not that bad. You're making it out to be worse than it is."

She might have been right, I guess. And physically, I was loads better than years before. But I still did not like being around crowds. At school, I tried to stay under the radar. That's why I avoided football games, dances, all that stuff. Whether I liked it or not, I would forever be the girl from *The Incident.* People were always going to think of me as that girl. I just wanted a nice, quiet, normal life with my haunted garden. That was good enough for me. "Thanks, but I'm just really not up for it. And I'm really into my book." I was smack in the middle of *Station Eleven* by Emily St. John Mandel.

We met up with Floyd and Pops outside and as if my friends had been communicating with Floyd by some psychic connection, even he tried to get me to go. "Y'all coming to the fireworks?" He asked.

"What do you think, Baby Ruth," said Pops. "I'm game. We haven't been in a while."

I shook my head. "Come on, it'll be fun," said Floyd, waving his arm in an invitational sort of way.

Pops looked at me and I gave him a look I knew he'd notice and understand even if the others didn't. "Well, probably best not," he said with a bit of a fake laugh. "I'm a little buzzed right now, to be honest."

"I could drive," said Floyd. "I'm good. We can cram in the ole truck here and I'll chauffeur. I'd just need to swing by the house and drop the trailer back off."

"You mean I can drive, right dad?" said Deja. "Because, we weren't out here drinking beer for the last three hours," she added, waving her finger around at herself, Lexi, and me.

"I'm good," protested Floyd.

"Mm-hmm. I'm better. So, I'll handle the driving." She stuck out her hand and Floyd handed her the keys.

"Alright. You right, you right. Okay, well, look here, then. If she's driving, y'all are out of excuses," he said to Pops. "Let's all go."

"Nah, y'all head on off," said Pops. "Ruth and I are going to make a night of it here."

Floyd looked at me and realized I was starting to get a little embarrassed. "Alright," he said "no worries. It'd be a lot more fun if y'all were there, but alright. Maybe next year, huh?"

"Next year," I told him with a smile.

"Alright! I'm gonna hold you to it!" he said with a big smile and pointing at me. "Y'all heard her! I got witnesses! Next year she's committed." He started walking off backwards and gave us a friendly wave. "We'll see y'all. But remember! You agreed for next year, Ruth! You're coming with us next time."

Floyd headed for the driver's door, but Deja beat him to it. "Where you going?" she asked him.

"Oh, right, right. Damn, you turning into your mama, you know that?" And he walked around to the passenger side of the truck with his head a few inches lower.

"Mm-hmm," was all Deja replied as she got behind the steering wheel.

As they drove off down the gravel lane, I got a text from Lexi. *You're not mad, are you? Sorry about Floyd. You know he meant well, right?*

I know, I texted her back. *Not mad at all. Totally cool. Floyd is great.*

Pops and I made a go of it ourselves. We made a small bonfire out away from the barn and from the garden. "Check out what I got," he told me, carrying a box out of the garage. He had bought fireworks, including some sparklers.

"Aww, Pops. Thanks." I'd always been partial to the sparklers.

Pops was all smiles. "Let's light 'em up." He had bottle rockets, roman candles, spinners, and some others, which we proceeded to light up one after the other.

I even ended up having a couple of beers with Pops while we swirled our sparklers, careful not to burn ourselves with them. I made big O's while Pops tried to write our names as fast as he could to see if I could see the letters. I couldn't quite make them out, but I told a little white lie about it. "I see them!" I told him. Pops kept swirling that little stick of fire around fast as he could and laughed.

Afterwards, we sat on some old buckets Pops had pulled out by the bonfire. Good ole Pops had even thought to get marshmallows, graham crackers, and chocolate bars. And we made ourselves some s'mores, just like the old days.

"All we're missing now is some fresh bass," I told him.

"What's that?" he asked.

"Don't you remember that time we went camping?"

"Oh, yeah," he said, "fish and s'mores."

I smiled. "It was the best." The memory of that smell threatened to bring up another memory of gunfire and smoke, but I pushed it aside. There was no way I was going to let that memory ruin our night. "Thanks, Pops," I told him again. "This was really nice of you." Although I was a little sad he had already known I wouldn't go to the county celebration. He had prepared to celebrate at home. I felt guilty then, like I was holding him back in life a bit. There was no reason he couldn't go out and enjoy himself. Except that he was stuck here with me.

"Your mother would kill me if she knew I was letting you drink at this age," he told me with a grin as he sipped his beer.

"No, she wouldn't," I told him. "She'd be having one with us."

He looked off towards the cemetery. "Yeah, you're probably right." He grabbed another beer out of the bucket he had by us and popped its top. "Here's to you, hon!" He said, holding it up towards the cemetery. And then he set it on the ground. "She can come get it later," he said with a bit of a slur to his words. He was looking a little tipsy.

"You okay?" I asked him.

"Who, me? Sure, I'm okay. I'm as okay as can be." He looked back out to the cemetery. "I miss her, though. I know she cheated and all, but I still love her. You know that, right? I never stopped. Even though . . ."

"I know, Pops."

"You think that's bad?" he asked. "That she done what she did, and I'm still hung up on her."

Pops usually didn't talk about Mom with me. At least not like this. So I tried to measure my words. "No, Pops. I don't. It just means you loved her. And she loved you."

"Did she?" he asked. And in his eyes, I saw painful memories start to rise.

"She did, Pops. I swear it. We talked about you lots when you were on the road. I know she did wrong. But she really loved you. She talked about y'all dancing at some country bar."

I had a flash then, Mom and me dancing in the living room. She used to tell me about when she and Pops were dating and used to go to some country bar all time. Mom would wear her cowboy boots and a denim mini skirt. When I was little, she would occasionally fish them out of the closet and put on some music and we'd have ourselves a good ole fashion line dance, just the two of us. Mom loved to dance. There was the *Do Si Do*, *Electric Slide*, *Tush Push*, and the *Cowboy Chacha*. It wasn't just country music, either. Mom liked so many different types. We must have done the *Macarena* a thousand times. That was my favorite. She also liked *Walk it Out* by Unk, which always made me laugh.

"The Whiskey Top!" Pops said, remembering the name of the bar. "Yeah, we went out there all time when we were dating." I could see them. His big ole smile. Hers, too. And boy, I bet they were all over each other back then. *Ewww,* I thought, *I don't need to imagine that.* "Ran into ole Dale up there once or twice. He just kept staring at your mama." There was a bit of a pause there as he sipped his beer. "I should have seen it. I should have had it out with him back then about staring at her like he did. Maybe things would have been different."

"Yeah, but if we are always looking back at the what-ifs in life then we can't see the what is." I was apparently feeling pretty philosophical in my buzzed state. I thought maybe I should rephrase what I meant in more Pops' terms . . ., "Letting what-ifs pile up is like letting sludge pile up in an engine, Pops. Too much of it and the engine can't go anymore."

Pops smiled. "How'd you get so smart?" he asked me.

"Genetics," I told him. I wished I knew the words to make him feel better. I didn't, but I tried anyway. "She loved you, Pops. And she loved me. She screwed up royally but would have taken it back if she could have.

And when her mistakes get you down, just remember the dancing."

"Yeah . . .," said Pops. "She sure could move. She was so much fun, you know? And she was fearless, Ruth. She was. If she wanted to dance, she'd dance. If we were at an Applebee's and a song came on she liked and she felt like dancing, we'd dance. She didn't care if people looked at us funny or whispered. She just went for it."

"And you danced with her?" I asked.

"Of course, I did," he said with a fond smile.

"Not everyone would have, Pops. I hope you know that. A lot of guys probably would have been embarrassed and told her to stop making a scene or something. But you didn't. You danced. That's pretty cool."

He nodded his head. "I did, didn't I?" he laughed.

"And she loved you for it. I promise you she did."

"Well, I loved her, too," he added.

"I know. It sucks for both of us she's gone. You think you'll ever meet someone new?" I wanted him to be happy. Mom was gone. Nothing either of us could do about that. And she wouldn't want him to be alone forever like this. "The music's still playing, you know. Even though she's not here with us." *Jesus, beer makes me think I'm Socrates or something*, I thought.

I got the ole shoulder-roll. "I dunno. Maybe I'll find someone else to dance with one of these days. What about you? You should have gone out with your friends tonight, not staying home with your old man. You're seventeen, Ruth. The idea of you going out to some party and meeting a boy and all that . . . it scares the hell out of me. But the idea of you not getting to do those kinds of things . . . well, that scares me worse. You're only young once and these days will be gone before you know it. You gotta put yourself out there and just live. Screw 'em if people talk about ya. Life's short. You and I know that more than most."

I gave him a shoulder-roll of my own. "I know. But I'm happy, Pops. You don't have to worry about me."

He smiled. "Well, I hope so. That's all I want. That's the only thing I want in this world, really. Just make sure you get out and dance some before you're old. That's all I'm saying." He held up his beer and we cheered and clunked the cans. "To dancing!" he said.

"To dancing," I echoed.

I think we both staggered back into the house that night. The world was spinning a bit when I finally hit the bed. But it was a gentle spin, not the kind to make you hurl all over the place. I wasn't so sure about Pops.

Chapter 10

Muddy Water

I felt cold and wet. I couldn't catch my breath. I was in darkness. All the sound was muffled, even my own screams. I wanted to escape, but I couldn't. Something was holding me down, pressing me back every time I tried to get up. I couldn't breathe. I needed air. *Oh, God! Anything for a breath of air! Please!*

I jerked awake, my hands flailing as I gasped for air. But the air was there now. It tasted so clean and crisp as it filled my lungs. I hyperventilated, taking huge gasps. My heart was aching from thumping so hard. I looked around in the darkness, almost expecting a tide of water to rush into me like waves on some distant stormy shore. But there was none. I was home safe in my bed. My heart was pounding, and my hands were shaking. I breathed quickly, over and over again – in and out, in and out – until I started to calm down. *I'm safe, I'm safe, I'm safe,* I kept telling myself.

"What was that?!" I complained to myself. That was not a cool dream, whatever it was. Not at all.

I slid out of bed and immediately had this sick feeling in my stomach like I was about to hurl. Maybe I had drank too much after all. My neck was stiff as a board and I had this icky taste in my mouth, like foul smelling swamp water. I really thought I might throw up.

I'll never drink again, I told myself. *Well, at least not for a while.*

I walked down the hallway still feeling slightly drunk and descended the stairs carefully with one hand on the wall for support. Once down, I then passed through the kitchen and turned right into the single bathroom Pops and I shared in the little house. It still had the lime green tub and pink sink from the awesome seventies remodel.

I drank several handfuls of water from the sink faucet, but still had an odd queasy feeling so decided to go out to the garden.

The full moon's light poured in through the windows and by it I made my way into the kitchen and out the back door. I could have turned on the lights, of course, but Pops was sleeping, and I didn't want to wake him. Besides, my eyes were adjusted to the darkness and I didn't want the piercing light delving into my eyeballs after such a shocking dream. Better the gentle darkness as long as there was lots of sweet-smelling air to breathe.

I waded into the tall leaves of the old garden, making sure to keep on the small worn path I imagine the garden had long ago decided could remain if only to keep those pesky humans out of the way. Maybe they remembered the farmer and his fire and salt. Maybe they remembered Eddie with his weed eater and mower. But whatever the case, they left enough room for someone to get out the back door and out to the cemetery, if only barely.

I felt like I could sense their mood sometimes and if I accidentally stepped on one of the flowers, it was like having an angry aunt side-eye you as you sat on her nice clean furniture. It was a *you better be careful over there,* kind of vibe. They had never hurt me, except that one time with the spike, which of course turned out to be a good thing, but I'd learned to walk the path they left uncovered so as not to offend.

This night, they were swaying a bit unnaturally given there was no breeze. They did that sometimes, I had come to notice. "Hi," I said quietly. "Don't mind me. I'm just having a weird night." By now, we had become more or less comfortable in our relationship, although I still didn't understand it. Was the garden haunted by Lilith? Were the flowers alive? Had the two merged into some new entity? So many questions with no answers.

Regardless of what was happening out there behind the old house, the garden had come to accept me, and I think maybe even enjoyed my company . . . as long as I wasn't being moody. I think it could tell when I was and didn't like any negative vibes. I don't think it minded if I was sad or upset, but if I was angry or just being in a bit of a bratty mood, I got the distinct impression it would rather I take my moodiness elsewhere. I had learned to pick up on the body language of the flowers if that makes any sense.

I was also still a little scared of the place given its supernatural mysteries and didn't want to risk upsetting it. I know that sounds strange, but sometimes fear is just good common sense, especially when dealing with something I can't even begin to understand. If a giant lion suddenly moved in with us and decided it was cool hanging out with me, I still wouldn't poke it with a stick when I was bored because it might rip my face off. Same thing with a supernatural garden. It made me feel special I got to be there, but caution was always high on the list. I'd seen it suffocate plant eating bugs. Granted, they were a lot smaller than me, but still . . . foxgloves got pretty big and I wasn't interested in testing the limits of the garden in any sort of negative way.

That night, I got a sense the garden was a little uneasy, but not about me. "You, too, huh?" I asked. "I just had the worst dream." There was a fog setting in and I could hear frogs and crickets off in the distance. And despite it being July, there was a chill in the air that didn't feel normal. It made me shiver a bit.

I sensed something from the garden, then. *Bad air,* it seemed to say.

Yes, somehow that felt appropriate. "Yeah, bad air," I said aloud. And the flowers seemed to hum their approval that I had understood them. I had spent years learning to listen to them by this point. And there was something in the air. Not a smell, but a feeling that was riding the wind. Something wasn't right. I breathed slowly and deeply in the garden as my mind and thoughts settled. I felt the familiar calmness, but it was tainted by its uneasiness as well. It was listening, I realized. To what, I didn't know. But the garden was listening.

Suddenly, a little breeze passed through the flowers. It sent another shiver through me, and this time I noticed the flowers seemed to shiver, also. That's when I knew something was really out of sorts. "What is that?" I asked.

And I sensed an answer I didn't much like to hear. *Death.*

I looked off into the distance where the dead lay in their slumber in the cemetery. And for perhaps the first time since we'd moved out to the little farmhouse, I felt scared.

The flowers seemed to close up on themselves and shrivel down a bit, kind of like when they squeezed a bug, except now it was almost like the entire garden was shrinking inward. I'd never seen them do that before. They didn't completely disappear or anything, but they noticeably retracted. Whatever it was they had sensed, they didn't like it and were recoiling from it.

I suddenly felt alone in the garden, which was very unusual and made the night appear all the more creepy around me. I sluggishly pulled myself back inside, giving one last look over my shoulder to the darkness beyond.

I went to the bathroom and one of Eddie's old memories reared its head. *James Monroe was only the 5th U.S. President, but he was the third one to die on the 4th of July. John Adams and Thomas Jefferson* (The Shakespeare chair thief, if you recall) *and James Monroe, three of the first five U.S. Presidents, all died on the Fourth of July. President Zachary Taylor died July 9, 1850 from food poisoning he got from cherries and iced milk he enjoyed on his Fourth of July celebration.*

Ugh, please shut up, Eddie, I thought. This was not what I wanted to be thinking about at that particular moment. Eddie wasn't actually talking to me, of course. It was just some strong memory he had attaching itself to me like a parasite. It weirded me out sometimes when his old memories seemed to well up in my mind like water from an underground spring because I knew they weren't my own. It was like having a total stranger walk up to you and start telling you just weird, random facts. But they were talking to you in your voice. Like, imagine someone you never met just started talking away to you, but everything they were saying sounded just like it was from your voice. It's like that in my head when this stuff happens. It's creepy. It was his memories, but they came through as thoughts in my voice in my head. And it seemed a pretty bad omen that it was about this death stuff on the Fourth of July.

I crawled back in bed to attempt to get some sleep, but I had the strangest dream. I dreamed I was back outside in the garden looking up at the night sky, but it wasn't a normal night sky anymore. It was Van Gogh's *Starry Night*. The stars were shining but they looked like they were an oil painting. The entire sky seemed to swirl around and around slowly, like the painting had come to life. And then poof! Pow! Poof again. Little splashes of color exploded in the distance like fireworks.

At first it was pretty, and I was even enjoying the unique beauty of it. But then something changed. The sky darkened, the lights blinked out. And then it started coming at me like I was Chicken Little, and the sky was falling. It was closing in, the swirls of paint getting bigger and closer. And it began to shimmer, like moonlight off water. It shimmered, like the way Lilith shimmered on rare occasions. It shimmered as the dead. And there was something there . . . something hiding beneath the paint. I couldn't quite see it, but I had the feeling that whatever it was – whoever it was - saw me.

Chapter 11

The Beast

Morning found me, confused and without a good night's rest, but the slight nausea I'd had the night before had passed and I felt a bit more like myself again. But I still remembered the part of the dream with the strange night sky.

I grabbed a cup of coffee from Pops' coffee maker and stepped out into the garden. Pops was gone, either in the barn or out to the cemetery. I wondered if he had a hangover. I thought about going to find him, but I was nursing a bit of a headache myself. Although I wasn't sure if it was from the beer or the weird dreams or both.

When we moved in, Pops had picked up an old metal table and two chairs someone had thrown out by the side of the road. A couple of the metal prongs had rusted and were likely scratching the hell out anyone who sat on them. But Pops fixed them up easy enough with his metal grinder. Then he painted them with some epoxy black paint, and we had ourselves free patio furniture. They were small and fit perfectly between the back door and the garden without intruding upon the flowers' space.

I took a seat in the chair I'd claimed for myself (Pops almost never sat in his, but it was there nonetheless if he ever wanted it) and then I proceeded to be typical weird me and talked to the flowers. "Morning." They were acting just like regular flowers now. They usually did during the day. "That was a pretty weird night, wasn't it?" I felt no response. Part of me felt a little rejected, like they were keeping secrets from me. "You're not much help, you know. I know you know something." I sipped my coffee. It tasted a little funny, like dirty or something. And I realized it was probably me, not the coffee. I smacked my lips trying to evict the memory of the taste of swamp water from my dream. I don't think it was really there, but it was so strong in my memory it felt like it was. "Bleck," I said, "I'm going to need something stronger than this. I feel like crap."

Something brushed against my foot and I looked down to see one of the leaves bending itself over on its stalk and onto my flip flop, which I noticed was in pretty poor condition. The flip flop, I mean. I had no idea what it was doing. It almost seemed like it was trying to pat me or something. "If that's supposed to be comforting then we need to talk about your social skills," I opined. But it made me smile nonetheless.

I watched as it righted itself and sort of shuttered a little, like a teeny, tiny dog shaking off water after a bath. And then it looked all normal again, as though nothing had happened.

"That's a pretty neat trick," I said. "I have no idea how you do stuff like that, but it's neat." I closed my eyes and took a deep breath. I heard a chirp above me and looked up. "Hey, Ruby," I said with a smile. "Long time no see." Apparently, she didn't share the sentiment, however, as she flew off. "Fine, be that way."

In the silence that followed, I tried to sense the garden, from the flowers on top to the roots deep in the soil. And I smiled. I could hear them. Well, sort of. They were waiting for the sun. That's all I was really able to pick up. The garden was waiting for the warmth of the sun. I opened my eyes and checked the weather on my iPhone. "The weather says it's going to be partly cloudy until around noon. Then it's going to be sunny later today. You'll get lots of sun then."

The flowers buzzed as if in applause.

My head felt inflated two sizes. I loved having this secret with the garden. And part of me was looking forward to the sun's rays just as the garden was. I was feeling better already. Nothing chased away the blues like a warm, sunny day in which one had nothing to do but relax.

I could have just sat right there in the garden all day and read with the flowers. But no, I thought, I should get out and do something. And besides, I had another old friend I hadn't spent much time with lately. I'd been sitting at home all week. Today was a good day to take the Beast out for a spin. Some good old-fashioned horsepower growling in my ears as the wind whirled my hair around sounded like a pretty good idea.

The Beast was a creature of Pops' own making, a monster worthy of Dr. Frankenstein himself. It was originally born a stately 1978 series two Jaguar XJ6. It's original inline six-cylinder engine had suffered catastrophic failure during the prior summer, as those old engines tended to do when they get over-worked in the Texas heat. After Pops delivered the bad news to the owner the man offered the car as parts to Pops for five hundred dollars, exclaiming he was done sinking money into that money pit.

Pops wouldn't have admitted it to many people, but he had always liked the look of the cars, just not the electrical or mechanical systems always full of gremlins. But the body and interior were in good condition with very minor rust. It needed new floor pans, but that was simple enough. So Pops, whose eyes no doubt fell to an engine sitting at the back of the workshop as he pondered the possibilities, suddenly had an idea, one which was blasphemous to both European car lovers and American muscle enthusiasts alike.

Pops often toured the junkyards for parts when he needed them and some months prior to the Beast's demise in its first life he'd come across a butt ugly 1973 Pontiac Catalina wagon, banana yellow complete with the wood siding. Clark Griswold would have been proud. The car's axle had broken among several other ailments and it sat rusting in the yard. But under that aircraft carrier it called a hood was a Pontiac 400 V8 engine, the same behemoth which powered GTOs and Trans Ams back in the day. He had looked it over and found it was in surprisingly good condition. Pops had nothing to do with it at the time, but when he inquired about it and was told it could be had for four hundred dollars if he'd take it out himself, he jumped on the deal.

He'd been tinkering with it for months and was sure it was now ready to go, but he didn't have anything to put it in. He'd long wanted a classic GTO for himself, but everything was way too expensive, even without an engine. So when the Jaguar came through the shop with the bad engine, he decided to create the monstrosity known as the Beast. He even cut open the hood and added a blower. I think he did that purely out of boredom. It was completely illogical putting that much muscle into a British four door sedan. He had to re-do the brakes, suspension, differential, the whole shebang to make it work worth a flip. But he loved every minute of fixing that car up. Anything to keep his mind busy. And thus, Pops' monster was born.

And on my seventeenth birthday, Pops gave it to me. It suited me perfectly, I thought. It was a freak just like me. It scared old people when I hit the gas and the engine roared as the tires squealed. More than one concerned parent chastised Pops for putting me in "that death trap of a car." It had no airbags, of course, hardly any safety equipment at all other than its massive pounds of metal. But Pops knew me. He knew I might have some fun with it, but I wouldn't go crazy. Well, maybe just a little. Pops had also seen fit to load it up with a used ten-inch subwoofer in the trunk and an upgraded sound system he'd scavenged from the parts yard. It was loud and I loved it.

I jumped in the Beast, fired it up, and turned up the radio. Once I hit Twin Rivers, I made a B-Line for Starbucks where I purchased a ridiculously fattening, yet delicious, coffee with whip cream and chocolate. The giant coffee in all its several hundred calorie glory finally chased away that awful phantom taste that had been plaguing me since the night before. If only we could get a Starbucks in Foxglove, I thought. I'd be there every day.

I sat there enjoying my drink when my phone rang. Deja. I would have invited her to come with me, but she always went to Church on Sundays and then she and her folks would go out to eat afterward, so I knew she was busy. Which was why I was a little surprised when she called. "Hey, what's up?" I asked.

"Just chillin' with the fam," she said. "You?"

"I'm up in Twin Rivers getting me Starbucks."

"Girl, you drove all the way out there again just for some coffee?"

"Yup, and it was so worth it. I'm enjoying it as we speak."

She laughed, "You should just invest in a better coffee machine at home. Hey, but guess what?"

"What?"

"You know Emily Tolliver?"

"Yes, of course." *Meh . . . she called me Quasimodo in the bathroom that one time,* I thought. *Not a fan.*

"There's this rumor going 'round that she's missing," said Deja.

"Missing?" I asked. "Since when?"

"Apparently just last night. I saw her, too. She was up at the fireworks show with Miranda and Amy. But apparently she hasn't been home yet."

I was playing with the straw of my drink, scooping whip cream with it as I talked "So? That's like, not even one day. That doesn't really sound like 'missing' to me."

"I know," she said. "It's probably nothing, but her mom is freaking out. She was calling her all last night and her phone is going straight to voicemail. So this morning she put out a blast on Facebook to everybody asking if anyone knew where she was and to tell her to call or come home. That was this morning. But now people are saying nobody can find her. Her parents and some others from their church have been out all morning looking for her."

I suddenly had a bad feeling. I remembered that eerie dread last night that woke me up. And the weird things in the garden last night. *Nah,* I thought. "But she drove last night, right?"

"Yeah, probably."

"So, if her car isn't at the field anymore, then she probably just went somewhere. Hell, she could around here in Twin Rivers or something."

"Maybe," said Deja. "Keep an eye out, I guess. And if you do see her, tell her to call her mom. She's like having a meltdown or something."

"Yeah, okay, I will."

"Well, shoot, girl, I gotta go. My mom's giving me crazy eyes."

I heard her mom in the background, "Don't you be telling people I'm giving you crazy eyes."

"But you are givin' me crazy eyes. Ruth, I'll talk to you later."

After we hung up, I went on to the mall. I liked Twin Rivers because nobody really knew me. I could walk around without getting stared at. I would have drove around and looked around for Emily's car, except I didn't really know what she drove. It was a red Hyundai, I remembered that much, but I wouldn't recognize it even if I parked right next to it. I'd never really paid much attention to Emily after our falling out. But I did keep my eyes open inside the mall just in case. I bought myself some new flip flops and a cute bracelet at a kiosk.

She probably went to some guy's house and had a wild night and slept in, I thought. People our age were starting to do things like that. I envied them a bit. I bet her mom would be pissed. Still, though, the whole thing with the garden the previous night kept creeping back in my mind. I wasn't Emily's friend, but I did hope she was okay. Once she showed back up, then I could go back to thinking about how much I didn't like her.

Chapter 12

Hide and Seek

When I got home, I grabbed my iPad with its Kindle app so I could go read in the garden. The flowers had gotten their fill of sunshine and now rested comfortably as dusk set on. They looked beautiful and peaceful. It would have been a great day if Deja hadn't started me to worrying about whether or not Emily's being missing had anything to do with the odd goings on of the night before. It wasn't her fault, of course. She had no way to know about my restless night.

When it started getting dark and the mosquitos started buzzing around my ears, I went in and started some dinner. Turkey chili sounded pretty good. And as the last of the light faded, Pops finally came in from whatever project he'd been working on in the barn.

"I got it running!" he told me.

"Got what running?"

"That old Honda motorcycle."

"Oh, the one Mr. Cockrell dropped off a few weeks back?"

"Yeah. I knew it just needed the carbs cleaned and some plugs and wires. All I need now is to make sure the brakes are working right, and I might can take it for a spin tomorrow. I don't think he'd mind."

"Wear a helmet," I reminded him. "You have responsibilities, remember?" And I pointed to myself in case he forgot.

"Yeah, yeah, I'll be safe. I'm not going to ride it too fast or anything. I just want to make sure it's running right before I deliver it to him. I'll probably just drive it over to his place. He'd get a kick out of that, I bet."

"Well, good for you, Pops." He went to the fridge and fished out a diet Coke. "No beer?" I asked.

"Oh, God. Don't get me started. Do you know how much water I had to drink this morning before my head quit hurting?"

I smiled. "I think I overdid it last night, too, and slept horribly."

Pops laughed. "See, that was my master plan. I made sure to give you just enough so that you wouldn't want anymore. That's good parenting, right there."

I chuckled. "Sure, Pops. Well, it worked. I'm going to stick with my tea for a while, thank you very much."

That night, I had a good night's rest thankfully, with nothing out of the ordinary. At least, nothing I remembered. And on Monday morning, I texted Deja to see if Emily Tolliver had shown back up.

She hadn't.

Oh, crap, I thought.

I read for a bit and then helped Pops with weed eating the cemetery. We had two weed eaters going but it still took the rest of the morning to do just half of the cemetery. I could never quite master getting the strings on my weed eater to work properly and I kept having to stop and pull them out or re-do them. Pops was a pro, though, and flitted around like a hummingbird from one tombstone to the next – zip, zip, zip – and they were done. Finally taking pity on my ineptitude, he told me not to worry about finishing and that he would take care of the rest.

The garden didn't like the weed eaters. It still remembered Eddie and his loud machines that cut and rent asunder. I made sure to keep a distance when I had a weed eater on me. Once Pops had suggested widening the path in the garden and he headed that way with one. But I made sure to stop him and kindly asked him to leave the garden to me. "It's my special place," I told him. "And it's perfect just like it is." So, he left it be. I think I earned some additional brownie points that day with the garden.

It was getting close to lunch, so I figured I'd go see what we had to make something, but just as I put my weed eater away for the day, Deja called. "Hey," I answered. "Any news?" This whole Emily Tolliver missing thing was starting to bother me.

"No. Hey, what are you doing right now? You busy?"

"No, just finished helping Pops. Why, want to go do something?"

"Actually," she said, "I was wondering if you wanted to go join the search?"'

"What search? There's a search?"

"Girl, you have got to get on Facebook. I keep forgetting you don't see any of those postings. This is like a big deal now. The police are involved and everything."

"So soon? I thought they had a forty-eight-hour rule or something."

"Well, if they do, they waived it. People are talking like something bad has happened. She had her car so maybe she just decided to go out of town or something, but it's pretty strange she wouldn't at least call her parents or anyone like this. People were out yesterday and then more this morning. But now they got those Equusearch people in town. You know, the ones you see on the news sometimes? They're having a meeting at noon to organize an official search."

"Oh, wow," I said. "That's not good."

"Nope," she said. "I was wondering if you could come pick me up and we could go volunteer? Lexi is heading out there, too, and can meet us up."

"Yeah, for sure," I said. I didn't like the idea of getting around the crowd, of course, but this was kind of serious. "I can come grab you now if you want."

Twenty minutes later several heads turned as the Beast pulled up to the church. The parking lot was almost full. There was a tent set up with people sitting in chairs and stacks of paper. A woman in a bright yellow T-shirt was giving out instructions . . .

"Remember, we want to be an asset, not a liability," she was saying. "It's hot out here so if you're a walker, make sure to hydrate often. We have lots of water available," and she pointed to big stack of water bottles. "Now, remember, drivers, don't drive distracted. We recommend at least two people per car, one to drive and the other to look around. The last thing we want is to cause an accident out there. As y'all know, we're mainly trying to see if we can find Emily's car. There's a description on the flyer with a picture of the make and model. She has a bright yellow sunflower bumper sticker on the right side of the bumper if it's still there, but it might be peeled off, so if you see a car that looks like it might be hers, even if it doesn't have a bumper sticker with a flower on it, call it in. It's very important that if you see it, you call it in. If it's parked somewhere, don't go messing with it. Just call it in and let law enforcement know. Now, does everybody understand that?"

Everyone was nodding. Lexi saw us and came over. "You have to sign up," she told us. And we saw there was a line up to the folks sitting in the chairs. "You sign in and they give you a pink bracelet," she said, showing us her paper bracelet on her wrist. "It's so they can try to keep everybody organized."

Lexi had already arranged to go with a couple of guys from school so after we signed in and got our bracelets, Deja and I jumped back in the Beast. "Where should we look?" she asked.

"I don't know. I mean, the last place she was seen was down at the fairgrounds, right?"

"Yeah, but there's been lots of people out there already," said Deja.

"There's a lot of country roads around there, though," I added. She agreed so we decided to start cruising the roads. It was a hot, muggy day, but otherwise pretty nice. We rolled the windows down and I slowly drove along while Deja kept an eye out. A couple of times we stopped the car to check things out. There were a few times we saw tire tracks in the mud by the road, but we realized after about the third time that it was probably other searchers who had been out this way pulling off the road to either check something out or turn around. And there were several other vehicles we passed out doing the same thing we were. After about two hours and the gas getting low, we decided to call it.

"Maybe she ran away or something," said Deja.

I had my growing doubts for a few reasons, most of which I couldn't tell her. *The Rule* and all. But it was still possible. "Yeah. Who knows? Maybe she had stuff going on at home and just wanted to get away for a while or something."

We called Lexi and her group was about done, too, so we all decided to meet up at the Dairy Queen back on Main Street. "You going to be okay?" she asked me.

"Sure," I told her. "I see everyone at school. It's not a big deal." Although it kind of was. These social interactions never seemed to go real well for me. I often would catch someone staring at me out of the corner of their eye or whispering something from a distance. It just made me uncomfortable. But I could play it off for a little while for the sake of my friends. And a sundae with chocolate syrup sounded pretty good. As long as it had no bananas since *The Incident* had ruined bananas for me. And Dairy Queen had surprisingly good tacos. I had skipped lunch, after all. Part of me felt a little guilty about the idea of enjoying an ice cream sundae and a few tacos while Emily was missing and possibly . . . well, you know. But we didn't know anything for sure. And a girl's still gotta eat.

Lexi was with Jackson Haynes and Patrick Elliott. Deja had mentioned Lexi and Patrick had recently started talking. I always thought he was kind of an idiot, but admittedly didn't really know him all that well. He was definitely a class clown, though, always joking and, from what I heard, barely passed last year.

But what I was not expecting was to see Miranda and her boyfriend, Nate, at another table along with Amy Choi and *ugh* . . . Logan Wallis, the boy who had kissed me under the bleachers sophomore year. *Oh, great,* I thought. *Of course, they're here.* I could see the bracelets on their wrists indicating they had also been out searching.

Miranda gave me a contemptuous look when I walked in and whispered something to Amy, who then also looked over at me. I didn't hear what they said, but Miranda apparently thought herself funny as she chuckled. For once, I guessed Amy wasn't playing follow the leader as she just shrugged whatever Miranda had said off, to the slight disappointment of the Queen Bee. Logan just seemed to be staring off into space.

Deja heard Miranda's laughter as we sat down, looked at her, looked at me, then looked back at her and said, "I know you not talkin' 'bout my friend over there."

Lexi, Patrick, and Jackson were now paying attention as well. "What?" asked Lexi, looking over to Miranda and Amy's table.

Jackson and Patrick both looked uncomfortable. I don't think they much liked the idea of being pushed into a confrontation with the other table. "Everything's fine," I said. Then I looked at Deja with my serious face and said more quietly . . ., "It's fine."

"Mm-hmm," she answered. She capitulated reluctantly but cast an eye back at the other table just in case they had more to say. They didn't. They might be the popular clique, but they were well aware Deja Lucas had a razor-sharp tongue and she was not afraid to use it. She wasn't a mean person by nature, which was really a good thing for us all. Because when put to the task, she could bring a grown man to tears just by the verbal thrashing she could unleash. She had the innate ability to quickly identify that thing that someone else was insecure about and just humiliate people who thought they could match wits with her in an argument. It was pretty brutal on the rare occasions she let it loose.

"Y'all gonna come out tomorrow?" asked Patrick, with that silly grin he perpetually had that apparently Lexi found cute.

"Hopefully she turns up tonight," said Deja. "But if she doesn't, yeah, I'll try to make it. That's if my taxi lady here doesn't mind," she said with a big smile.

"I don't mind," I said quietly.

"That car's so badass," said Jackson, looking out the window at the Beast.

"Yeah, how many horses that thing got?" asked Patrick.

I shrugged. "I think about four hundred."

"Damn," said Jackson. "That thing's a Beast." That actually made me smile.

Lexi and Deja both laughed, too. "That's what she calls it!" said Lexi.

"No way," said Jackson. I nodded. "Well, I see why. It's so cool. Your dad fixed it up, right?"

"Yeah."

"Man, you gotta take us for a ride someday. I've always liked your car."

It was nice to have a pretty normal conversation with a group of kids my age for once. We chatted about cars and Patrick swore his truck could take the Beast, to which I politely explained only in his dreams, but I wasn't willing to race him like he wanted. We also talked about Emily and where we might check out tomorrow if she still didn't turn up later that night. As I ate my sundae, though, I noticed both the guys looking at me a bit.

"Hey, what's up with your hand?" asked Patrick. I had been holding the sundae up with my left hand, not even thinking about the little white ringlets which, like a blue-ringed octopus, scattered across my palm. "What are those circle thingies?" And he pointed to them with the straw from his drink.

"Dude," said Lexi.

"What? I'm just asking."

"I don't really know," I told him. "Something bit me out in the garden one day. I didn't even see what it was. But after the bite healed, it left these on my hand, like an allergic reaction or something but they never went away."

"That's so freaky," said Patrick.

"They're kind of cool," said Jackson. "It's kind of like henna."

Huh, I hadn't thought of them like that before, I thought. To me, they just looked like a bunch of weird splotches.

"What about your head? Does it hurt? You know, the bullet or whatever?"

"Pat, man . . .," Jackson said. "Why would you ask her that?"

"Because I'm curious. Can we see the scar?"

"Boy, you need to work on your EQ," Deja told him. "Don't make me come across this table at you."

"It doesn't hurt," I said, and reluctantly lifted my bangs so he could see it.

"Aww, is that all? I thought it would look a lot worse, to be honest." He actually seemed a little disappointed, which made me feel better.

"Well, it's been a few years, you know . . . so it's fading a bit," I told him. "It sucks that it messed up my motor skills and stuff, but other than that it doesn't really bother me. I forget it's there sometimes, to be honest."

"You seem to walk just fine," said Jackson.

"I do, mainly," I agreed. "It's gotten a lot better over the years."

"Man, if I had a bullet in my head, I'd be telling everybody," said Patrick. "That's gangster." I just rolled my eyes. He was annoying as hell, but I had to admit his big grin was starting to get a little infectious. I found myself smiling.

"Patrick, you stupid," said Deja, but she was smiling a little, too.

"Ignore him," said Lexi. "Patrick thinks any scar is cool."

"Hell, yeah," he said. "Check this out," and he lifted his shirt to reveal a long scar around his chest and stomach."

"Ew, gross!" I heard Miranda say from the other table.

"Oh, wow," I said. It was huge! It looked like a miniature Grand Canyon running along his torso. "What happened there?"

"Bobbed wire," he explained. "My brother and I made a fort when we were little and used some old bobbed wire we found on it. I was up on the roof playing around and slipped. I reached out to grab hold of something but slid down the wire a bit. It got me good. Mine's way bigger than yours," he added proudly. And as much as I couldn't believe it, I pretty much decided then and there that I liked Patrick Elliott after all. Not in any kind of romantic way. I still thought he was an idiot. But he was a likeable enough idiot, I supposed. And suddenly, my Harry Potter scar didn't seem all that bad compared to what he had going on.

I was surprised how long we stayed talking to the boys. It turned out they were decent enough guys. Jackson sure had a lot of questions about our old farmhouse and Pops' car hobby. He even seemed pretty interested in the garden, which surprised me given not many guys I had ever known would care much about such things.

"Hey, do you think I could ride with you tomorrow if you go looking again?" asked Jackson. "I'd like to cruise around in the Beast."

"Yeah, me, too," said Patrick. "It's pretty sweet. I can drive if you want."

"Well, I'm not going to let you drive it," I told Patrick. "Because I'm sure you'd try to race it around or something. But sure, if you guys want to come with us tomorrow, I'm cool with it."

"Awesome!" said Lexi. And we made plans to meet back up at the Dairy Queen in the morning.

"She'll probably come home tonight, I bet," said Jackson. "At least, hopefully."

"Do y'all think anything bad has happened to her?" asked Lexi.

"Don't know," said Jackson. "But the longer she's missing, the worse the odds."

"I hope she's okay," said Lexi.

"Me, too," I agreed. And I meant it. Even if Emily was kind of an ass sometimes towards me.

After we left and I was driving Deja back home, she said, "I think Jackson likes you."

"Nah," I said. "He just likes my car."

"Mm-hmm," was all she replied with a coy smile on her lips.

Chapter 13

Starry Night

That night the dream returned. It started out much the way the last one did. I was down in the garden and then looked up to see the night sky. And again, it was like Van Gogh's famous painting come to life. In the sky something changed. It seemed to be melting. Then, like someone had tipped over a bucket, down came all the colors in a deluge. I closed my eyes and put my arms over my head expecting to get smashed or drenched by oil paint. But nothing seemed to happen. I gingerly opened my eyes and saw I wasn't in the garden anymore.

Now I was standing by some sort of pond or lake. As I looked around me, I saw all the world was now an oil pointing. Everything except myself looked like an artist had just brought it into creation with the stroke of a brush. But it was still alive . . . moving like the natural would. Despite its odd appearance, I had the strangest impression that I knew where I was. To the right of me there was a wall of trees and underbrush, but it opened up just here where there was a long dip in the land that met concrete down below. It then ran into a large concrete culvert. To the left of me, the culvert poked back out of the little hill I was upon and emptied into what looked like the little lake.

I know this place, I thought. I was standing on the levee that ran just outside of town, looking out over one of the water retention basins in the county. This one was just half a mile or so from the fairgrounds. I'd been four-wheeling out here before with Deja and her dad.

A few feet below was the concrete drainage culvert that diverted water here to the basin. And as I looked out over the basin, to the left a bit the water churned and began to swirl like a whirlpool. And then the color changed, from the deep brown and purplish water a red hue began to emerge, brighter and brighter. I took a few steps down the embankment for a better look. But still, I needed to get closer. And then it took on a form.

"Oh, no," I whispered. It looked like a . . . I leaned forward just a bit more to try to get a better look, lost my footing, and fell into the painting of the water. It didn't feel like water. I felt cold, but not wet. It moved around me in a way that made it look like how it might look if I was swimming through it. Only I wasn't really moving – the scenery was.

I sank down into the basin, and there before me the painting of a car revealed itself. It was a red four-door sitting upon the muddy silt. The driver window was down about a fourth of the way. Protruding from it was a slender forearm that appeared to be both floating yet frozen in time. And upon the wrist I could see a watch. As I moved closer, I could see it was still working, the second hand sweeping smoothly away. Upon the face of the dial was a sunflower and the hands of the watch seemed to grow from its center. It was not a simple, basic sunflower, though. I recognized it as one from Van Gogh's famous painting, with the dark yellows, browns, crimson, and the edges of the petals wild and unkempt. And then I heard it . . . *tick, tick, tick* . . . it began to echo all around me, the only sound to be heard.

There was a face on the other side of the window, a painting of a girl perhaps deep asleep. While her face was still, her strawberry blond hair of fine brushstrokes floated lazily in the water. "Emily," I whispered. But she didn't respond. The ticking continued. "What is this?" I asked her and this alien world around me. Still no response. *Tick, tick, tick* . . . It was getting louder now, and I was only getting more confused by the second. A painting of a box turtle swam by me, its beady little eye looking at me as if to say *what are you doing down here? And why are you not part of the painting?* I tentatively reached out to touch Emily's hand. "Emily," I said again.

The painting of the girl came alive. Her eyes opened and she turned towards me. Red paint ran down the other side of her face. In her eyes, I saw she was in pain. *Ruth.* I heard it clear as day in my mind.

And then I woke up, my heart pounding and my body shaking. I sat up in bed, my eyes darting around the room expecting to see her standing in front, those sad eyes pleading for help. But there was nothing, just an empty room cast in the moonlight.

Chapter 14

A Historical Excursion with Vincent Van Gogh

Oh, God, I thought, *Emily's dead.* She somehow drowned in her car and I just dreamed it. But what a weird way to dream it . . . like a painting. It was very different than other dreams I had in the past. And she looked at me. That was so weird. *Wow,* I thought to myself. *This is really trippy.* And I didn't do acid or anything. I feel like I need to put that out there. Because I think if I did acid, and did way too much, that might kind of explain what happened. But no, no acid.

This was new territory. I'd dreamed of people's memories before. I had even dreamed of people's deaths, like Mr. Lancaster, but not like this. *She couldn't have seen me, right?* I thought. The dreams were always just what had happened. How could she look at me if I wasn't there when it happened? Never once before had anyone in one of my dreams ever acknowledged me as though they could see me. And I don't mind saying it had freaked me right the hell out.

I couldn't stop shaking. I spent the rest of that sleepless night jumping at shadows and any weird noises, rattled practically out of my bones. Part of me was scared that if I fell asleep again, I'd dream about her again. But another part of me kind of wanted to do just that. I mean, this was really fascinating stuff happening. I kept thinking to myself, *did she see me? How?* And if she was out there in the basin by the levee, how had nobody found her? Everyone had been out looking for her and I'm sure people probably went right down that levee, probably half a dozen times by now. Did they go right past her? I guessed that if she had driven her car down the levee for some reason and somehow crashed into the basin, it was certainly possible nobody could see it down in the water. I wasn't sure how deep it was out there, but in the dream, it had seemed pretty deep.

I also couldn't get the painting stuff out of my head. Why was I dreaming in oil paints? And what was up with the Van Gogh imagery? I tried to put it together, like it was all some bizarre cosmic puzzle.

Among Eddie's old books I had plunked down in my closet was a book about Vincent Van Gogh. More specifically, the former caretaker had a 1966 edited selection of letters by Van Gogh between him and his brother Theo which also included numerous pictures of his paintings that followed the timeline of the letters. I went through it a bit, marveled for the hundredth time at some of the paintings as well, and just let it all soak in.

Thoughts came to me. Perhaps not entirely rational, but some of what was happening just seemed to have these odd little threads connecting to each other as I sometimes felt occurred in life. *Alright Emily,* I thought to myself, *you want to get metaphysical and supernatural? Let's do it.* I needed to just relax and let the events of the world happening around me soak in. As I lay there in bed looking over all his old paintings and letters, I began to ponder the unlikely ways Vincent Van Gogh, Lilith, Emily, this town, and even I were all connected through long, loopy threads of time and coincidence.

There is a little-known theory about Van Gogh's death. And interestingly, if true, Van Gogh painted a portrait of his killer just before he died. And you'll never believe who may have been the culprit.

Yes, yes, Van Gogh shot himself and died by suicide. I'm not saying he didn't. But it's the why he shot himself that I find interesting. People say he went crazy, but a few historians have noted that perhaps his insanity was medically related. More to the point, perhaps he was one of the many people who took powerful medications only to find the cure worse than the disease.

I grabbed my iPad, sat up, and started searching a bit. Van Gogh had Temporal Lobe Epilepsy and took a medicine called digitalis to combat the seizures. Too much of digitalis can cause hallucinations and nausea, among other things. It can also cause xanthopsia, a condition where one's vision becomes heavily tainted in yellow. Some believe Van Gogh's legendary "Yellow Period" may have been the result of the side effects of digitalis poisoning. Another known side effect is light corona whereby lights often take on a halo effect around them, particularly at night.

Van Gogh became enamored with wheat fields in all their yellow and green glory and it's rather interesting to me that at least part of the reason why may have been because of his epilepsy medication. He may have just been tripping on digitalis, basically. How very progressive of him.

Digitalis is also what killed Lilith. You see, digitalis is made from foxglove flowers, whose scientific name is *digitalis purpurea.* Lilith, like poor Marie Curie and her beloved radium, had died of a very slow poisoning that had taken years to finally claim her. And, perhaps, so too did Vincent. He dutifully took his medicine and the seizures waned, but so, too, did his mental health. He suffered from insomnia and nausea and the only person he was close to was his brother, Theo. On December 23, 1888, after receiving news from his brother that Theo was engaged and after also having an argument with fellow artist and roommate Gauguin, Vincent took a razor to his left ear sheared part, or nearly all of it, off.

Popular history says he presented it to a prostitute named Rachel as a token of his passionate devotion. Another account is that he gave the ear to a maid named Gabrielle who worked at the brothel, but not as a prostitute. Early Christmas present? A little creepy, there Vincent. But maybe there was more to it. Gabrielle was said to have had significant scarring on her arms from a rabid dog attack when she was a child, the wounds having been cauterized by an iron poker heated upon an open flame. I guess that's what passed for good health care in those days.

Some say Van Gogh gave her his ear in an expression of empathy. *You are scarred but not alone.* Something along those lines. People who knew him reported Vincent wasn't exactly a very nice person. They all thought he was a little nuts. And he probably was to a degree, but his mind was like a bendy river that ran deep, full of strong currents swirling about like his brushstrokes. So maybe that was his way of trying to reach out to someone, the offering of his literal self to a woman. Also very progressive of him, if true. Crazy is also a fair assessment, but only to the extent that we use the term as a catch-all for mental health issues we find difficult to understand. Some of the most interesting people who have lived likely fall into such a category in one form or another.

Two years after the ear slicing incident, Van Gogh left the inn on that fateful day in Auvers-sur-Oise, France on July 27, 1890 and went out to the wheat field where he shot himself in the chest with a revolver. Not progressive, Vincent. Very anti-progressive, actually.

As I thought about these things that night (trying to avoid sleep as best I could), I felt an odd kinship with the artist because he didn't die from that bullet, either, at least not right away. Had it happened in our modern era of medicine he likely would have survived just as I did instead of pulling a Garfield. He lay out in that field for hours until he finally realized death was apparently occupied elsewhere. So, he finally picked himself up and trudged back to the inn late that night. He walked upstairs to his room and fell into bed where sleep apparently was also off on holiday with death as neither would find him for quite some time.

He must have made some terrible noises for upon hearing all the moaning and groaning coming from his room, the innkeeper and his daughter checked in on

Vincent to inquire if he was ill. They found him there in bed, curled up in agony, bleeding all over their good sheets. When they frantically asked what happened, he remarked, "I've tried to kill myself." The innkeeper's daughter, who was thirteen at the time, the same age as me when my life got turned upside down, stayed with him through the night expecting he'd die at any moment, but death was still out of town.

The next morning Vincent's friend and physician Dr. Paul-Ferdinand Gachet arrived and patched him up best he could. He told Vincent he'd do all he could to save his life, but Vincent responded, "I hope not or I'll just have to do it over again if I live." Or so one version of the story goes.

Thereafter, the doctor announced he believed it was a lost cause. "If he wants to die then he will probably die."

Vincent's brother, Theo, arrived later in the day by train and together he and the innkeeper's daughter stayed with Vincent through the next night when, finally, death got around to picking him up.

One of the last paintings Van Gogh had done was of Dr. Gachet, the very same who'd tried to mend his wound. In the painting the good doctor wore a button-down heavy coat, a tan cap, with his elbow resting on two books and his hand holding his head in thought. In front of him is a modest bouquet of purple foxglove flowers, from whence came digitalis and, perhaps, some of Van Gogh's madness.

And so perhaps the same flowers who killed the farmer's wife (Lilith) also may have contributed to the death of the artist (Van Gogh). Then some farmers named a town after the flowers and over a hundred years later a girl drowned in her car while one of Van Gogh's sunflowers ticked away eternity's time on her wrist there in the dark of her watery grave.

Jesus, I thought to myself, *Neil was right.* Neil deGrasse Tyson once said "We are all connected; to each other, biologically. To the earth, chemically. To the rest of the universe atomically.*"* I couldn't help but to keep thinking there was some odd pattern taking shape before me. But I couldn't make heads or tails of it. I just jumbled my brain up good trying. And what difference did it make? If the dream was true, then Emily was dead. She'd been dead all this time, just as the garden had foretold on the Fourth of July.

Oh, I realized, *the levee . . . I get it. I know why she was probably out there.* It would have been the perfect out of the way place to watch the fireworks away from the crowds. She would have had a direct view. So that's why she might have been driving on it. And it's so narrow, all it would take is a slip of the wheel and you could end up in the basin, especially at night. *Poor*

Emily, I thought. *What a sad accident.* Maybe this was why I was dreaming of her. Maybe in some cosmic way, Emily was reaching out because she wanted to be found.

As I went to the bathroom to do my business before going back to bed, I began to ponder what Harry would have thought about it all. Harry Truman, I mean.

Truman had philosophized on the matter of ghosts on occasion. Our 33rd President was convinced the White House was haunted. He wrote a letter September 9, 1946 to his wife Bess. Part of it read:

Night before last I went to bed at nine o'clock after shutting all my doors. At four o'clock I was awakened by three distinct knocks on my bedroom door. I jumped up and put on my bathrobe, opened the door, and no one there. Went out and looked up and down the hall, looked into your room and Margie's. Still no one. Went back to bed after locking the doors and there were footsteps in your room whose door I'd just left open. Jumped and looked and no one there! The damned place is haunted sure as shootin'. Secret service said not even a watchman was up here at that hour.

Maybe it was Lincoln knocking. Some say he did that. Several people have claimed to see Abraham Lincoln's ghost after he died. Winston Churchill once stated he exited his bath in the Lincoln Room one night, naked and smoking a cigar (as one imagines Churchill often did), only to find Abraham Lincoln leaning against the fireplace. According to Winston, he greeted the President's Ghost, "Good evening, Mr. President. You seem to have me at a disadvantage." Winston claims Lincoln smiled and then disappeared. Churchill refused to ever sleep in the Lincoln Room again.

Eleanor Roosevelt used the Lincoln Bedroom as her study and quipped in 1932 that she had a distinct feeling there was somebody always in that room. Her staff member, Mary Eban, claimed to have seen Lincoln in there as well. Theodore Roosevelt is said to have seen him, as did Roosevelt's personal valet who is said to have run screaming from the White House in pure terror. Grace Coolidge claimed to see him, and so, too, Queen Wilhelmina of the Netherlands. She claimed someone was knocking on her door as she slept in the Lincoln bedroom one night. When she got up and opened the door, Lincoln was standing before her. She was so shocked, she fainted immediately. And when she awoke, he was gone. Dwight D. Eisenhower claimed he once passed a man in the hall in the White House when he suddenly realized the man looked exactly like Lincoln. He turned immediately after passing the man to get another look, but there was no one there.

I'm having an Eddie moment, I realized. I was starting to go down the rabbit hole of one of Eddie's weird conspiracy theories. I'm not saying they're right or wrong. I'm just saying Eddie may have a valid point that a lot of people who have lived or worked in the White House have claimed to see very similar things many years apart. I'm not even saying I believe it. I'm just saying Eddie believed it and that maybe I don't think Eddie was so crazy for believing it.

And then there was Emily . . . still out there, several feet underwater just sitting in her car – parked beneath the water and hidden from all these people trying to find her. What if they don't find her? I read a story about a woman who had been missing six years before a drought revealed her car in a bayou. She'd been there all that time, people coming and going on boats, and so many probably walked right past the spot on the bank who knows how many times. I couldn't get the image out of my head of Emily just rotting away out there and nobody knowing what happened to her. It would become like *The Incident,* but worse . . . a mystery with no answer. Her parents would be staying up at night wondering where she was and what had happened to her.

I knew I couldn't leave her out there, of course. But what to do? *The Rule,* I reminded myself.

I ended up getting upset at Emily, which probably wasn't fair seeing as how she apparently died in an accident, but still, there it was. The more I thought about it, the less fair it seemed that I should have to break *The Rule* for someone who didn't even like me. "This is bullshit," I quipped to absolutely nobody. "You were mean as hell to me. I don't owe you anything."

You owe her at least common decency, Ruth, I thought to myself.

Shut up, little voice. Nobody asked you.

I crawled back under the covers and pulled the sheets up over my head. "I don't have to do anything," I told the darkness. But only silence answered. *They'll find her on their own eventually.*

Will they? And how long will it take? What about her parents?

"Ugggghhh!!" I groaned in frustration, kicking and shaking my sheets. "I'm not telling anyone," I pouted. "I'm going to bed!" I attempted to do just that.

But I couldn't sleep. I kept thinking of the Emily I knew in first grade when another girl, Amaya, peed her pants and cried. Emily tried to make her feel better. "It's okay. I peed sometimes, too," she told the girl. Or the Emily in second grade who brought the silver dollar she'd found under her pillow to school for show and tell. "I lost my big tooth but look what I got from the tooth fairy," she told the class, pointing both to her new gapped smile and the big silver coin in her hand. Or the Emily who, in sixth grade, told me she wished she had brown skin like mine. "I think it's so pretty," she told me.

Dammit. Damn, damn, damn. I felt a cry coming on. *Nope. Nope, I'm not going to do it.* Why should I cry for Emily Tolliver? She thought I was a freak. She enjoyed making fun of me that day in the bathroom. Why should I feel so bad for her? *She called me Quasimodo!*

People say mean things, sometimes. She was once your friend.

Ah, dammit. And a few tears got past me. "Okay," I told the darkness. "Only a little cry." *And tomorrow I'll figure out how to tell people where she is.*

Chapter 15

Beneath the Levee

The trick was to not be the one to find her, I decided. I couldn't leave her where she was, but I also couldn't very well tell everyone I had a dream and knew where she was.

So, the next day, I picked up Deja, then Lexi, and then we headed up to the Dairy Queen to meet up with Patrick and Jackson.

"Can I drive?" asked Patrick.

"Umm, no," I said.

"Awww."

"Hey, you can sit up front," Deja told Jackson, moving to the back. I side-eyed her. "After all, you're the one who wanted to check out the car," she added.

"Thanks," he said with a smile as he slid into the passenger seat.

Jackson asked me several questions about the modification Pops had made to the car as we rode around for a bit, checking out back roads I'm sure we and dozens of others had already covered. We stopped several times to look around, but we were miles from the levee. "There's no way she's anywhere around here," said Patrick at one stop. "Everybody has looked everywhere. Let's head up the highway to one of the other towns and drive around there."

"Maybe we should just call it," said Lexi. "I bet she's long gone – like probably drove out of state or something."

"Why don't we do this?" I suggested. "Let's just kind of backtrack. The last time anyone saw her or her car was on the Fourth, right?"

"Yeah," said Patrick. "She was at the fairgrounds earlier in the day, but I think she left before the fireworks, which is kind of odd."

"She probably met up with someone," said Lexi.

"Yeah, but the cops would already have that information. I'm sure they have her phone records and stuff," said Deja.

"That may take a while to get, though," said Jackson.

"Well, okay," I said. "So, if she left – she maybe went to go meet someone, right? In which case maybe someone did something to her. But if she just went off to be on her own, where's a place she might have gone around here that's kind of hidden, but that she could have driven to?"

"Well, that's kind of the obvious question," said Deja sarcastically. "But everybody's looked in those places."

"Maybe," I conceded. "But let's just drive back to the fairgrounds and start from there again. Maybe we'll think of some place we missed."

As we headed back out to the fairgrounds, I intentionally went the back way around to it that would take us near the levee. And as we approached the fairgrounds, the road went right over it. I slowed the car and looked down the levee. Way off in the distance I could see a bend that would take the levee around to the basin.

"Why are we stopped?" asked Patrick.

"Hey, yeah," said Lexi, looking the way I was looking. "What's down there?" she asked.

"The levee? Nah," said Deja. "Walkers already covered it."

"It won't hurt, right?" I suggested. And I turned the Beast onto the levee and started that way.

"I don't think you're allowed to drive on this," said Jackson. There was a fence to prevent cars from doing just that, but it was broken and had fallen over. It looked like it had been that way for many years.

"Probably not," I said. But the worn marks upon the levee indicated it had clearly been driven on many times. There were two distinct tracks going all the way down. As we crept along, I suggested, "What if Emily wanted to watch the fireworks, but away from everyone? Wouldn't this be a cool spot to go?" We rounded the bend and reached the clearing. I stopped the car, looking out on the basin, and asked, "What's this?"

"It's the drainage pond," said Patrick from the back seat. "It's got some big ole catfish in it. Lots of bass, too. It's a good fishing spot except for all the damn turtles that'll steal your bait. I been out here a few times." We all got out and had a look. Off to the right was a stretch of trees with dozens of egrets nesting. Out before us in the basin, we could see the triangular heads of a good half dozen turtles popping up along with circular ripples where fish were just barely breaking the surface of the water as they swam along.

Deja looked back on the other side at the drainage canal. "Fairgrounds would be off that way, right?" she asked.

"Yeah, I think so," said Jackson.

I tried to nonchalantly approach the edge towards the basin and just below was the concrete culvert jutting outward. As I did so, I saw just above it a large divot in the muddy soil. I looked back a bit the way we had come and could see the grass looked a bit pressed down, but not overly so. However, at the right angle, it did look like a line going down into the water and right where the water met the bank, the mud was definitely squished down a lot. My guess was that must have been where Emily's car went in. It must have been going backwards. I hadn't really doubted my dream, but actually standing there and knowing what was probably hiding just feet in front of me was still unnerving.

Jackson walked up to me. "It's pretty, huh?" he asked.

"Yeah," I said, still kind of looking at the line barely discernable leading down towards the muddy divot below. He looked down, too, but further right at the culvert. "So, I guess when it rains the water just kind of all runs down here, huh?" I suggested, acting like I didn't see anything out of the ordinary as I held a silent prayer on my lips that he did. I couldn't keep this charade going much longer before it would become too obvious. *C'mon, see it,* I thought, *see it, for Christ's sake.*

"Yeah," he explained. "So, lots of the water runs off the roads, you see, into ditches and then they lead over there," he said, pointing to the big ditch on the side, "then it all comes out here." He looked to the right where the birds were nesting in the tree. The he looked left. I could feel him pause as he tilted his head a little to get on the angle I had seen. "Hey . . .," he said, pointing at the near invisible line and the divot down below, "do you see that?"

About time, Sherlock! I looked again. "See what?"

"That," he said, and then he tilted my head a little with his hands gently. "You see it?"

"Yeah, it's like a line, right?"

"There's two of 'em."

I looked closer and he was right. Even I had missed that other one. Deja, Lexi, and Patrick walked over.

"What y'all lookin' at," asked Deja.

"Here, come stand right here," he told them. "Now look down that way. See that bit of mud down there that looks pressed down. Follow it back up with your eyes."

"I don't see anything," said Lexi.

"I see it," said Patrick, "and look here!" He walked down to it and moved some of the thick grass out of the way, revealing a much clearer divot in the dirt. "These are tire marks! And lookit, they go right in there," he said, pointing to the water below. "You don't think . . ."

"Mm-hmm," hummed Deja as she studied the scene closer.

"Shut up, guys," said Lexi.

"What?" asked Patrick.

"I know you're just trying to mess with us."

"No, we're not," said Patrick. "I'm being serious right now."

Lexi frowned at him. "Bull . . . you guys are trying to mess with us."

"No, I'm being totally serious," said Patrick. "That's tire marks. And they go right into there. You can see it! And they ain't that old."

"Mm-hmm . . . yeah, I see 'em, too," said Deja. "They do look like tire tracks, Lexi," she added with her eyebrows slightly raised.

Lexi looked worried now. "So . . . what do we do?"

"I guess we call someone," said Jackson.

"But what if y'all are wrong and that's really just nothin'?" Lexi asked. The others just looked at each other, uncertainty on each of their faces.

"But what if you're right?" I asked quietly. "I think they look like tire marks, too, now that I'm seeing it."

Patrick was staring at the water. "Y'all see that, too?" he asked, pointing.

"See what?" asked Deja.

"Look at the water close. See that rainbow tint to it. That's oil or gas or something in the water."

We all looked closer and saw as he saw, rainbow oily slick glinting in the sunlight. "This water's so polluted, though, that could be from anything," suggested Jackson. "But yeah, that plus tire tracks . . . man, I don't know. We may have found something here. Probably not, but maybe, right?"

"Well, even if it's nothing we're not going to get in some kind of trouble for just doing what they told us to do, right?" asked Deja. "I mean, they said 'if you see something, call it in.' Well, we see something, don't we? We all standing here sayin' we see it. It don't mean we know what we're seein'. But I'm looking at what you're looking at and it sure looks like tire marks going right into the water to me. And like you say, there's some kind of oil or gas around the water here. I mean, how do you explain that? There's no logical reason there should be any tire marks right here. How deep you think this thing is?"

"It's pretty deep," said Patrick. "After one of them hurricanes a few years back they came out here and made it deeper. I've been out here when the water is low, and it gets a lot lower than this. I'd guess this is probably nine feet or so."

"That'd be deep enough to cover a car," said Jackson. "I'm a little worried if we call someone, though, you might get a ticket or something, Ruth, for driving your car on the levee. Maybe we should park it back on the road?"

"Hell, we don't have to call someone to find out if there's something here. I can just jump in and see," said Patrick. "I ain't scared." And he started taking off his shirt and boots, not a care in the world about everyone seeing his scar. *I could learn a thing or two from Patrick*, I thought.

"You can't be serious," said Lexi.

"Sure, I can," he said back.

"There's snakes and stuff in there," said Deja.

"They ain't going to bother me. All the racket we been making, they're long gone anyway. I go swimming down at the river all the time and never had a problem. I seen plenty of snakes out there, too, but they just take off soon as they hear you."

"You sure, Pat?" asked Jackson.

"Yeah, ain't no thing but a chicken wing, man. I got this." And in lickety-split fashion, he had his jeans off and was down to his underwear.

"Oh, Lord," said Deja. "Boy, you better keep your drawers on. I ain't trying to see your white ass mooning me. Or other things." Patrick did a little dance for everyone in his underwear. "Oh, Lord, help me Jesus," said Deja. "This boy crazy."

Patrick started down the steep bank. "Be careful," said Lexi. And, as if on cue, he slipped, slid down a foot, tried to stand up, but then tilted right over and in, much like I had in my dream. "Patrick!" she yelled.

His head popped up immediately, "Damn, that's slippery," he said.

"Are you okay?" she asked.

"Yeah, I'm fine. Caught my toe on something coming in, but it's fine. Y'all come on in, the water's nice," he said with that big grin. "It's deep, too. I ain't even touching bottom." He slapped the water towards us as though he were playing in a pool, but we were way too high for it to reach.

"Just hurry up," said Lexi. "I can't believe you're in there. Is your foot bleeding?"

"I don't know. Probably," He smiled and then went under. He was down a good thirty seconds before his head popped back up. He wasn't smiling anymore.

"See anything?" Lexi asked. But he was gone again, back down.

"Why's he going down again?" she asked.

"Man, he's going to mess with us, watch," said Jackson. "I'll bet you five dollars he comes up saying he sees something."

This time it seemed like at least a minute before he popped back up again, although it was probably still just a few seconds. "Holy shit!" he said, his eyes wide.

"See, I told you," Jackson said.

"Na-uh," said Lexi. "Don't B.S., Pat."

"I swear to God her car's in here," he said.

"Don't be lyin', Patrick Elliott," said Deja in warning. "This ain't no joke."

"I'm not. Y'all, I swear to God. I'm not playing. Her car is seriously right here!" he said, pointing out in front of him. "Look . . .," and with that he swam forward a bit and then stopped. He was no longer swimming or treading water and he was raised slightly more out of the water, with his chest on up now out of the water. "I'm standing on her car right now," he told us. "It's right here. I swear to God. I swear it. I am not lying. I'm standing on it."

"No way," said Lexi. But the color drained from her face.

"Oh, wow," I said. And I wasn't just faking surprise. My heart was beating fast and had risen a couple of inches in my chest. I didn't think the dream was false, not after seeing the tire marks and oil slick, but it was still a shock to see this play out before me as it was.

Deja looked at me. "You think he's telling the truth?" I looked back at her and nodded. She went back to the Beast and pulled out her phone. "Oh, Lord," she said.

A half hour later, the top of the levee was buzzing with lights, emergency vehicles, and two tow trucks. The sheriff's office came out first since we were outside city limits. They immediately kicked us off the levee and told us not to call anyone or text about it. But it was way too late for that. Patrick, Lexi, even Deja had started texting people immediately after we had called 911. Word was already out well before the first sheriff's car arrived.

Before we knew it, we were back on the road watching and a news helicopter flew over our heads. They even called paramedics who came out to clean and patch up Patrick's big toe he'd sliced open on his slip into the basin.

"Seriously?" he had asked. "All this for a little cut on my toe?"

"No reason to take chances, son," said Billy Crutcher. The local police had arrived just after the sheriff's office. "It was a brave thing you did. You should have called us first, but still, good job." He looked over at me. "Ruth, you doing alright?"

"Sure," I told him.

He nodded his head. "Well, good to see ya, although I wish it was under better circumstances."

"Yup," I agreed. I still saw Billy around town now and then, of course, but it had been a while.

"That's Channel Two News!" said Patrick, his eyes careened up to the topaz sky. "We're going to be on the news!"

"I expect so," confirmed Billy. "If some news folks try to talk to y'all, please don't say anything until we've had a chance to talk to the family, okay? Emily's parents don't know anything about this just yet."

"You think she's in the car?" Lexi asked quietly.

"I don't know," Billy said. "I expect so."

"You know she is," Patrick said to Lexi. "She must have done like what Ruth said, driven out here to watch the fireworks and then missed the curve in the levee or something and slipped off of it in the dark." Billy looked at me with an interested eye.

Shut up, Patrick.

"Poor Emily," said Lexi.

Poor Emily, I silently agreed. But at least she was found. That was something, I guessed.

"And you found her, girl," Deja told me. Billy was still looking at me.

"No, not at all. Jackson did. I totally missed the tracks. I would have gone right by it."

"Patrick found her," said Jackson. "We all didn't even know if we were really seeing something or not. Not until Patrick jumped in and found the car."

"Well, sounds like you all found her," said Billy, and thankfully he stopped looking my way. "But Patrick . . ."

"Yes, sir?" asked Patrick.

"You did good today. You all did but jumping in that water to find her car. That was something. I'm going to make sure to tell your dad the same next time I see him." Billy and Patrick's dad were old friends.

"Way to go Patrick," I added.

"Yeah, way to go," said Jackson.

And Lexi was looking at Patrick like he was the cover of a romance novel written just for her.

While we talked Billy's radio went off. "Hey, Billy," said a voice.

"I'm here," he replied.

"Can you call on down to the auto parts store and see if they have a car cover we can use? Girl's in here. We need to cover this up when we put it on the flatbed. They don't want to remove her for crime scene folks."

"Damn," said Patrick.

"Yeah, I'll check with 'em," said Billy.

"So, she is in the car," said Jackson.

"I can't believe this right here," said Deja. "This crazy."

"Y'all weren't supposed to hear that, so remember, don't talk to anybody about this until we've had time to talk to her family," said Billy.

"Oh, Lord," said Deja, looking down the road. I followed her gaze and my heart sank. I didn't even have to recognize the car to know that Deja did. She knew who was coming down the road.

"What is it?" asked Billy, turning to look at the gold minivan rapidly approaching. "Aww, damn." He recognized it, too.

"What?" asked Patrick.

"That's Emily's mom's car, right there coming," Deja said. Billy got back on his radio to warn everyone.

Chapter 16

Please Don't Park on the Dead

It had taken a few days for police to do whatever they were doing, but by Thursday the arrangements were made, and the funeral scheduled for Saturday at one.

Bill Baker called and talked to Pops about it. "We're going to have a big turnout, I suspect," he said. "May even have some news folks. Any chance you can get out there and mow, maybe spruce the place up the day before?" he asked Pops.

"Sure thing," Pops promised. "We'll have it fixed up."

"I know you'll have it real nice," Mr. Baker said. He had come to think of Pops as the greatest thing since sliced bread. Pops and I had done wonders already to the cemetery over the years. Where before the grass and weeds were pouring out all over the place, monuments hidden by prickly lettuce and crab grass, we mowed, trimmed, and poisoned them into submission during our tenure. Now the place had nice clean lines along the winding roadway and curbs. And you could actually read the monuments, including some flat ones a lot folks probably didn't know were even there.

And the ants . . . oh, my Lord there were so many ant beds before we poisoned a good many out. We had a real heavy rain once years back when there were still hundreds of ant mounds all over the place. The rain left big patches of standing water out there in the cemetery. I remember looking out over it all and asking Pops "Hey, what's all that rust looking stuff floating around all over the place out there?" It looked kind of like brown seafoam or something.

He took a look. Then he took another, longer one. "That's fire ants."

"No!" I said, staring back at it all. "But they're floating. They can do that?"

"They're doing it," said Pops.

I had put on my rain boots as I had to get a closer look. And sure as shootin', Pops was right. That "rusty" looking stuff was actually millions and millions of fire ants huddled together, like life rafts abandoning a cruise ship or something. They were holding on to one another and floating the water, like a bunch of drunk college kids floating the Guadalupe. You wouldn't want one of those rafts of pain floating up to your bare leg, that was for sure. We still haven't god rid of all of them, of course. I doubt that's even possible. But Pops and I have done a pretty bang up job of getting rid of most of the fire ant mounds that used to dot the cemetery every five feet or so, it seemed. Now there were just a few about, and we regularly dusted them with Borax which kept the infestation under control.

Anyway, Deja had called me that Friday. "Hey, you're going to the funeral, right?"

"Well, sort of. I'm going to help out with the burial part, but I'm not going to the wake."

"You're skipping the service?" she asked. "Why?"

"Oh, you know. I don't really like that kind of thing after Mom."

"Oh," she said. "Sorry. I should have realized."

"No, it's fine. I just don't really want to sit through another one of those things. And Emily and I weren't really all that close, you know?" Plus, I didn't want to get too close. I was already having crazy dreams about Emily. I could only imagine what might happen if I got up close to her.

Deja paused on the other end of the line. "She should have been nicer to you. I understand."

"It is what it is," I told her. "I feel horrible for her. I just don't think we were that close is all."

We talked a bit about everything and then again about how crazy it was Emily Tolliver was gone. Deja summed it up towards the end of our conversation. "This is so crazy. I guess we all forget how fragile life is sometimes."

"Yeah," I told her. Although in my mind I was thinking, *I don't forget.* Watching Mom's life just slip away in moments was indelibly etched into my memory.

"Well, I'll see you tomorrow. You're up for talking and hanging out after the funeral and stuff, right?"

"Yeah, sure. It's just the service part I don't really like."

"Good. Because I gave Jackson your phone number."

"You did what now?"

"Now don't get mad or anything. He called me and asked for it. I think he just wants to make sure you're doing okay."

"Why wouldn't I be doing okay?" I asked. My defensiveness was pretty much automatic after all these years.

"Well, we did just find our dead classmate, Ruth. It's kind of a horrible thing. I know you're a tough girl and all, but I'm a little wigged out myself about it. So is Lexi. It's not every day someone you grew up with just up and dies like this."

"Yeah, I guess you're right," I told her. "I don't know . . . I guess after what happened with Mom and all . . . just nothing surprises me all that much anymore. Anything can happen to anyone, you know? Good things. Bad things. Anything can happen at any time, really."

"Yeah, but just because bad things happen sometimes doesn't mean they're normal, right? I mean, it's like school shootings or global pandemics, that kind of stuff. We hear about this sad and horrible stuff so much that we start thinking, like, that it's normal or something. But it isn't. You know I love you, right? You're like a sister to me. I just don't want to see you get jaded on the world or something. I hate what that asshole did to you and your mom. He was an evil SOB, but you know most people ain't like that. What he did ain't normal. Emily dying by this accident ain't normal, either."

"I know," I told her. "I hope I don't seem all callous or something. I care. I do. But you got to accept the things you can't change, right?"

"Yeah, but also to know the difference about what you can't change and what you can. I've been watching you, hanging out with us and Pat and Jackson and all . . . I like seeing this part of you, you know? You're like, coming out of your shell. And you see how they act around you now, right? They're not staring or anything anymore. Now you're just normal ole Ruth to them. And I think Jackson is into you."

"He's into my car," I corrected.

"Girl, you know that's just an excuse. He may like your car, but he clearly likes you, too. You know he ain't ask me for your number *just* to check up on you."

"I guess," I told her. After we talked, I thought about what she was saying and tried to take it to heart. *Maybe I should try to be more empathetic,* I thought to myself. I knew I had kind of walled myself off since *The Incident* and that it was kind of a defensive mechanism. But people sucked sometimes. I guess just sometimes was the operative word, though. And Jackson and Patrick had ended up being really nice so far. *We'll see,* I thought.

Normally the funeral home handled all the set-up and Pops just dug the grave then filled it back in, but we both decided to help out since there were so many people. We both skipped the wake, however. It was just as well as the chapel must have been packed with pretty much everyone from school. Emily was pretty popular, after all. And even people who didn't really know her all that well were attending her funeral. Maybe to pay their respects or maybe just to be part of the event this had seemed to become. I wasn't sure.

We could tell when the service ended because a long line of cars began snaking its way from the church in town down Old Cemetery Road our way. I'd never seen so many cars for one funeral. The local police were here to help control traffic, but they had their hands full, so Mr. Baker had asked Pops and I to help out with parking, which suited us just fine as we also wanted to make sure nobody messed up the landscaping Pops and I had worked so hard on the last few years, but it was no easy task given how many people were arriving.

A silver Volkswagon Jetta pulled up and I pointed towards a spot. Miranda Bennett, Amy Choi, and Amy's younger brother Kai stepped out. Amy looked striking today in her black dress with her jet-black hair which had been dyed pink at the edges. *That seems a little inappropriate,* I thought. I didn't know much about Kai, except that he was shy, skinny, and from what little I had heard about him, pretty smart. Unlike his sister, who had become a bit of a party animal, Kai was the nerdy academic who, kind of like me, only hung out with a couple of friends and pretty much kept to himself.

Miranda was wearing an elegant black dress with lace at the top and bottom. I hated how good she looked in that thing. And she was wearing what I could only assume was her mother's extra set of pearls. Or maybe she had her own. I had to stifle the eye roll I wanted to give.

Miranda took a quick look at me. "Hi, Ruth," she said awkwardly. No little snide jokes today, I guessed.

"Hi."

Amy muttered to Kai, "Come on." She grabbed his hand in an older sister sort of fashion and as she did, I noticed a splash of color . . . reds, blues, and greens, on her wrist in the form of a wristwatch. Then she gently pulled him by the hand, and he trailed behind her like a silent shadow.

After most folks had parked and found their way to the grave, I decided my services were no longer needed and was about to head back to the house for a nice glass of iced tea in the garden. But something stopped me.

Down the lane I saw a shimmer. It couldn't have been Lilith . . . not way out here. I usually only saw her shimmer in the garden around dusk. This shimmer was appearing in the middle of the day.

It was difficult to make out, but it appeared to be moving away from me with the current of the crowd. It disappeared. Only to reappear further down the lane where it seemed to stop.

No way. Curiosity got the better of me. I followed. I'd never seen a shimmer quite like this. Lilith's was almost invisible. Even Mr. Lancaster, that day when Adam and I had played catch, had a shimmer that was barely noticeable, almost foggy in a way, as though nothing but a trick of the light. What I was seeing now was more animated and substantial than ones I had seen before. I had to wonder if other people wouldn't be able to see it, too.

It disappeared as I neared again, but then I saw it reappear off towards the burial service. *Well, this is different,* I thought. But then again, I talked to killer flowers like we were old friends. So maybe this wasn't so strange after all. At least not for me.

I hadn't planned on attending the service, so I wasn't dressed properly for it, but I meandered up to the outskirts of the gathering. It was all too familiar. The same preacher who, several years ago, had eulogized Mom was giving practically the same speech again. Emily's mom was being comforted by another woman who looked similar, possibly her sister. Her dad stood beside the women, patting his wife gently, his eyes bloodshot and red.

Pretty much everyone from school was there. Miranda was standing with her boyfriend, Nate, who had found her in the crowd. Next to her Kai appeared to have his phone out and was playing a video game. *Classy,* I thought. Next to him was Amy and Logan Wallis, who was now holding her hand. *Ugh, Logan.*

They didn't seem to notice me there in the back, which was fine by me.

Most everyone else was listening solemnly, crying softly or just watching the coffin or their shoes sadly. *This is depressing,* I thought. *And this is why I don't like funerals.* I was about to turn and leave when the shimmer reappeared . . . right next to Miranda. It flickered a moment, then was gone.

I wonder if that's you, Emily, I thought to myself. But then I thought, *what are you doing, Ruth? You're breaking* The Rule. *Go home already.*

I turned to walk away, but I had taken mere steps when the shimmer reappeared . . . only inches from my face. "Whoa!" I whispered, taking a few steps back in surprise. It flickered . . . strangely. "What the . . ."

A guy named Alex from school turned and looked at me with a disapproving look. Apparently, he was the only one to hear me back there behind the gathering.

I waved my hand a bit and whispered to him, "Sorry. Wasp." He turned back around and shook his head.

I took that as my cue to make a hasty retreat and turned and started walking away. This was exactly what I didn't want to have happen. I didn't want to look like some crazy person in front of other people. It was bad enough people knew I'd been there when we found Emily at the levee.

As I was walking across the cemetery towards home, the shimmer reappeared right in front of me as if to block my way. I stopped dead in my tracks. It started flickering again.

"Nope," I said aloud, but quietly, turning my head back to the service to make sure I was far enough away that nobody could hear me or see this one-sided conversation. "Just . . . no. I'm not doing this. Go away." I closed my eyes and went right through the shimmer. But that stupid shimmer kept popping up around me. Flicker, flicker . . . again and again it appeared, like a puppy tagging along wanting its treat.

Flicker, flicker. "Stop it," I whispered. But it just kept blipping in and out. "Ugh, you're so annoying! Go away." *My life could not get any weirder right now,* I thought to myself.

When I reached the house, the shimmer was still trailing me, fading in and out like a mirage, but definitely following me and still flickering like a bad light bulb. By now, I was both really kind of scared but also a little angry. I had never seen a shimmer act like this. And as I passed through the garden, I said out loud, "Don't let her in."

I had no idea what I was thinking when I said it, and mostly I thought it an empty ploy, but something happened. The shimmer, which had been following right next to me, popped like a bubble and was gone. I stopped and turned around. *Wait, what just happened?* For a second, I was worried something horrible had just occurred. If that shimmer was Emily Tolliver, and I was certainly convinced by that moment it was, did I just accidentally exorcise her or something? But then I saw the shimmer reappear several feet outside the garden. It was flickering weakly and looked like it was struggling to stay visible.

Whoa, I thought. *Did the flowers do that?* I figured of course they must have, but I had no idea they could do something like this. But then again, I had no idea a dead person could do what Emily was apparently doing. Assuming this shimmer was Emily or some part of her. So this was new on several levels.

I also suddenly realized how bold it had been to utter what I'd said. I had never said something to the flowers that might be construed as an "order" before, and I wondered if I'd overstepped. The garden was a special place. And as I'd seen myself, a powerful place. It was not a place or a thing or whatever it was to be trifled with.

"Sorry," I said to the garden. "She's kind of freaking me out, though." *Was it a she? An it? No idea.* The flowers seemed to hum. They were curious about what was happening. Admittedly, so was I. I walked to the edge of the garden and just stood there looking at the shimmer.

Flicker, flicker, it continued weakly.

"What are you?" I asked.

It moved around in a chaotic sort of circle – blink, blink. There was a halogen bulb out in the barn with a bad ballast . . . this shimmer reminded me of it. Blink, blink, flicker, flicker.

And then it was gone.

I stood watching for a few minutes to see if it came back, but it didn't seem to reappear.

That was too weird, I thought as I went inside the house.

Chapter 17

Rumors

The knock at the back door some fifteen minutes later caused my heart to leap up in my chest. As I looked through the window, I saw Deja and Lexi standing by my little table in the garden. Deja must have seen the clear relief wash over my face because as I opened the door she asked "You okay? You looking a little jumpy."

"Yeah, I'm good," I said. "Just having a weird day is all."

"Aren't we all," said Lexi.

"You believe all these people?" asked Deja. "It's the middle of summer but it feels like a pep rally or something down there with everybody. A really depressing ass pep rally, though."

"Service over?" I asked.

"Pretty much. A lot of people are still hanging around, but I don't know why. Saw your dad still down there. Patrick pissed him off good. He peeled out in the grass with that stupid truck of his. I thought your dad was going to yank him clean out of his driver window for a second."

"That idiot," I said.

"Hey . . .," Lexi started in defense.

"Did he mess the grass up?" I interrupted.

Deja pulled out her phone and showed me a picture of two huge gouges. "Aww, Patrick!" I said.

"Pretty much," she agreed. Lexi gave her a look. "What? You know he was actin' a fool, girl. And that's your man. You need to talk to that boy."

"He's not my man," she said.

"Mm-hmm," Deja said dubiously.

"Well, okay, he's sort of my man. I mean, I guess we're dating now. But you have to give him a break, okay? He only sped off 'cause he got nervous is all," she defended. "Julie Schmidt kept bugging him about finding the car."

"Well that's a good thing, right? That Patrick found it." I said.

"You would think!" Lexi replied.

"Some people talking some ole bullshit," said Deja.

"About what? Patrick?"

"Apparently Miranda was saying it was awfully strange that Patrick jumped in the basin and found the car," said Lexi.

"You're kidding," I said. *Dammit.* "What's strange about it? It's not like he randomly jumped in. We all saw the tire marks."

"I know," said Lexi. "But then Julie started in about how Patrick wouldn't have really jumped in unless he already knew the car was there."

"That's stupid."

"Mm-hmm," agreed Deja. "Nobody's listening to that girl. She's got nothin' better to do than try to stir up some crazy rumor."

"Well, most people think it's great we found her car and everything," said Lexi. "But yeah, Patrick got really mad at Julie. She basically called him a liar in front of several people. I told her she didn't know what she was talking about and that she was being totally ridiculous, but Patrick left mad and kind of sped out."

"Well, I kind of know how he feels," I added. "It sucks when people start making stuff up about you."

"If people 'round here don't have any drama, they'll just make some," added Deja. "Everybody's talking now about why Emily was out on the levee and was she really there alone, blah, blah, blah. Just a regular ole accident where somebody died apparently just isn't exciting enough for some, so now here comes the rumors."

"Like what?" I asked.

"Like Emily must have been out there to meet someone or something. That seems to be the big one," said Deja.

"Yeah," agreed Lexi. "I mean, I kind of get it, though, right? It is a little strange she was all the way out there by herself."

"Maybe she just wanted some time alone," I suggested.

"That's what I think," agreed Deja. "I don't know why that's so hard for people to understand. If I had a car, I'd probably go on long drives by myself, too."

"I do," I said. "I go all the time."

"Yeah, but on the levee," remarked Lexi, "at night?"

"Well, no, of course not. That was a little odd," I agreed.

"Yeah, it's weird she would go out there alone just before the fireworks got started," said Lexi. "She was at the fairgrounds before that, we know that, so she literally left right before the fireworks. We don't know if she went straight to the levee or just ended up there later that night, but why'd she leave before the fireworks got started?" There was a slight pause before she added, "You don't think she killed herself, do you?"

"Why would she do that?" I asked.

"I don't know. She was an artist, right? You know, sometimes creative people like that are just . . . I don't know . . . extra sensitive to things and stuff. Maybe she drove into the basin on purpose?"

"I don't think so," said Deja. "There's easier ways to check out other than driving your car off a levee if that's what she wanted to do. Plus, they're saying the car was going backwards, like she was trying to reverse back to the street but went off the side. I straight up think it was just an accident."

"Yeah," I agreed. "Hey, what did you mean about her being an artist?" I asked.

"You didn't know? Wow, Ruth, you really don't pay much attention to other people, huh?"

"Well, she wasn't exactly all that nice to me."

"I know, but still . . . Emily was like a legit, straight up artist. She was into painting, sculpting, and some other artsy stuff . . . glass stuff," said Lexi. "She was really good. She won some big prize at the county fair last year for some porcelain thing she made with metal all in it – even won some scholarship money for it. She made jewelry and stuff, too. I saw some of her necklaces. They were pretty . . . like glass bead things with gold shaped in them. She was talking about selling them and I was totally going to buy one."

"It's sad, y'all," said Deja. "That girl had talent. And now she's gone. She should have never been driving out on that levee at night, I know that much."

"Yup," I had to agree. "Even in the daylight it was kind of scary driving on it."

"I guess we'll never know why she went out there," said Lexi.

"Anyway . . . can we talk about something other than Emily? That's all anybody's been talking about lately. Let's go do something tomorrow – like out of town for once," said Deja.

"We could go to Twin Rivers," I suggested. "I need a Starbucks fix." That was the closest one and it was still about a forty-minute drive.

"I just want to get out of town. I am tired of Dairy Queen, y'all. I don't care where we go," added Deja.

"Is it cool if the boys come?" Lexi asked both of us.

"Cool with me," said Deja.

"Same here," I agreed. "Although I may give Pat a piece of my mind about him messing up my cemetery."

"No, don't," she said. "He didn't mean it. You know, Pat acts like he's so tough and doesn't care what anybody thinks all the time, but he's really a sweet guy. And he likes y'all. He was so proud we all helped find Emily together, you know? I mean, it's a big deal to him. Now people like Miranda and Julie are trying to make it into some kind of bad thing. It bothers him.

Jackson and he are good friends, but I don't think he really has a lot of other friends. And, like I said, he really likes y'all. I seriously think it would hurt his feelings if you get all mad at him, Ruth."

"Okay," I said. "I mean, I'm not *really* mad at him. Grass grows back and all. Pat's cool. I like him."

"Really?" she asked with a big smile.

"Yeah . . . I can see why you like him. He's a nice guy. Plus, he has a scar way bigger than me," I added with a smile of my own.

"Yes, he does," agreed Deja. "He looks like he got in a sword fight and lost," she said.

"Honestly, when he showed us that thing . . . that was probably the first time in forever I really thought *okay, maybe mine isn't really such a big deal.'"*

"Oh, totally," said Lexi. "Pat thinks his is great. He'll show it to anyone. He doesn't even need to know them, and he'll still show them."

"You need to be more like Pat," Deja told me.

Oh, my God, she might be right, I thought.

"I can't believe I just said that," she added. "And what, do tell, do you think of Mr. Jackson Haynes, Ruth?" she asked with a coy smile.

"He's cool, too," I replied nonchalantly.

"Mm-hmm."

"Do you like Jackson!?" asked Lexi, looking at Deja, then me, and positively beaming at this point.

"I didn't say that!"

"But she didn't deny it, either, now did she?" quipped Deja faster than a greased bullet.

"Y'all quit. I said he's cool, too, alright? That's all."

"Well, I think he likes you. Y'all would make a cute couple," suggested Lexi. "And he's really nice."

We said our farewells with plans for the next day and then the girls headed out the back door towards the cemetery where I presumed Lexi had driven them given Deja didn't have a car. Floyd had mentioned to Pops he was planning on gifting Deja the Mustang when it was done, but she didn't know that, and I didn't ever tell her as I didn't want to spoil the surprise.

"Mind the flowers!" I told them as they walked the narrow path to the gate like a couple of tightrope walkers.

"We know, we know," said Deja.

"What is up with that girl and her garden?" asked Lexi, who probably thought she was too far away for me to hear.

"Girl's got issues," said Deja. "She did get shot in the head, remember?" But she wasn't trying to whisper, and she turned and gave me a wave with a smile. She knew I could hear them. But that was one of the things I liked best about Deja. You didn't have to worry about her talking behind your back. She wouldn't say anything behind your back that she wouldn't also say right to your face. And if she had something to say, she would always let you know. Deja trying to stifle her opinion was like Lexi trying not to let out that goofy laugh of hers. Neither of them could do it even if they tried. Maybe for a short span of time, but then it would build up and erupt like a volcano. If Deja clammed up for a week, she'd probably blow up and vent all at once. The thought was frightening. And who knows what Lexi would do. She'd probably pass out or pass wind if she tried to hold her silly laugh in. They were who they were, eccentricities and all. Kind of like me. *I have the most awesome friends,* I thought to myself.

Chapter 18

Time will Tell

Tick, tick, tick. . .

"Ugh, quit it," I said in my dream. What was this infernal ticking noise? I couldn't see anything, just pitch blackness. But that stupid ticking noise wouldn't stop. Couldn't I just have my own nice dream, maybe about being on a tropical beach somewhere with a cute guy (Jackson perhaps?) whose only desire was to fetch me whatever I requested? "More tea, Ruth?"

"Why, yes, please. On second thought, how about a lychee margarita?" And off he'd run to fetch it while I lounged in my chair with a good book. Lexi once made us lychee margaritas when her parents were out of town one Saturday. They were pretty darn good. Her mom's favorite, apparently.

But no, of course it couldn't be that easy. I had to sit in the dark and listen to this invisible clock tick away eternity for no apparent reason. It reminded me of Spanish class with Mr. Mack, the last class of the day, waiting for that last half hour of time to go by. If you ever get diagnosed with a terminal disease and are told you don't have long to live, you should move to Foxglove, Texas and take Mr. Mack's ninth period Spanish class, because every second of that thing feels like an eternity.

What? I asked the darkness. *What is up with this stupid ticking noise!? Will you please shut up, already?*

Slowly, the volume of the ticking receded a bit, but in a way, it became clearer, like the sound was getting tuned in better by an old radio. And then I saw light. I groaned. *Oh, come on. I'd really rather not.* But it didn't matter. My world faded away and like a camera coming back into focus, I saw a memory that was not my own.

I saw it as though I were looking through Emily's eyes. She was working on something. It looked like a small copper disc, but she was affixing wire to it in intricate shapes, bending them around curves and back again with a pair of tweezers. She must have been wearing some kind of magnifying glass visor because it was up close and delicate work. After a while, I could see what the shapes were that she was making. They were boats . . . tiny little boats.

There appeared to be eight total, four on the left and four on the right. The ones on the right were so tiny I couldn't imagine how she was even able to manipulate such tiny pieces of wire into such shapes. And they appeared to be on the water as Emily had made what looked like tiny little waves. While the other four boats appeared to be close and sitting on land . . . a beach, maybe.

As Emily turned her head, I could see she was comparing the tiny creation on the disc to a printout of a painting she was using for reference. Below it was listed *Saintes-Marie*. It appeared to be another Van Gogh painting. *Of course, it is,* I thought to myself, *more Van Gogh oddness.*

I watched, somewhat bored but also a bit curious. Why make it so small? And why was there a hole in the middle of the disc? Back and forth she went, comparing her creation to the painting.

After setting another miniscule piece of wire in place, she pulled close a little plastic container, like what one would use to take a teaspoon of medicine from. It had just a smidge of bright red paint or something it. Emily dipped the tiniest paint brush I had ever seen into it and when she withdrew it, what must have been only a few drops of paint were on it, but it looked grainy and watery. She then proceeded to paint just one small part of the nearest boat. At this rate, it would take hours to finish whatever it was she was making.

After the first brush stroke and the paint went on, she manipulated it to remain in between the single form of wire she had created for that one small area. Then she drew back and admired her work.

Tick, tick, tick.

The dream seemed to skip ahead in time. Where were we? We were no longer in her room. This room was much bigger with a row of windows, and there was a steel box in front of us. I could hear the sound of gas and flame, like a furnace.

The disc was all painted now and Emily had put it aside and picked up what looked like a large pair of metal salad tongs. She then used them to pick up some strange, tiny tripod of metal. As she turned, I saw she was not alone.

"You ready?" asked a man with a jovial round face. I recognized him . . . Coach Van. He was the art teacher up at the high school. He also coached volleyball.

"Yup," she said. Coach Van opened the door and I could now see it looked like a miniature oven. Well, more like a volcano. The inside was glowing bright orange and, in the dream, I imagined I felt radiating heat against my face. Emily used the metal tongs to place the tripod inside the little oven. Then she switched it out for what looked like a metal spatula which she used to lift the disc like a pancake. She then steadily moved it towards the oven. For a moment, her hand became shaky and the disc threatened to slide off, but Coach Van reached out and gently steadied her arm. She smiled awkwardly at him and he smiled back reassuringly. "You got it," he told her. Together, they placed the disc inside the oven on top of the tripod. Coach Van closed the door. "That's going to be a good one."

"As long as it doesn't curl up or crack," she said.

"It won't," he said. "You enameled the underside well enough. It'll hold up. Just take your time layering.

That's where you make or break a piece. The wire is thinner than the dial, so they may cool at different rates. Just go slow."

"I hope it'll be okay," she said. "I've already spent hours on this one. Like, hours."

They both took off their gloves and peered into the tiny window of the oven. The enamel was just bubbling now and melting into smooth glass.

"These cloisonné dials are so beautiful," he told her.

"Yeah," she agreed. "I never would have thought of this as a medium. It's really cool."

"I used to love those vintage pocket watches Waltham used to make with beautiful porcelain dials. I still have a few at home. They're getting rarer and rarer to find without cracks. Not many companies use enamel anymore."

"I know, and they're so expensive. Which is great! I have to say this is probably the first time my hobby has actually started paying me anything. I used to make those necklaces, but they would only sell for like fifteen or twenty dollars, which was barely above cost. These things make way more money."

"How are sales?" he asked.

"They're good. I mean, we can only make one at a time right now and all, but we're getting anywhere from several hundred all the way up to a well over a thousand dollars each for 'em."

"Whew," he whistled. "Think you can make me one?"

She did an *I dunno* shoulder-role. "I'd have to ask the boss about that one. I just do the dials."

He smiled. "Well, do that. I really would like one. I could pay for the parts and all, maybe even add in a little profit to boot. But I can't swing a thousand dollars, I'm afraid. I have a teacher's salary, remember. But these are just so cool."

"I'll see what I can do," she promised. "I'll definitely make you a dial, at least."

"Well, that's the best part, isn't it?" he said with a smile. "I'd be thrilled with just one of those. But one in a watch I could wear would be so awesome." They looked back into the oven. "It's ready," he said.

And then I woke up. I was back in my room, nothing but the faint hint of moonlight through the window to illuminate the dark.

I wanted to just roll back over and go to sleep, but I couldn't. My mind was caught up in Emily's memory. *Huh,* I thought to myself, stretching out and slightly annoyed at losing yet another good night's sleep to interruptions of other people's memories. This is what happened when I got too close to dead folks. I started dreaming some of their old memories. Following that shimmer on the day of the funeral up to the service had brought me closer than I had intended to get, so now came the dreams.

The memory settled a bit, like water clearing as silt settles. Watches. She was making a fancy watch dial. That would explain the hole in the middle and the small size of that disc. And it would also help explain this annoying ticking that seemed to invade my mind of late.

It seemed like an awful lot of work to make something like that, though. Why not just buy something off eBay or Amazon? They had every kind of design of watch a human could think of on there. But then again, Emily was an artist. And she'd said they were selling for hundreds of dollars, some even over a thousand. Was that each? *Wow.* I had to admit I was impressed. This was a whole different side of Emily I never knew. Of course, I didn't even know she painted.

Suddenly, I felt a bit of heel. I had summed Emily up as only those not so great parts I had seen on rare occasions, like in the bathroom those years ago. But there was more to her than that. She'd been a regular girl just like me. She had her own hopes, fears, and aspirations. I hadn't been treating her very nice. Well, her shimmer at least, whatever that was. I'd been acting like a brat. A scared, rude brat. And I resigned myself that I would have to do better. This was no way to treat the memory of a girl I had grown up with and once been friends with. I had no idea what happened when we died. Maybe she was long gone and all I was seeing were echoes and memories. But maybe part of her was still around, scared, wanting help. And if I was the only one who could see her, I'd turned my back on her. *Not very nice, Ruth,* said my inner voice.

Hey, she was mean to me first, remember? I reminded it.

Still . . .

I went to the bathroom to splash water on my face. Suddenly, another useless fact popped into my head. *The unofficial watch of U.S. Presidents is the Vulcain Cricket, the first mechanical alarm wristwatch first introduced in 1947 and worn by Harry Truman. Since then almost every U.S. President has been gifted a Cricket after they are sworn into office.*

I don't care, Eddie. Please keep your useless facts to yourself. Eddie's memories were like pimples . . . popping up when you least expected them and annoyingly difficult to forget about once they were there.

Chapter 19

Coffee is Essential

The next day I picked up Deja and we met up with Lexi, Patrick, and Jackson at the Dairy Queen. I was starting to feel like an Uber driver having them all pack into my car again. Still, it was nice to socialize with someone other than just Lexi and Deja for a change.

"Release the Kracken!" Patrick demanded with delight as we roared down the backroads in the Beast on our way to Twin Rivers. I decided to oblige and opened up the gas a bit. "Hell, yeah!" he exuberantly exclaimed in joyful approval.

It was the kind of hot, muggy day that made me thankful for air conditioning in the old car. The upgraded stereo system was coming in handy, too. I was letting Jackson thumb through my music stations on Pandora to find something to listen to when Kacey Musgraves' rendition of Neon Moon with Brooks & Dunn began to play.

"Oh, leave it here!" said Patrick. "This is a good one." And he began to sing, "When the sun goes down, on my side of town . . ." As the song progressed, we all sort of raised our eyebrows and looked at one another. Patrick was good. Really good. He had that southern drawl and smooth voice like so many popular country singers.

"Damn, Pat . . .," said Lexi, "I didn't know you could sing like that."

He just smiled his big goofy grin and kept singing. As the song kept going, we eventually found ourselves all singing . . ., "If you lose your one and only, there's always room here for the lonely, to watch your broken dreams dance in and out of the beams of a neon moon." Jackson was pretty much as bad as I was at singing, which made me feel better, because Deja and Lexi were both also pretty good.

The impromptu sing-along continued on our way to Twin Rivers and I found myself smiling and laughing, particularly as we did our rendition of *Thrift Shop* by Macklemore.

After several more minutes of impromptu karaoke, conversation returned. "Did y'all see Amy's brother playing that video game all during the service?" asked Jackson at one point.

"Yeah, that was pretty rude," said Lexi.

"And Amy just let him," agreed Jackson. "That was supposed to be one of her best friends, but she looked like she was on a date or something standing there holding hands with Logan the whole time while her brother played games."

"Hey, didn't you make out with Logan once?" Lexi asked me.

You did not just say that! I thought. "It wasn't really making out. We kissed. Once. For, like, a second. We don't even talk anymore."

"Oh, yeah, I remember hearing about that," said Pat with a laugh. "Man, he got ripped on for that."

It got uncomfortably quiet for a moment. Deja broke the silence. "So Pat, which one of your cousins is your favorite uncle?"

"Huh?"

"I'm just curious who peed in your family's gene pool. I mean, clearly, you're missing some brain cells or something. It must be a genetic thing, right?"

He seemed to think a moment. "I don't get it," he told her.

"You stupid," she summarized. And in the rearview mirror I could see was giving him that *and I mean it* look. She then looked at Lexi, "That's your man. Mm-hmm."

"Pat . . .," Lexi whispered to him, shaking his arm a little and looking towards me, "you hurt her feelings."

I just pretended not to hear her, but finally Pat caught on, "Aww, my bad," he said, immediately flushing and clearly embarrassed. "I'm sorry, Ruth. I didn't mean nothin' by it." He looked like a mouse caught in a maze, unsure of which way to turn. He looked quickly to Lexi for help, but she just rolled her eyes, so he tried his best solo, "Deja's right. Sometimes I just say stupid things without even thinking. I'm really sorry."

"It's cool, Pat," I told him. "I know you didn't mean anything bad by it and I'm sure it's true, anyway. He probably did get made fun of and all."

"Only 'cause people just don't know you that well," he tried to explain. "I mean, you're awesome! It's just most people don't know it, you know?"

"But we know it," said Jackson. I felt myself blush a little.

"Mm-hmm," I heard from Deja in the back. I wasn't sure if she was responding to Pat's explanation, agreeing with Jackson, or implying something else. Normally I could expertly read her *Mm-hmms,* but that one may have had a few meanings behind it.

"It was mainly Miranda and Amy anyway," said Pat. He didn't mention Emily, but I was sure if the other two had made fun of Logan, Emily had as well.

"Ooh, I can't stand them two," said Deja, "always acting like a couple of spoiled princesses. And I know we're not supposed to talk bad of the dead and all, but y'all know Emily was like that, too," she added. "She wasn't as bad as those other two, though."

"I don't know," said Pat. "Emily was always cool to me. I think she was way better than Miranda and Amy are."

"Bro, you know she talked about you behind your back, right?" said Jackson.

"Seriously?" Pat asked.

"Yeah, but only when the other two did."

"Which, let me guess, was pretty much all the time, right?" asked Deja.

"Well, yeah, I guess," said Jackson. "They're just like that."

"Like, what kind of stuff did they say?" asked Pat.

"Just the same stuff they say about everyone. Making fun of whatever little thing they find funny," said Jackson.

"So, like what?" pressed Patrick.

"Like, how you're loud, and silly, and kind of crazy . . .," added Jackson. There were almost certainly other, meaner things they said, but he didn't want to go there.

Pat looked a little hurt as it was. "Well, I guess they got me there."

"Which is why we think you're awesome, Pat!" said Lexi cuddled up next to him and kissing him on the cheek. "And you're handsome, funny, and brave."

"And I think you might be the best singer I've ever heard in real life," I added.

"Yeah, I'll give you that one," agreed Deja. "Boy, I would have never guessed you could sing like that. And you know I wouldn't say it if it wasn't true. I don't give compliments that ain't earned. Nah, uh. Not how I was raised. I'm gonna say it how I see it and tell it like it is 'til it ain't. That's just me. And you got some pipes on you. Where'd you learn to sing like that?"

His face reddened. "I dunno. Church, maybe?"

"Church!" Deja gawked. "You're kidding me."

"No," he replied. "I go regular. I sing in the choir down at First Baptist."

Deja laughed. "I'll be damned. I sing in the choir at First United!" she added. "Good for you, Pat. I'm going to invite you to my church one of these Sundays. Ooh, I'd love to see the look on their faces when you start belting out some vocals like you just did. It'll blow their minds."

Pat was all smiles, too. "My grandpa was a really good singer and a fiddler. Maybe I take after him."

"Well, you can come sing with me any time," she told him. "Just try to think before you speak, mmkay?"

"Yeah, my bad," he said again. Lexi pat his hand, reassuringly.

"You're alright," Deja told him. "We cool. I just ain't good at keeping my mouth shut, neither. If somebody says something about one of my girls, I'm gonna be on it."

"And don't sweat what Miranda or Amy may say," said Jackson. "They do that to everyone. I doubt Amy even means it. She used to be pretty cool, too, but I think her parents' divorce did a number on her." He turned in his seat and faced them. "You remember her in middle school . . . what a little bookworm she was? Now look at her. She went crazy after her mom and dad broke up. And you see how her brother is, right? He's like super withdrawn and hardly talks to anyone. And Miranda . . . well, Miranda's always been Miranda, I guess."

"Miranda's like that because of her mom," added Lexi.

"What do you mean?" asked Jackson. "I've met her mom. She seems nice, always so polished and . . . what's the word . . . sophisticated, I guess."

"Nah, that lady's just stuck up," said Patrick. "I've met her a couple times. Both times her nose looked like an ole ski ramp the way she was looking down on me. And I'm taller than she is! It's like she's some physics wizard . . . looking down on everyone even if they're taller than she is. I don't like that lady."

"Well, I'm just saying she carries herself well, I guess," Jackson tried to explain. "She always looks and acts so proper, you know what I mean?"

"No, no. Pat is totally right," said Lexi. "I could tell you stories about Mrs. Bennett. I was in Girl Scouts with Miranda when we were little, and her mom was the troupe leader. And, Oh My God, that woman . . . she had a comment for every little thing. And you know, those snide comments that, like, two-faced people always say, things like 'Oh, that's a cute outfit you have on today, Miss Lexi. Don't you think it'd look nicer if you fixed your collar and tried to wear it right, though?' Just stuff like that. And she always called us Miss. Miss Lexi, Miss Sarah, Miss Jennifer . . . I remember I wore some ribbon in my hair one time and she was all 'Miss Lexi, aren't we maybe a bit old for ribbons in our hair?' Then the other girls made fun of me for it. My mom was pissed when I told her about it. I was seven! There's something wrong with that woman, I'm telling you. And she was non-stop nit-picking Miranda about everything . . . the way she ate, the way she talked, how she sat, just nothing was ever good enough. She had something to say about anything and everything. I don't know how Miranda deals with it, to be honest. I can't imagine living with that woman. She's a nutcase."

"Well, Miranda's basically turning into her mom," added Deja. "I can't hardly tell the two of them apart when they're together. They walk alike, talk alike, act alike . . . it's like Miranda is a damn clone or something of her mom. It's just weird."

"Sounds sad, actually," I muttered.

"Well, I don't think either Miranda or her mom likes me at all," said Pat with a laugh.

"No, probably not," said Lexi with a smile. "And that's a good thing, Pat. I don't know what kind of guy Miranda's mom is ever going to think is good enough for her little princess, but I'm sure it's not a guy I'd ever want to hang out with."

"Mm-hmm, I know that's right," agreed Deja. "And sad or not it's no reason for her to act like she does to everyone else," she said directed towards me. "I mean girl, let's be real. You been through more than anyone else I have ever known, but you're still cool as hell. So that girl has no excuse."

"Yeah, Ruth," said Pat. "You should have been hanging out with us years ago. You're good people."

I laughed. "Thanks, Pat. You are, too." Out of the corner of my eye I saw Jackson looking at me with a smile on his lips. *That dimple,* I thought . . . *he has such a cute dimple on his cheek when he smiles.*

I hadn't felt so normal in years. We spent the day in Twin Rivers going to the mall, eating junk food in the food court, and then went to a park with a pond that had about a thousand turtles in it we fed our leftover lunch to.

"Hey," whispered Jackson next to me on the bank of the pond. "Any chance you'd like to hang out with me some time?"

"We are hanging out," I stupidly said, not picking up on what he was asking at first.

"No, I mean, like, just us. You want to maybe go do something tomorrow afternoon? I got a summer job down at the dollar store, but I get off at three and could swing by your place around four, maybe?"

Is he asking me out? I thought.

Yes, dummy, replied the little voice in my mind. *Now would be a good time to say yes.*

"Yeah, sure," I said. *Holy crap,* I thought. *I have a date!*

Chapter 20

The Old Oak Tree

Tick, tick, tick . . .
Nope, go away.
Tick, tick, tick . . .
I mean it. Quit.
Tick, tick, tick . . .

The dream began with the same eerie ticking noise I had heard when I dreamed about Emily in her car. Except this time, when my eyes opened in the dream, a landscape appeared. A solitary tree stood before me. I looked around and it was as though I were yet again inside a painting inside my dream. There was a bench under the tree and upon it was a shadow. It looked like a pendant. I looked up, and there hanging from the branch of the tree was a rope with a noose tied around it. *Well, I don't like the look of that,* I thought.

I looked around but didn't see anyone. There was a trail nearby, brownish black but of some sort of synthetic material, not dirt. Like grains of sand, a million tiny brushstrokes established the form of the trail as it ran both backward towards some woods and forwards into a greater expanse of clearing. Looking that way, I could see picnic tables and a trash can. I reached up for the rope and tried to grab it, but it just faded through my fingers.

The ticking continued.

"Is someone here?" I asked the emptiness.

Tick, tick, tick . . .

"Enough with the damn ticking noise, already."

I began to hear a slight noise. It sounded like . . . crying?

"Emily?" I asked.

I'm sorry! The thought came to me in my own voice in my mind but was not my own. *I'm so sorry!*

Upon the shadow of the noose on the bench, a form appeared. I looked up but saw no one. The rope had disappeared, yet its shadow still remained and showed someone standing on the bench. Arms reached out to the side. Shadowy hands grasped the shadowy circle and placed it over the head.

Wait, stop, I thought. "Emily?" I asked. But how could it be Emily? She was already dead. *Oh, no. What if this is someone else and I'm dreaming of them like I dreamed of Emily?*

"Don't do it!" I said. I climbed up on the bench but there was no one there. Yet when I looked down, the shadow continued towards its intention. "Wait! Don't!"

I'm sorry. The feet stepped off the bench.

The ticking stopped.

I awoke. And after a momentary pause for reflection, I told my ceiling, "Well, that sucked."

Chapter 21

So You Think You Can Paint

I awoke in the morning, safe and sound under my covers. I sighed. Somewhere out there in the world, close by given I had picked it up in a dream, there was probably a body hanging in a tree just waiting to be discovered if it hadn't already. *Well, it won't be me finding it this time,* I thought. *Once was enough for me. I guess we're going to be having another funeral soon.*

The last time I'd dreamed about something like that was the night Emily died. I felt pretty sure someone had died last night. But something felt off about it. I couldn't put my finger on it. While it was a dream very similar to other deaths I'd dreamed about before, this one felt less tangible. I didn't actually see someone die, did I? It was just a shadow. Why would I only see a shadow with nobody there? *Something isn't right.*

Oh, forget it, I told myself. *This is why you have* The Rule*, Ruth, remember?* I reminded myself. *So, you don't drive yourself completely crazy with thoughts like this. Someone got depressed and killed themselves last night. It's sad and it sucks, but it's done and there's nothing you can do about it now. So just get on with your day.*

I was already feeling anxious enough as it was, what with my first date ever in about seven hours. *How sad is that,* I thought? Most girls my age had already had a few boyfriends over the years. Some were even in what many would consider long-term relationships. *Hey, better late than never.* Not that I was thinking Jackson and I were going to end up in a relationship or something. I mean, it was just a date. But still. He was awfully cute. *That dimple . . .*

After brushing my teeth and my hair (admittedly far more thoroughly than I usually did), I still had several hours to kill. Part of me wondered if I should jump in the Beast and go for a drive, maybe see if anything was happening in town like, oh, I don't know, news about someone dying last night.

Nope, none of my business. Go read a book, Ruth. So, I picked up my iPad and I went to the garden to try to find a new novel to read. Several looked promising, but I was too distracted to read. *Dammit,* I thought, switching over to Safari and then going to the local news website. Would there be anything in there about someone hanging themselves last night? Probably not. Most suicides didn't end up in the newspaper, I had learned after working at the cemetery. Police and news were usually pretty respectful about things like that.

I didn't find anything in the paper that stood out. *Who was it?* I wondered. God, I hoped it wasn't anyone I knew. Had to be close, though, for it to reach my dreams. *Poor guy or girl or whoever.*

I kept thinking about the conversation we had in the car about Emily, Miranda, Amy, and basically the whole situation. *Don't be anyone I know,* I thought again. I of course wasn't a close friend of Emily's or anything, but I was beginning to understand that she, I guess like so many people, was a multi-faceted person and I was only seeing one side of her when she was hanging out with Miranda and Amy, probably trying to impress her Queen Bee friend, Miranda.

I was sad I hadn't gotten to know her other sides. She'd been so talented, artistically. That miniature painting of the boats on the watch dial . . . how in the world did she do that? And in glass, no less. It was really something. I wished I could do something like that. And the more I thought about it I began to feel infused with an odd pent-up energy, like I needed to be doing something creative. And I needed to get my mind off that sad dream. So, I figured maybe I could try a little art. I wasn't sure why, I had never really felt the urge like this before, but hey, I had time to kill. Why not?

I had a full art kit in my closet, with paints, four canvases, and brushes. I think Mrs. Jenkins, my eighth-grade teacher, had given them to Pops thinking art might be a good outlet for me after *The Incident.*

Wow, these are pretty old, I thought as I examined the tubes. But I had never opened any of them and they were all still sealed with a little metal cover on each end that had to be punctured by a little spikey thing in the cap to open, so I figured they were probably okay.

Next, I grabbed a pencil, a large eraser, and, having pretty much no idea what I was really doing, I took it all out to the garden. I didn't have an easel, so I just took the other chair that was out there and put one of the larger canvases up on the armrests. There wasn't much of a breeze, so it seemed to work okay. Then I sat down in the other chair and looked at my blank canvas. *Alright . . . I got my canvas, my paint, a big glass of mint iced tea . . . now what do I do? What am I going to paint?*

Probably because I lacked originality, I decided to paint, what else, the garden. At first, I was going to try to sketch it out with the pencil. But then I realized I really didn't need to. As I looked out over it, I realized that abstractly it just seemed like just a bunch of various colors all bumping into one another. It suddenly dawned on me that maybe an impressionist painting might not be so impossible to try. Just throw down some of the colors I could see in the garden and see what happens.

I lost track of time. Hours slipped by and I barely even noticed. It was pretty Zen-like being out there, just dabbing more color here and there. The flowers seemed to hum quietly in my mind. They liked having their portrait made. Or maybe they just liked me admiring them for hours. Whatever the case, I sensed something akin to satisfaction from them . . . maybe even pride. It made me smile. It was such a pretty day, too. It'd been a scorcher of a summer so far, but today wasn't so bad and the sun felt nice as it arched overhead signifying noon.

I leaned back and looked at my creation. I couldn't believe what was in front of my eyes. By no means was it anything as good as Van Gogh or even Emily would have done, but I had a real painting. It actually looked like the garden. It was so pretty. I couldn't believe I made it. I took a moment just to take it in. *Wow,* I thought, *I didn't know I could do that.* And maybe I couldn't. I wasn't sure if what I'd just done was me or a product of Emily's memory. But it didn't matter. A painting of my favorite place in the world was sitting there in front of me. And my hands had done it. I felt amazing.

I heard chirping overhead and looked up to see Ruby on the roof staring down at me. "Hey, you," I said. Maybe she was admiring my painting. "What do you think?"

She flew away. "You know, I don't even know why I bother trying to talk to you," I called after her.

"What about y'all?" I asked the flowers, turning the painting around as though they had eyes to see. Whether they could or not, they hummed approval nonetheless. "Thanks," I said. "What do stupid birds know anyway, right?" I stared at the painting a moment. *It's missing something.* "Oh, I have to sign it," I said. And I found the tiniest little brush in the kit which I dipped in black and then signed my name to it. "There, now we're done."

I took a long drought of my tea, finishing it off, and then a deep breath. After another moment of self-appreciation, I closed my eyes and tried to envision Emily working on the dial again. Working on such a small and confined area seemed significantly harder than the painting I had just done on a broad canvas. All those tiny little pieces of wire that had to be bent just so and placed together to make the pattern. Then the enameling and the firing. Each layer had to be gently applied, fired, and then a new layer applied on top. No, I was sure not ready to try something like that. Even with Emily's memories apparently amping up my artistic abilities, that seemed way out of my league.

As I thought about her working in the memory, I tried to intentionally lose myself in it to see if anything new would pop in my head. I seemed better at picking up old memories when I didn't try to extract something. Often, things just popped in my head when I was completely spacing out and not really thinking about anything.

This is probably too much information, but Eddie's weird presidential facts were always popping in my head in the bathroom, which was always a little weird. But I guess I did my best spacing out in there. And, although I don't like to think about it, I had a strong suspicion that's where Eddie did most of his reading. So that's probably why I picked up on his old memories so much in that particular room of the house. Admittedly, the thought sometimes creeped me out. It was almost like we were still living with the guy in a way.

I thought about Emily and her art, but I also let myself just kind of think about nothing . . . just float above her memory without trying to pull anything from it. Let something pop out on its own if it wanted to. I felt a churning in my thoughts. Several of the tidbits I'd discerned just sort of clicked like little Legos snapping together. All the weird art memories I was having of Emily, the strange way I'd seen the location of her car in my dream as if though it was an animated oil painting, and even the painting I'd just done of the flowers . . . they all seemed to coalesce into an idea of sorts. This was the same sort of way Lilith's history came together in my mind. Kind of like the enamel powder Emily worked with . . . when it reached the right temperature, all the little individual grains just sort of melted together to form a larger design.

I looked at the foxgloves I had painted, then I thought about the foxgloves in the jar on the table in Van Gogh's famous painting of Dr. Gachet. What was this incessant feeling that there was some whisper in the universe trying to tell me something and I was missing it? Why were the dreams I had of Emily all about this art stuff? And why was I thinking about Van Gogh again? I mean, I liked art as much as the next person, but I wasn't normally all into it. And this nagging thought in my head was like a bee buzzing around, its bzzz, bzzz was starting to drive my batty.

What is it? I asked the void. *What am I missing?* The melting of various thoughts began. I knew Emily had been recreating Van Gogh's art in glass on watch dials. It wasn't just the boats on the one dial I had seen. There had also been the sunflower on her watch. My guess was she had made several or more such pieces.

Despite knowing I really shouldn't delve into her life or death like I was doing, I had to admit there was a bit of a sense of pride in putting some pieces together. I was getting pretty good at picking things up, I thought. This was kind of cool. I really didn't have any huge interest in the stuff Eddie's old memories jammed into my head unbidden, but I was finding this information pretty fascinating. I didn't even wear a watch or anything. I just used my phone to tell the time. But still, here was this whole art thing I had never even thought of before. And looking at the painting in front of me I'd unbelievably just made, I suddenly felt a part of it. I felt the joy of creation, the satisfaction that something beautiful was wrought by my hands. *This must be what Pops feels like when those old engines fire up after so many years of brokenness,* I thought.

Okay, if Emily was making the dials, who was making the rest? Working on something that detailed and with so many parts would be difficult. So that meant someone who knew how to do that would have been working with Emily to put her dials on a movement, add hands, put it in a case, and make the whole thing look and work right so they could sell them for top dollar. It seemed obvious by Coach Van asking for one in the dream of the memory that he wasn't her partner. But someone was. So, who was the *boss* she had asked about?

There was still that something gnawing at me. Something just didn't feel right. *Let it go,* I told myself. *The Rule, remember?* I was breaking my own rule by even letting myself get caught up in all these things about Emily's life. I was letting Emily's memories, and her talent, drag me to places I'd promised myself I wouldn't go. I did not want to slip up and start having everyone think I was totally out of my mind. It was bad enough I sometimes spoke out loud to the garden. I really needed to be more careful about that. Although Pops was really the only one who might accidentally overhear me, and I don't think he would have thought much of it if I just explained that was my way of talking to myself.

Still, the questions and curiosity were popping up in my mind like the shimmer had on the day of the funeral – persistently there and hard to ignore. I found myself wanting to know what had happened. Why was she out there on the levee that night? Was she really just out there by herself to watch the fireworks? I had to agree with Deja and Lexi's assessment . . . that just seemed off.

You're straying from The Rule, I thought to myself.

Yeah, but you knew Emily, countered the little voice. *That makes this different.*

Does it?

Well, does it feel different?

The little guy had me there. It did. It wasn't some stranger who had died that I was being curious about. This was a girl I'd known since grade school. And sure, we hadn't been all that close lately, but was it so wrong to be drawn to her life and death when it was someone I had grown up with like this?

I'd been so embarrassed and paranoid about being ridiculed or feeling like a freak around other people for so long, I'd crawled into a little shell like a turtle, hiding away from everyone except my two closest friends and Pops. This internal place I'd retreated to may have sheltered me and made me feel safe like the turtle's shell, but it also held me back.

It was time to stop giving a damn what people said or thought about me and just live my life how I wanted to. And if people called me a freak, so what? I only had one more year of high school anyway. After that, there was a great big ole world waiting for me. I could be whoever I wanted to be. *Unlike Emily*, I suddenly thought to myself. Her options had been closed now. Like Mom, she'd run out of road. And she'd been so young, like me.

Something had to change. I decided I certainly wasn't going to tell anybody about my dreams or the shimmers, but I would try to stop cutting myself off from everyone, including Emily, like I had always done.

I picked up my painting and prepared to head inside. But then I stopped and said quietly to the garden. "If she comes back, you can let her in if you're okay with it. I should be nicer to her."

And I felt something emanate from the garden. It felt like maybe it was considering what I'd said but wasn't sure what it wanted to do about it. I definitely sensed that the garden itself had an opinion on this particular matter. Was it being protective of me? I wasn't completely positive, as with all things with the garden, nothing it conveyed was ever really said, only felt. But as I pondered it, I thought that was what I was feeling. The garden had been attacked a few times throughout the years, first by the farmer and then by Eddie. It was a survivor, strange though it was. And I think it saw me as kind of the same way, like I was a wounded duckling that it had taken under its wing. We had a kinship. I had to admit the feeling brought a bit of warm joy to my heart. "Aww," I said to it. "Thank you. You're such a good friend." And I went inside as the flowers hummed and swayed gently on a breeze that wasn't there.

Chapter 22

Cloisonné

It was one thirty and I still had a couple of hours before Jackson was due to come by, so whether it was boredom or continued curiosity, I decided to research more about what Emily had been doing.

Enameling had been around for thousands of years. It involved using glass and metal oxides which were mixed into an enamel paste and then fired to about a thousand degrees, causing it to liquefy and bond to metal.

Enamel watch dials, such as found on old pocket watches or luxury wristwatches, required multiple layers of enamel powdered or otherwise evenly applied onto metal, usually copper or silver. Each layer was applied and fired separately. The thicker one tried to make any single layer of enamel for any one firing, the more likely it would be that it would crack or not look right. However, the more layers, the more depth and luster the enamel would have. Only with perfect balance could a perfect result be achieved. It was, by all accounts, a very time-consuming medium and apparently very difficult to get right.

And if all that wasn't difficult enough, I then learned Emily wasn't just making enamel dials, she was doing cloisonné enameling, which went several steps further in that each section of the dial was separated by tiny bits of wire hand bent and placed just so to keep each little color of enamel separated from other colors. For instance, a flower design would require each petal to be formed of its own wire. Each section of whatever design was sought would have to be painstakingly mapped out with miniscule strands of wire for each color and section. This upped the level of difficulty and, at least for watch dials, increased the rarity.

As I killed an hour or so surfing the internet on this strange world of watchmaking, I learned luxury watches with cloisonné dials sometimes could sell for astronomical prices. Some of the rarest were by brands such as Rolex and Vacheron Constantin with dials by famous cloisonné artists such as Nelly Richard, Marguerite Koch, and Carlo Poluzzi. Looking through eBay I found a few cloisonné dial watches going for anywhere from two thousand dollars to several that were listed for around seven to ten thousand by such brands as Omega, Longines, and Franck Muller. I even saw one by Patek Philippe going for a hundred and forty thousand dollars. I couldn't believe it. For a watch! Like, that you put on your wrist and wear around to see what time it is . . . which a five-dollar quartz watch would do just as easily. *That's a house,* I thought. *Who would spend enough money to buy a house on a watch? Rich people, I guess.*

As I clicked through the listings, I came upon one that was just unbelievable. There before me, with a *Buy it Now* price of four thousand dollars, was a cloisonné watch upon the dial of which was a blood-red background with a snaking tree branch full of white flowers. I'd seen something very similar recently. *No way,* I thought to myself. I clicked on the listing and then knew it was much more than a coincidence. The seller's name was listed as *Mugunghwa.* And below the name it listed a city and State. *Foxglove, Texas.*

"I'll be damned," I said out loud.

I searched online for *Van Gogh Almonds.* I could vaguely remember the almonds part from prior reviews of his artwork. There was one in particular I was looking for . . . and there it was . . . Van Gogh's *Red Blossoming Almond Tree.* Emily had made that dial. There was not a doubt in my mind. So, who was selling it?

I figured it was a shot in the dark, but I Googled the seller's name, Mugunghwa. And I got a hit.

Mugunghwa wasn't a person at all. It was a flower, *Hibiscus syriacus,* the national flower of South Korea.

Oh, now that's interesting, I thought. And one of my own memories came back to me, that of Amy Choi's wrist with a splash of color upon it at Emily's funeral. "Ha!" I said proudly, "found you!"

Chapter 23

Merry Go Round

I heard the knocking at the back door. *He's in the garden?* I asked myself. *Why is he out there?*

I opened the door and there was Jackson. "Hey," he said with that smile of his.

"Hey."

"Hope you don't mind me coming to the back door. Lexi had told me you were always out there so if I came over to just walk on back and I'd probably find you at the table out here."

"Well, normally that's true. I was outside earlier."

"That's a hell of a garden you got there," he said, thumbing back towards the flowers. I was picking up a distinct *who's this guy?* coming from the garden, however.

"Yeah, thanks. Well, come on in." I gave him the quick tour of the house.

"Is it cool I'm in here while your dad's out?" he asked.

"Yeah, of course. Why wouldn't it be?" I said.

"Oh, okay," said Jackson. "I don't know. Some dads might not be cool with it, is all."

Oh, yeah, right. I'd never had a guy over before so hadn't even thought about it until just then. Would Pops freak out if he saw Jackson in here? Pops was probably in the barn, but I hadn't seen him in hours. I doubted he'd care. Pops trusted me. If anything, he'd probably be happy to see me hanging out with a boy for once.

"Nah, we're good. Although we should probably head out."

"Yeah, sure," he said. "So . . . where do you want to go?" I had been wondering that same thing. There weren't many places to go around Foxglove and sitting up at the Dairy Queen seemed like an invitation for gossip and not overly exciting. DQ had some decent coffee . . . Mocha Moolatte wasn't bad . . . but it still wasn't Starbucks. Suddenly, an image flickered in my mind. The dream . . . a park bench beneath an old Oak. I shook it off. "Wherever," I responded. "Maybe just go for a drive?"

"Sure," he said.

For once, he drove, and I enjoyed riding in his old Chevy Truck. It was pretty beat up, but it was clean and smelled like Febreeze. *Aww, did he clean his truck?* I wondered. It certainly looked like it had just had a good wipe-down.

We headed for Main Street in town and cruised past the old shops and stores. In the sixties these would have been all full . . . dress shops, beauty salon, hardware store, toy store, you name it. But these days, more than half were closed. Some had been closed for decades, a few others finished off by Covid in 2020. *Stupid pandemics.*

The other half that remained consisted of mundane things that could still survive in a small town notwithstanding the Amazon and Walmarts of the world. There was still a beauty shop Ms. Shirley owned. She pretty much cut most everyone's hair in town, guys and gals. We had a thrift store, two antique stores which both took consignments and whose owners were two sisters rumored to have hated each other since they were kids. I really don't know how either one of them even stayed open as I couldn't imagine they had much business. There was an auto supply store and Pops was one of its best customers. But not much else.

Kacey Musgraves was on the radio again aptly singing about the Merry Go Round of life. "Are you playing her just for me?" I asked.

"Well, I like her, too," said Jackson.

He's really making an effort here, I thought. *Clean truck, playing the music he knows I like. This guy's making a pretty good impression, I have to say.* Kacey's song aptly fit the state of the town in a lot of ways. *This could be our town's theme song,* I thought to myself as we passed the many dilapidated old buildings.

"Want to stop in for an ice cream or something?" Jackson asked as we neared the red football shaped logo with "DQ".

"Nah, maybe later."

Past the Dairy Queen was the turnoff to head out of town, and as we neared it, I saw something glinting. At first, I thought it was a play of light off the windshield, but then I realized what it was . . . a shimmer. The shimmer. And it was right in the middle of the turnoff. *I thought you'd gone for good.* I straightened up a little in my seat and tried to get a better look. If the shimmer was indeed Emily, or some echo of her, it certainly picked an interesting time to pop back up. *Bad timing, girl,* I thought to myself. *Or is it? What are you up to over there?*

"You up for a drive out of town?" I asked.

"Yeah, sure," said Jackson, taking the right turn and heading out.

A few miles down the road we hit a "T". A right turn would take us back into town, ironically right back on Main Street eventually, and a left turn would take us truly out of Foxglove. I saw the shimmer appear far down the left road. Jackson, apparently already noticing me look that way, automatically took the left.

"We could head out to Twin Rivers if you want," he suggested. "I know you like the Starbucks out there, right?"

"Yeah, sounds good," I agreed. "I'm always up for a good Mocha Frappuccino. If I don't get my Starbucks fix, I go into withdrawals."

He laughed. "Well, we don't want that. Let's go get you a cup."

Why did you have to appear again when I'm out with Jackson? I thought. *All this time when I was alone and you could have shown up, but now? You pick now?* Amazingly, though, I was kind of glad it was back. For better or worse, I didn't want to leave things with this odd shimmer that might be Emily in the way we last departed.

As we headed to Twin Rivers, I kept my eyes open for any sign of the shimmer. I just hoped it didn't suddenly appear in the truck next to me or something. The last thing I needed was to jump, make a scene, and start looking like the crazy girl in front of Jackson.

"You okay?" he asked. "You look, I don't know, nervous or something."

"Me? Nah, I'm good." *The Bones* by Maren Morris started playing on the radio and I turned the volume up. "I love this one," I told him, trying to look more normal and relaxed.

"Me, too," he agreed.

His air conditioning was on high but apparently low on coolant or just generally worn down as it was doing a mediocre job of cooling us. "Can I roll down the window?" I asked.

"Sure," he said. "Actually, I always do. My a/c doesn't work all that great. I just figured you wouldn't want to. You know, girls are always worried about their hair and stuff."

"I'm trying not to worry so much about stuff like that anymore these days," I told him. I knew the wind would blow my bangs about, revealing my scar, but I decided it would be better to have messy hair than be all sweaty. Besides, Jackson had already seen my forehead.

He followed suit, rolling down his window and taking off the ballcap he'd been wearing to reveal a mop of hair. "Ahh, much better," he said. *Damn, I do like that smile,* I thought. *I hope he doesn't pull a Logan on me.*

"You should bring the truck by the barn sometime. I bet Pops could get your a/c sorted out for you no problem."

"Seriously?" he asked.

"Yeah. Pops is genius on stuff like that. You might have to buy the parts, though, if it needs something."

"Cool. I'll do that," he said. "It's just kind of gotten worse and worse."

"Probably just a Freon leak," I said off-hand.

"You know a lot about cars?" he asked.

"Not really. Not like Pops."

"Well, your dad seems like he's kind of a car guru."

"He is," I said. "It's just kind of his thing."

It was a pretty straight shot to Twin Rivers on the county road, but all of a sudden, the shimmer appeared again up ahead. It was in front of an old worn out sign that read "Old Oak Park, 1.2 miles".

I remembered my odd dream. *Oh,* I thought. I wasn't so sure about this whole *follow the shimmer* idea given that dream. I had dreamed of someone hanging themselves in a tree the night before and it sure looked like it was in a park. I didn't want to end up going there and finding some dead person. Not again. There would be no way I could explain that. But surely if there was a dead person out there, someone else would have found them by now, right? It was already nearing four in the afternoon.

And you never actually saw the person, the little voice reminded.

True. If the shimmer wanted me to see something in the park, this was not really a great time. But I'd told myself that if it appeared again, I'd be nicer and wouldn't just ignore it like I had. The park was coming up quick and I needed to make a decision. I saw the shimmer ahead at the turn-off . . . it was flickering wildly.

Dammit. Okay. But there better not be another dead person waiting for me in there, I thought.

"Hey, Jackson," I ventured, "you up for a walk in the park?"

Chapter 24

A Walk Beneath the Wood

The afternoon heat was laid on us thick as cake icing, but Jackson didn't seem to mind too much as we walked. There was a long walking trail that surrounded the diameter of the park and dipped into the woods for a long stretch, then down by the river before circling back. In the morning and evenings many a jogger could be found as it was quite popular, but today the park was mostly empty save for a few moms with little kids running around and playing. A young man was also in the center clearing area playing a game of catch the Frisbee with his dog, who was exuberantly jumping up and down each time the man was getting ready to throw, then would chase after it with what was clearly a huge dog smile on its snout.

Jackson was taller than I thought. He kind of towered over me as we walked. I couldn't think of much to say. Apparently, neither could Jackson. "That dog can jump!" He ventured with a smile as we watched the dog sail into the air and chomp down on the Frisbee. Part of me immediately thought of Benny as he jumped at Dale those many years ago. *Damn, he was a good dog.* But then I chastised myself. *Stop thinking about the damn Incident, Ruth, and try to enjoy your date.*

"Yeah," I replied, "and fast, too." I had thought about asking Pops about getting another dog, but wasn't sure how the garden would react. It might be time, though. I'd just have to make sure it didn't dig in the garden or try to eat the poisonous flowers. And then there was the unusual concern the flowers might eat the dog instead.

Another awkward silence spilled over us as we continued to walk the path. *Where is that darn shimmer?* I wondered. *She brought me out here, so what's the deal?*

"So, what all do you like to do for fun and stuff?" Jackson asked.

I shoulder-rolled him by reflex. "Not a whole lot, I guess. I read a lot. And I help my dad out in the cemetery."

"And you garden, right?" he added.

"Well, not really."

"But you have that big flower garden in the back of your house . . ."

"Yeah, but it really just kind of takes care of itself. I don't have to do much."

"Oh, I think you're being too modest," he said with a knowing smile. "Gardens are hard to keep up. I know. My mom has a big ole vegetable garden. My dad gets out there all the time, too. They're both always out there working on it. Keeping up a garden like the one you have takes a lot of work."

Well, my garden is alive and consumed a dead woman named Lilith a hundred years ago, so now it has magic powers and can't die, I thought to myself. I laughed a little to myself at the thought of actually telling him that.

"What?" he asked.

"Oh, nothing. I do enjoy the garden, though, so thank you. It's nice of you to notice and to say." Another awkward silence threatened to intervene, so I beat it to the punch, "I've kind of started painting recently, too."

"Oh, yeah? I used to draw when I was younger."

"Like what?" I asked.

He paused a bit before responding, "Well, it's kind of nerdy, I guess. But I actually really liked comic books when I was younger and so I drew comics and stuff."

"Really . . . I would not have guessed you were a comic book artist."

"Well, I definitely wouldn't say I was much of an artist, but yeah, I used to draw stuff like that a lot."

"And you don't anymore?"

"Well, maybe sometimes." He was blushing a bit.

"Why are you embarrassed about that?" I asked. "I think it's cool." I wasn't really into comics, but I recognized a lot of people were and some of them were pretty neat. "I've seen some really good anime movies on Netflix," I added. They weren't comics, *per se,* but kind of similar.

"You watch anime?" he asked, shocked.

"Yeah, sure. Some of them are really good."

"Like which ones?" He seemed skeptical.

"Well," I thought. "There are lots that I like, actually. But I really liked *Spirited Away, Mary and the Witch's Flower*, and *A Silent Voice*. I literally cried when I watched *A Silent Voice*. It was kind of sad, but so sweet."

"Oh, I haven't seen that one," he said.

"Oh, you have to. It's so good. So, so good. It's all about the consequences of bullying and guilt . . . it's genius."

"I will watch it tonight," he replied. "Wow, I would have never guessed you liked anime. That's really cool."

"Well, see," I said. "We're just learning all sorts of interesting things about each other, aren't we?"

"Yeah, I guess so," he said. "That's totally awesome you like anime, I have to say. I don't think I know anyone else who has even seen those movies. *Spirited Away* is a classic. I've probably watched that one at least half a dozen times. You seen *Children of the Sea*?"

"Yup," I said.

"I liked that one, too. Wow, you really do watch them, huh?"

Well, I have no life, so I watch a lot of Netflix, I thought to myself. But again, not something I really needed to tell him out loud. "They remind me a lot of some of the fantasy series I read," I added.

"Like what kinds?" He asked.

We spent several more minutes talking about the books I liked and the shows we both watched. As we talked, the path entered the woods and above us a canopy provided some shade. Cicadas buzzed, birds flapped amongst the branches, and a rabbit took off from beneath some brush as we approached. "Oh, cool," he said. "You see that rabbit?"

"Neat," I replied, even though I saw rabbits all time out at the cemetery. I hadn't seen one with Jackson before, so it was still neat.

The awkward silence was finally gone as we walked and talked. And as we walked the path nearest to the river, his hand slipped into my good one. *Oh,* I thought, *okay, we're doing this?* And then we continued on as though it were totally normal.

As the path exited the woods we were once again out in the clearing on the back half of the trail. As we walked along, I noticed someone sitting at a bench near a tree up ahead with a notebook on their lap. As we got closer, he looked up at us and flipped a few pages on the notebook rapidly. I recognized him as Amy Choi's little brother, Kai.

Instinctively, I kind of pulled my hand back a bit. I wasn't even sure why except that I expected Jackson would want to let go of my hand when Kai saw us, probably not wanting anyone to see us walking together holding hands. But I was wrong. When I pulled my hand back a bit, he kept holding on to it. Then he gave me a little look to make sure I was okay with it. I was.

"Hey, Kai, what's up?" Jackson greeted him.

"Oh, hey," Kai said quietly. He looked at the two of us, hands together, with a slight bit of confusion on his face. His face looked gaunt.

"What you up to?" Jackson asked. Kai had a sketch in front of him and appeared to be drawing some sort of diagram and pictures. *But that's not the page he was on when he saw us,* I thought.

"Nothing much. Just sketching a little." He seemed to close the book a little, but as he did so, his hand flipped over revealing the watch on his wrist. I did a double-take when I saw it. *Holy crap!*

"Mununghwa," I said spontaneously.

Kai's eyes shot towards me and widened as Jackson turned to me at the same time, "Huh?" Jackson asked. "Munung . . . wha?" he laughed.

Kai, however, knew exactly what I had said and now looked like a deer caught in headlights. *Crap,* I thought to myself. *Why the hell did I just say that out loud? It just slipped out.*

"The flower," I said, trying to play it off a bit as I pointed to Kai's watch. "That's a hibiscus from Korea, right? I think it's called a Mununghwa . . . or something like that."

Kai was practically shaking. "Umm, yeah. How do you know that?"

"Oh," said Jackson, now leaning in and inspecting Kai's watch. "Wow, Ruth, you have really good eyes. I can barely even see that thing. She's like a professional botanist," he told Kai. "You should see the garden at her house. It's crazy. She has flowers taller than me. I'm totally serious. It's awesome."

I graciously accepted the unintended excuse from Jackson. "Oh," said Kai. He was still clearly unnerved, but he seemed to be less shocked. He stood up and stepped closer with his arm outstretched towards us to give us a better look at the dial. "Well, you're right," he said to me, "I can't believe you spotted that from there, but this is a Mununghwa flower. They're really popular in Korea."

The dial appeared to be black enamel with a burst of pink flower in the center with five large petals, each encircled in gold wire. The silver hands of the watch extended from what would have been the stigma of the flower. "It's beautiful," I told him. There was a memory welling up in me. A memory of me making this very watch, only me was Emily. It was odd, like a daydream. Part of me could see myself working on this very dial.

"Yeah, pretty cool," said Jackson, clearly only partially interested. "Your parents give you that or something?"

"Um, no, I made it," he replied.

"You made it?" asked Jackson, now more interested. "Like, you made the watch? How'd you make it?"

Kai withdrew his arm and closed his book fully. "Well, I mean I only really put all the parts together. Someone else made the dial."

Yup, I thought, *and I know who that someone else is. Or was.* I had just assumed it was Amy that Emily was in business with since they were friends and all. I didn't even think of Kai at the time. But now I saw it. Here was Mununghwa.

"Oh," said Jackson. "For a second there, I was about to be super impressed."

"Well, the movement is also really important," said Kai. "Everything has to fit right in order for it to work."

"Oh," said Jackson. "I don't know much about watches." The awkward silence had returned with a vengeance. "Well, cool seeing you and all," said Jackson.

"Yeah, you, too," said Kai. There was a backpack by the bench, and he picked it up and started shoving his notepad into it. As he did so, I caught a glimpse of something in the bottom of the bag. Rope.

Oh, Kai, I thought. *It's you. You're the shadow.* How had I not seen it? I looked closer at the tree and the bench. This was it. This was the place in my dream, the painting come to life. And Kai was the one who had killed himself. Only . . . he hadn't. Not yet. I didn't think this had ever happened before . . . me dreaming about someone dying before they died. Was even such a thing possible? Well, the dreams themselves were supposed to be impossible, but they were there nonetheless. Had Emily somehow painted this in my mind? *Oh, I'm going to get a headache thinking about this later,* I thought. *This is why she brought me here,* I thought.

"You want a ride or something?" I asked Kai.

Jackson looked a little surprised, but he didn't object. "Um, yeah, sure. We can give you a ride if you want."

"No, I'm good," Kai said dismissively.

But there was something about the way he said it that I didn't like. "How'd you get out here?" I asked.

"What do you mean?"

"I mean, you don't drive, right? Someone drop you off or something? Or did you walk all the way out here?"

He looked perturbed with a *why are you asking* expression. "Amy dropped me off. She's coming back to pick me up in a bit," he said.

He's lying, said the little voice.

"Well, do you feel like walking with us a bit?" I asked. Jackson was really looking confused now, but I pressed onward. "Your watch dial is cloisonné, right? That's so cool. I've been studying enameling."

"You have?" Kai asked.

"You have?" Jackson also asked.

"Yeah. What, a girl can't have hobbies?"

"I'm good," said Kai. "Amy will be out here in a while to get me."

Like hell she will, said the little voice. *She has no idea he's here. He's planning on doing something terrible. You know why the shimmer brought you here.*

I know, I know. Just chill, I'm working on it.

"Walk with us," I suggested. "I can tell you about my flowers."

Kai had a look on his face. It was a wounded animal kind of look. "I said no, okay? I'm sorry, but I'm good. Just . . . y'all have a nice walk and all, but I got some drawing and stuff to do."

"Ruth," suggested Jackson, "I think he wants to be left alone." He smiled at Kai and tried taking a few steps forward to walk on, but I stood firm.

"Call Amy," I told Jackson, still looking at Kai.

"What?"

I looked at Jackson. "You got her number, right?"

Jackson looked to me, then Kai, then back to me with a *what am I missing here?* look on his face. "Umm, yeah." He pulled his phone out.

Small town, I thought. *I figured he probably had it.*

"Why are you calling my sister!?" asked Kai.

"I just want to check and see when she's going to get here. It's hot out here. I just want to make sure you're not going to be stuck out here too long."

"I already told you I'm fine. It's none of your business!" he said.

Jackson looked at me, trying to figure out why the hell I was acting so weird about Kai. "You mind calling her?" I asked him.

He reluctantly started thumbing through his contacts to ring her. "What is your deal?" asked Kai, now watching Jackson's fingers in trepidation. "Look, fine, okay! If you want to give me a ride home or whatever, fine. Don't call my sister, though, okay? She's busy. She'll get pissed at me."

"Oh, okay," I told him. "I guess we shouldn't call her then," I said, now looking at Jackson. He paused, looked at me, then put his phone back in his pocket. "But you're coming with us, right?" I asked Kai.

"Yeah, I guess so," he said. "Jesus." We started walking a bit and he asked, "You guys aren't going to like drive me out to some back road and murder me or something, are you? Because you're acting kind of weird."

"I'm just worried about you," I told him.

"Okay . . . but why?" he asked.

Now what, Ruth? I thought. *You're breaking* The Rule *big time here.* But I couldn't stand by and do nothing. There was no way in hell I was leaving that park without Kai. I didn't know what happened with him and Emily or why he had that rope in his backpack, but he was coming with me if I had to tie him up with it and drag him out of here. He wasn't ending up in that tree on my watch. And clearly Emily didn't want him to do it, either. "You like flowers, don't you?"

"Um, I guess so," he said. "Why?"

"Because I'd like to show you my garden."

As we walked, Jackson leaned down and whispered to me, "What are we doing?"

"Helping," I whispered back. "I hope."

Chapter 25

The Hibiscus in the Garden

To his credit, Jackson didn't say a word as he drove me and Kai back to the farmhouse. I knew he was probably brimming with questions at this point, not the least of which was probably *Ruth, what the hell is going on?* But he just went with it in all its strangeness.

I was about to test the depth of his flexibility. When he pulled up to the house and we all got out, I said "Hey, Jackson, would you mind if Kai and I have a chat in the garden?"

"What do you mean?" he asked.

"Well, Pops is probably out in the barn," I said, pointing out that way. "Why don't you take the truck on out there and see if he can look at the a/c. I want to talk with Kai about something."

"Talk about what?" Kai asked.

"Flowers," I told him.

"Flowers?" he asked.

"Yeah, flowers. Remember? That's why I asked if you wanted to come check out the garden in the first place." Both the guys were looking at me like I was off my rocker, but I had a plan and they were both so confused at this point, neither one of them objected.

"Um, sure, I guess," said Jackson. "So, I just drive it over there?"

"Yeah," I affirmed. "Tell Pops I asked if he could just take a look at it for you."

Jackson reluctantly got back in his truck and then drove it off towards the barn.

"We've got some time," I told Kai. "Once Pops starts looking around under that hood, it's going to be a while."

Kai just looked at me awkwardly. "You're kind of weird," he said.

"You are not the first person to tell me that," I told him. "Now, grab your backpack and come with me."

He reluctantly complied. "Look, do you want something?" he asked as we rounded the house to the back and entered the garden.

"Yes. I told you, I want to show you the garden."

The flowers looked particularly stunning today, standing upright in colorful splendor. I sometimes forgot how beautiful they were given I was so used to them by now. "Well, okay, these are kind of cool," he said as we entered. The flowers, however, were humming concern.

Is he dangerous? I thought. I had assumed Emily's shimmering and the dream had led me to him to stop what it was it appeared he meant to do out there in the park. Did I have it wrong?

We sat down at the little table that was my favorite place in all the world. *What the hell do I tell this guy?* "I would like us to have a talk," I told him.

"Okay," he said. "About what?"

"About what you were doing out there in the park today."

He seemed annoyed with me. "What do you mean? I was just sketching and stuff. Why are you acting all weird? Why am I even here at your house?"

I looked steady at him. "Why, indeed? You sort of freaked out there when Jackson was going to call Amy, didn't you?"

"No," he said. "I just didn't want her to get mad is all."

I took a deep breath. "Amy doesn't know you were in the park, does she?"

Kai fiddled in his seat, shifting his body weight uncomfortably. "Yes . . . she dropped me off there."

"Did she?"

He wasn't making very good eye contact. "What do you want, Ruth? Is this because my sister is always so mean to you or something? Look, I'm sorry about that, okay? I know y'all have issues, or whatever, but I don't have anything to do with that."

"That's not what this is about," I told him.

"Then what?! What do you want!?"

I looked at the backpack down at his feet. "I want you to show me your notebook."

He rocked backwards in the chair. "Why?"

"Because I want to see what you were doing when we walked up to you."

"I told you, I was sketching some stuff for some future watch projects."

"Then show me," I dared.

"Fine," he said. He pulled out the notebook and flipped it open. "Look, see?" he challenged, turning the book around and showing me a sketch of a bird. He had drawn a circle around it, as it would appear once formed upon a dial, with a diagram for the placement of the cloisonné wires and colors.

I reached out to take the notebook up in my hands, but he pulled it back. "Why can't I see it?" I asked him.

"Because it's private," he said. "I'm just showing you so you'll leave me the hell alone about it."

"But that's not what you were working on earlier, is it?" I asked. "Show me that, Kai." And I tried to flip the pages forward.

He slammed the notebook shut. Then he grabbed his backpack and started shoving it back in. "This is stupid. I'm leaving," he told me. "Tell Jackson to drive me home, please."

I felt a slight breeze. And as I looked over, there inside the garden, just by the gate, was a shimmer. It wasn't Lilith. And I understood. This is why it had appeared today, and this was what she wanted. A memory came to me . . . maybe my own, maybe someone else's from the house or the cemetery. It was an old Johnny Cash song lyric . . . *for as sure as God made black and white, what is done in the dark will be brought to the light* . . . if Kai walked out of this garden right now, there was no telling what might happen to him later. *The Rule* be damned . . . I couldn't just let him leave without trying to help. "What does your suicide note say, Kai?" I asked.

He froze. Then he stared at me, angry red, teary eyes. "What?" he quietly asked.

I looked into those eyes and beyond. I saw his anger, but it wasn't directed at me. It was directed at himself. "What does it say? Does it apologize for what happened to Emily?"

He began visibly shaking. "How . . . what do you mean?"

"I know something bad happened out there on the levee and that you blame yourself for it. I'm not trying to accuse you of anything. My heart tells me that whatever happened, you didn't mean it." If Emily had wanted vengeance of a sort, I figured she would have just let him do what he was already planning on doing without intervention. She must have wanted me to stop him. Otherwise, why the dreams? Why had the shimmer appeared earlier today and why was it here now? "Just sit down, take a deep breath, and breathe, Kai. You have a lot of pain in your heart right now. I can see it. I can feel it. Just talk to me."

He sat down. There was a long pause and I felt a calming hum from the garden. I hoped Kai felt it, too. "I don't know what you're talking about," he said. But he said it without conviction.

I stared intently at him. "Yes, you do. It's eating you alive, isn't it?"

"No," he tried to say.

"Yes, it is," I told him. "It's been eating you up, all this guilt and hurt. So much so, there is hardly anything left, is there?" I tried to give him a comforting look. "You look like you're hurting, Kai. That's why you were out there today, isn't it? You just want it to stop?" A long pause ensued.

Finally, he spoke. "How can you tell?" he asked.

"I just see it in your eyes," I told him. "I've had some hurt, too, along the way. Maybe hurt see hurt easier than others." I never did stop thinking about all the things I could have done differently that night Mom died. How many times had I thought to myself, *if I'd only . . .*

A tear fell down his cheek. "I didn't mean it," he all but whispered.

I reached out with the hand the garden had helped heal all those years ago, and I took his hand in mind. "Close your eyes," I told him. He did. "Now just breathe." He took a deep breath. Then another. I did the same. I could smell the flowers. I could hear them in my mind humming softly.

I opened my eyes and Kai was looking at me. He looked much calmer now, but the pretense erased from his face revealed the pain within him. His eyes were pools of deep-filled sorrow. He looked so tired suddenly. "What happened?" I asked him.

His hand began to shake a bit and his voice was broken as he quietly said, "I can't . . ."

"Nothing can be worse than what you were already about to do today," I told him softly. "And I'm not here to hurt you. I know you don't know me. But I want to help you if I can."

"Why?" he asked.

"Because I don't think you meant to hurt Emily. I don't know what happened, but my heart tells me you didn't mean for it to happen."

"I didn't," he quietly sobbed. And after another quiet moment, he began, "We were going to watch the fireworks together . . ."

As he told the tale, something most unusual happened. Although unusual things happening in the garden no longer surprised me. I began to see his words, yet

another painting forming in my mind . . . a waking
dream.

Chapter 26

The Waking Dream

Emily was driving slowly along the levee with Kai in the passenger seat as they rounded the bend and disappeared from view of the road. "Just up here," he told her.

"This doesn't seem very safe," she said. "I hope I can back us out of here okay."

"It'll be worth it," he promised, "just trust me. There's a big opening in the trees up here." As stated, a clearing opened on either side of the levee. To the left was the basin, and to the right, a very large drainage ditch which snaked back up towards the fairgrounds, although they were hidden from view by dense wood. "We'll have a great view of the fireworks from here," he said. "They'll pop up right over those trees," and he indicated the tree-line off in the direction of the drainage ditch.

Emily put her car in park and turned off the ignition. "Okay, so are you going to tell me what's in the bag and why we drove out to the middle of nowhere to watch the fireworks?" she asked.

He had a smile plastered on his face. "Yeah, follow me," and he got out of the car and stepped in front to the hood where the headlights remained on, illuminating the empty levee. Emily hesitatingly followed. Kai opened up the bag and placed three plastic lights on the hood of the car which he turned on. They looked like candle lights that would be found at a fancy dinner, except they were plastic. They mimicked the glow of a flame, though, as he turned each on. Next, he withdrew a bottle of champagne. "Ta-da," he said. "Amy got it for me. That's why I wanted to come out here just the two of us."

"Oh, nice," she replied.

He popped the cork with a loud *pop!* "We're celebrating," he announced, taking a big swig.

"We are? And what are we celebrating this evening . . . the Fourth?"

"More than just that. For starters, this . . .," he said, fishing a stack of hundred-dollar bills from his pocket. "An even thousand," he said proudly, handing them over to her. "Each. And that's after I put some aside for expenses for the next one." He raised the bottle and took a big gulp.

She stared at the stack of hundred-dollar bills, fanning them out in her hands with a smile. "Oh, wow. A thousand dollars each!? How!? How much did we get for that one?"

"Twenty-five hundred even," he said with a big grin.

"No way," she said, still holding the money in disbelief. "This is so great. I can buy a kiln!"

"Yeah, that'd actually be a good investment," Kai agreed. "You may need it soon. I wouldn't be surprised if we start getting some special orders at this rate."

"Oh, it'd be so nice to have one of my own. No more having to drive up to the school and begging Coach Van to help me. You know they won't even let me up there unless he's there supervising? I've felt so bad for him always having to stay late. He even came in on some Saturdays for me. That reminds me . . . we need to do something really nice for him. He asked about maybe getting a watch for himself. Do you think we can make one for him?"

"Well, I guess so. But you know they're worth a lot of money. You don't just want to give him one, do you?"

"I mean, yeah, a little. He's done a lot for us." Kai looked skeptical, though. "How about this? What if he pays for the parts? How much would that be?" she asked.

"It just depends . . . the movement is probably the most expensive thing if we go Swiss. If he wants a good ETA one, it'd be three hundred or so. But if he doesn't care about that we could just get a cheap Seiko NH35 for like forty bucks. They're actually really reliable. I've modded a bunch of watches with those and never had any problems with them, but they only beat at twenty-one thousand six hundred instead of twenty-eight thousand eight hundred, so the sweep of the second hand won't be as smooth. He might not care, but a collector would. Let's see . . . a decent case is about sixty dollars. Regular hands, only about thirty dollars. Blued-steel ones would cost about two hundred, though. And they're sometimes hard to get. AR coated sapphire crystal, about thirty bucks. Leather strap, thirty bucks for a cheapy, a hundred or more for premium. So, with all the bells and whistles, I guess parts would be about five hundred. But if he's fine with the cheaper stuff, only about a hundred and fifty. The dial is then whatever you and he come up with."

"Oh, that's not so bad, then," Emily said. "Let me ask him which way he wants to go on it, fancy or cheaper."

"Okay, but we can't be giving away a bunch of these for cost. That's why I don't really want anyone knowing what we're doing. All of yours and Amy's friends will want deals, especially if they find out how much we're selling them for on eBay. They'll probably just turn around and sell them anyway and we need to be making some money on these."

"I know," she agreed. "But hey, I made one for Amy for free so you could give her one for her birthday, remember? I just think we kind of owe Coach Van. He's spent a lot of time helping me on these and we wouldn't have been able to make them without his help."

"Okay," he agreed. "You're right. But just for him, okay? I don't want people at school getting all mad at us when we won't give them a deal or something just so they can flip it online. Plus, we're starting to have a brand here and I don't want that to get messed up if other people start trying to sell our stuff."

He handed her the bottle and she took a drink. "You're getting pretty serious about this, huh?"

"I am," he said. "This could be big for us. Twenty-five hundred is the most we've gotten so far, but I think we can still make even more."

He sat down next to her and rolled up his sleeve to reveal their latest creation. "Like this one . . . check out what I finished today. Almond blossoms." He took it off and handed it to her as she handed him back the champagne.

"Oh, it turned out great. This red background just pops. I'm glad I went with the darker red. And I like the hands you used with the little circle thingies. I love it. Man, though, this one was such a pain in the ass. It took me three tries to get this stupid tree branch to look right. And all these flowers . . . they look so small now that it's all done, but they were such a pain. So does this one have a Swiss movement or cheaper one?"

"Swiss, of course," he said. "I went with another ETA 2892A2. They're getting hard to find, though. I could get a clone, but it's not the same and would really hurt the value. I was actually thinking of trying out a Miyota 9015 . . . that's a Japanese movement but one that still has a higher beat per hour, but I think we just need to stick with Swiss, you know? That's what buyers want. And for the hands, I went with the actual heat-blued Breguet style hands for this one, not those fake painted ones. It's more expensive, but a real collector is going to like that, I think. It's just that kind of little extra detail that I think will get us even more money for this one. I listed it today for four thousand," he said with a smile.

"Four thousand!? Do you really think anyone will pay that much?"

"Yeah. That dial is amazing. It's stunning. I'm telling you, you can't just find stuff like this anywhere. I would love to keep this one for myself. I mean, I would like to keep all of them, of course. But this one . . . it's your best yet. It's so beautiful." Emily couldn't help but smile at Kai's exuberance. He sure loved this stuff. "And did you see the review the last guy left? He said it was the most beautiful watch he has ever owned, even better than his Rolex Daytona. I think we can definitely get more for this one with everything we did to it. We should launch our own website. We may end up getting ten grand someday soon for each one," he mused as he sipped and talked.

"No way," Emily said with a dismissive laugh. She handed the watch back to him and he buckled it back on his wrist.

"No, really," he said. And he stared at her intently. "You and me. We can do this," he said, holding his wrist back up to display their creation. "These are special. Every one of these you make . . . they're beautiful works of art."

"Ten grand?" she mused. "That's a lot of money. Like a lot, a lot."

"I know. I told you there were people out there who were willing to pay this kind of money for these. You didn't believe me, huh?"

"I mean, I did, but ten thousand dollars? I never thought you meant that kind of money. If we started making that much . . . even four thousand would be crazy. I could literally rent myself an actual studio. I could just paint all day like as my full-time job after graduation if we ever made that kind of money."

"We can do it," he said. "We just need some more good ideas." As they waited for the fireworks show to begin, they sipped upon the champagne generously and talked about their future plans. "We should do ships," he suggested after more than half the bottle was gone. "Ships sell really well."

"I can make ships," she told him.

"Ulysse Nardin did some cloisonné ships. They sell for tons. And animals! Lots of the animal ones, like unicorns, and birds. We could do some smaller ones for women. I think birds would be really good! We could do a whole line of different types."

They drank, talked, laughed, and planned. "Birds would be cool," she told him. "I like anything with bright colors. What about a Flamingo!"

"Oh, totally," he said. "That'd really pop."

"And parrots."

"Yeah, that's brilliant. Parrots. Can you do that, though? That'd be a lot of feathers."

"I can do it," she confidently replied.

"And a blue jay!"

"A robin!" she added.

"They're going to be awesome," he said. "We're going to sell them left and right. What if we tried adding gemstones? Do you think we can figure out how to add diamonds and emeralds and stuff?" he asked.

"Maybe," she said. "Let's not get too carried away."

Emily looked down and saw the champagne bottle was almost gone. Then she saw a spark in the sky. A tiny flare rose above the trees in the distance. "Oh, look! It's starting!"

The fireworks began, bright explosions in the sky of gold, orange, purple, green, and blue. They watched and drank, finishing off the bottle. As the crescendo erupted, Kai reached over and kissed Emily.

She wasn't expecting it, but she hesitatingly kissed him back. At first. But then he tried to lean her back on the hood of the car and put his hands in intimate places. Emily retracted. "Wait . . .," She tried to lean back up, but he was pressing her down, trying to kiss her more urgently. She pushed him back. "Kai, stop." She leaned up again, pushing him back. "We can't be doing that."

"Why?" he asked.

"Because . . . I mean, lots of reasons. You're Amy's little brother, for one. And I'm older than you."

"By, like, two years. That doesn't matter."

"Well, it kind of does," she said.

"In five years it won't make any difference at all."

"Five years?" She tried to massage her forehead. Her vision was getting pretty blurry.

He stared at her longingly. "I love you," he said, leaning in towards her.

She leaned away. "What?"

"I love you," he said again. "I've been in love with you since forever."

"Wait . . .," she said, sliding off the hood of the car and standing up. Her vision was spinning now from all the champagne. Kai stood as well and walked towards her to put his arm around her waist, but she pulled away and stepped back. "Just wait," she told him. "Jesus, I think I drank too much."

"Well, sit back down," he suggested. And he stepped towards her again as though to help her, but she backed away further.

"No, no," she said as she stepped back a little.

"Come on, don't weird out about it. It's a perfect night. I just thought this was the right time to tell you. I've been wanting to tell you for the longest. You're awesome, Emily. You're so beautiful and talented . . .," He took another step towards her and she held her arm up for him to stop. He reached for it as though to hold her hand.

She stepped back again. "It's just . . .," she began to say.

. . . But then she was gone . . .

Kai heard grass whisp, a thumping noise, then a hard whack, and then a splash, all within seconds. "Emily?" he asked in confusion. He walked to the edge of the steep embankment overhanging the large concrete culvert that led the water from the drainage ditch down into the basin. "Emily?" He asked again, looking down and expecting to see her below, probably standing right next to the embankment in a few inches of water, mad her shoes were wet.

But he couldn't see anything. "Oh, crap," he said, pulling his phone out quickly and turning on the flashlight which he then beamed down into the water below. There were circle swirls and little waves lapping the embankment as though a large stone had just been plunked into the water, but nothing more. He stared in shock and disbelief for a few seconds.

Then he cried "Emily!!" He tossed his phone on the ground, threw his wallet beside it, undid the buckle of the watch, and threw that down as well. "Oh, my God," he said as he half stepped, half slid, down the slick grass of the embankment. "Emily!"

When he reached the concrete culvert, he used it like a small diving board and jumped into the murky water, still wearing his shoes, blue jeans, and other clothing.

He didn't think the water was that deep. He half expected to land in only three or four feet of water, but instead he sank deep. His feet didn't even touch the bottom as he quickly pulled himself back up. "Oh!" he yelped in surprise at the water's deepness.

The water soaked quickly into his clothes, sucking them to his skin and weighing him down quickly. But he was in a panic now and paid little heed. He dove. He could see nothing in the water. The night was as a blanket of darkness covering the basin now that the fireworks were over. Only the occasional blinking of light denoted other fireworks far in the distance, but in the water of the basin, all was quiet black.

Kai rose again, struggling to tread water as the weight of his clothes and shoes tried to pull him back down. "No!" he rasped to the indifferent water around him. "No!" He dove again, this time swimming deeper, his hands outstretched, sweeping back and forth, searching for any part of her to grab on to. But each time he caught nothing but weeds, rotten leaves, wood, and grime. He rose again. He dove again. He rose again. And he dove again.

The minutes ticked by. He struggled to tread water as he became exhausted. "Please no," he began to sob. "Emily!" He yelled, circling round and looking every which way. "No, no, no . . .," he swam back to the bank and crawled up it, then turned back to the water before him. "Emily!" he yelled again. But the water was still and there was no sign of her.

He crawled back onto the levee and reached for his phone. Who should he call? 911? His thumb hovered over the numbers, water droplets splashing upon the lit screen. Instead, he closed the numbers and opened contacts. First on the list was Amy. And he pressed the call button.

The dream faded a bit, but was not all the way gone, as I heard Kai's voice across the table in the garden. "I tried to find her," he told me. "If I could have just gotten her out of the water. It was an accident. I swear to God it was an accident."

I knew he was telling me the truth. I had seen it as he spoke it. Although had I not seen it, I probably would have had doubts. What a freak accident it was. And how did Emily's car eventually end up in the basin with her inside?

I looked past him towards the garden. The shimmer was gone, but in my heart, I felt I knew why it had appeared. I suspected that had Jackson and I not gone to the park today, Kai would have finished his note. And right about now, as the sun began to dip with the onset of dusk and the few people who were also in the park today left, he would have set up that rope he brought in his backpack, climbed that bench, and bid farewell to the world. He must have walked all the way out there earlier in the day to do just that.

Emily didn't want that. That's what the dream and the shimmer had been about. "I believe you," I told him. "It really wasn't your fault, Kai."

He was still crying softly. "But it was. She stepped back to get away from me. She was trying to get away from me because I'd kissed her. If I hadn't reached out to try to grab her hand . . ."

"Kai, I was out there on the basin, you know, when Patrick and them found her."

"I know," he said.

"It's super steep. Patrick literally fell in, too. And that was in broad daylight."

"He did?" he asked.

"Yes, and he was looking where he was going, but he still slipped and fell right in. He even cut up his toe doing it. The paramedics had to bandage him up."

"I didn't know that," said Kai.

"That spot where all this happened, it's so steep and slippery around that culvert area."

He wiped his nose a little. "Yeah, I remember that much."

"I don't get it, though. Why didn't you call the police?" He shifted uneasily in his chair. "I don't think you're lying to me or anything. I really don't. But I'm still confused how Emily ended up in her car and all that."

"I should have called the cops," he said. "I guess I was scared. I didn't know what to do. So, I just called Amy. I told her what had happened, where I was and all, and how to get there. And she told me to just stay right there and keep looking for Emily. She made me swear I wouldn't call anyone else and that I would just wait for her."

"Amy was the one who pushed Emily's car in?" I asked.

He nodded, and again the dream seemed to swirl and come alive and I saw what he spoke.

It wasn't just Amy who had come when he called. Logan Wallis was with her, too.

"Did you find her?" Amy asked when she arrived.

"No," Kai answered. He pointed to the water. "She's still in there. I couldn't find her."

"How long has she been in there?!" asked Logan.

"Since right when I called you," said Kai.

"Damn, Amy, we have to call the cops. She's drowned."

"No, not yet," said Amy.

"Not yet?" he asked. "Amy, it's already been like fifteen minutes. We have to get someone out here."

"Just wait!" she told him. Then she set her eyes intently on Kai. "It was an accident, right, Kai?" she asked him pressingly.

"Yes, of course."

"Amy, we can't not call the cops," said Logan. "We could get in trouble, too."

Kai inferred the worst from what Logan had said and the way his sister was looking at him. "Wait, what do you mean by *too*? It was an accident! She was backing up and just fell."

"Yeah, well, you can just tell that to the cops, okay?" said Logan, skeptically.

"No," Amy said resolutely. Logan was fishing his phone out of his pocket anyway. Kai was shaking, both from the wet and from fear of what was about to happen. "No!" she told him again, walking up to him and snatching his phone.

"Amy, we have to," he told her.

She bit her lip. "We need to find her."

"What?" Logan asked.

"We need to get in there and find her!" she said, pointing to the water below. "She might still be alive."

"She's not," Logan said, incredulously. "It's been fifteen minutes already! I'm sorry, but she's dead, man. She's drowned."

"We don't know that. Just look for her."

"Are you serious right now? You want me to get in there?"

"Yes!" she demanded. "She could still be alive. We can't just stand here." She spun around on Kai. "Why did you get out? I told you to keep looking for her. Get back in there and find her!"

"I tried," he started to explain.

"Well, try harder!" Kai dutifully obeyed, shedding his shoes and his shirt this time slowly.

"This is crazy," said Logan.

"Crazy is us standing here while Emily drowns." Amy was also shedding her shoes and over clothes.

"You seriously want us to get in there? In the dark? And try to find her in that," he said, pointing to the inky water below.

"You got me the champagne, right?" she asked him.

"What?" he asked.

"The champagne. I asked you to get it for me and you did, right?"

"Yeah, so?"

"So, I gave it to him and that's what they drank out here. If Kai's right and Emily got drunk and fell into this thing . . . who do you think they're going to blame for giving her the alcohol?"

Logan's face paled. "He gave it to her," he said, pointing at Kai.

"Yeah, after we gave it to him."

"I can't get in any trouble for that," he said.

"Are you sure? Because I'm not. But if Emily's still alive, none of that matters, right? So, let's just find her." She turned on the flashlight of her iPhone and Logan's, and then she set them down on the slope of the bank so they shined their light downward. Then she took Kai's phone and did the same thing. "I'm going in," she told Logan. "Help us look." And she turned and started heading down the bank with Kai. She paused as Kai went back into the water. And she turned and looked at Logan. "She might still be alive. Come on!"

"I don't know," he said.

"Please, Logan." And as Kai began swimming under the water searching for Emily, she added softer and more urgent. "He's my little brother. I'm begging you. We don't know she isn't still alive."

Logan shook his head but started taking off his shirt. "This is so bad," he said. "This is just so messed up." But he then joined them in the water. "We can try looking right here, but if we don't find her soon, this is pointless. She's drowned, Amy. And if she's drifted further out into this thing, we're not going to find her. It will take divers and professionals."

"We have to try," she told him. "There's still a chance."

Logan was the most powerful swimmer of the three, and he dove with broad arms sweeping through the water. A few feet away, Amy did as well.

Barely a minute after starting their search, Logan surfaced with a strained expression. "I got her," he said. "Help!" he spurted. He struggled with the weight of something and with Amy's help they managed to get back to the bank. Then all three of them worked together to pull her out.

"Oh, man," he said as they shined a light on Emily's ghostly white face. "Emily?" Logan tried as he pat her face. She had been pale in life but now looked like the porcelain she often created. And as he pat her face, he noticed something oozing down her hair. It looked like mud at first, until he touched it and his hand came away crimson red. "What the hell?" he asked. "It's blood. Why is she bleeding?" He looked at Kai in shock. "Why is she bleeding!? Dude, did you hit her?"

"What?" Kai asked. "No! I think she hit her head on the culvert or something when she fell."

"Yeah, whatever," Logan replied. He quickly turned and washed the blood off his hand in the water below. Then he turned back on Kai, "What'd you do, hit her with that champagne bottle or something?" he accused, pointing towards the bottle back up on Emily's hood.

"I didn't hit her!" Kai yelled angrily.

"Shut up," Amy told both of them.

"I didn't!"

"Okay, just keep your voice down, dammit. Be quiet!"

"Look at the blood," Logan told Amy. "He killed her!"

"No, I didn't!" Kai spat back.

"Be quiet!" she said to them again. "I see it, okay? She could have easily hit her head just like he's saying." Logan shook his head but said nothing. "Quick," said Amy, "help me turn her on her side."

"What for?" asked Logan.

"Just help me." And they rolled Emily on her side. Amy then began smacking her back hard. Water dribbled out of Emily's mouth, but nothing more. She rolled her back flat. "Do either of you know CPR?"

"CPR!?" replied Logan, "Amy, look at her. She's dead." Amy tried anyway and began her best efforts of chest compressions. "Amy!" said Logan.

"Shut up," she told him. She tried blowing air into Emily's mouth, but still nothing was working. Kai was watching intently and saying little prayers while Amy kept trying for several minutes before Logan spoke again. "She's gone, Amy. She was gone before we even got here. We need to call someone already."

Amy sat back and put her arm over her mouth. "Dammit," she said quietly. "Dammit!" she cursed again, more loudly.

"Now can we call somebody?" asked Logan.

She paused. "Just let me think," she said.

"It's okay," said Kai. "Amy, let's make the call. I'll just tell them what happened."

"Just shut up a second," she told him. "I just want to think a minute."

Firework noises still popped far in the distance. After a moment, Amy stood up and looked back down the levee to see if there were any cars. But she couldn't see past the bend, which was good, as it meant anyone down at the road probably couldn't see them. "Okay, look," she said. "This was an accident. There's no reason anyone needs to know any of us were ever here."

"What are you talking about?" asked Logan.

"I'm saying Emily drowned, right? Why does anyone ever have to know Kai was here with her or that we came out here? Nobody needs to know that."

"So what? She just came out by herself and fell in? That doesn't even make any sense."

"But she did fall in," said Kai.

"I'm not talking to you," Logan warned him.

Amy looked at Emily's car still parked on the levee. "Okay, she didn't just fall in, then. She had a car accident."

Logan caught on to what she was indicating. "I'm not doing that." He looked at Amy and then Kai. "This is all your fault!" he told Kai. "I don't know what happened out here, but I think you and Emily got into some kind of argument and you hit her with something. Probably that stupid bottle up there, and that's how she ended up in here bleeding and drowning," he snapped at Kai.

"That's not what happened," Kai angrily replied as he stood up looking like he was ready to hit Logan.

"Just you try it," said Logan. "Unlike Emily, I hit back."

"Stop it!" said Amy. "It was an accident! I already told you what happened, Logan. They were both drinking, and she just lost her balance."

"Then why couldn't he find her? She was right there!" he said pointing to the water. "I found her right away. I doubt he even tried."

"I tried!" said Kai. "I did try." He looked to both Amy and Logan, "I didn't do anything to her! It was an accident."

"Then that's all you need to explain to the cops, isn't it!? Why should we do anything to make it look like it happened some other way?" He looked at Amy, "If it was really an accident then he won't get in trouble."

"We gave them the bottle, Logan."

"You gave them the bottle," he said. "You asked me for a favor, and I gave it to you. You're the one that gave it to him," he said, pointing at Kai forcefully. "That's on you."

"It's on us. Look, I don't know what will happen if we try to explain all this, okay, but do you really want to take the risk? Why does anyone need to know we were here? It's not going to change what happened. Look, you don't even have to do anything, Logan. You've already done so much by finding her. But you're right, okay? She's dead. Emily's dead and there's nothing any of us can do to change it. Why does anyone have to know any of us were here?" she asked again. "They don't! It won't change anything." Logan didn't speak, but he was listening and thinking. "I'm not asking you to do anything else," she promised him. "Just let me handle it. All I need from you is for you to just go and wait for us in the car."

"And what are you going to do?" he asked.

"I'm going to put her in her car and push it," she said. "Then there won't be any doubts from anyone about whether or not this was an accident if they find her in her car, alone, in this water thing. People accidentally drive into water things all the time, right? I hear about it all the time. They'll find her and just immediately say it was an accident, and then we won't have to try to convince anyone or explain things to prove it was an accident."

Logan paced a bit in frustration. "Isn't that like, desecrating a corpse or something? It's a crime, isn't it? And destruction of her car, or whatever."

"Who's going to know?" she asked. "I'm not asking you to help me," she told him. "I'll do it. All I'm asking is for you to wait for me in the car and not tell anyone about this."

He considered. "Fine," he decided. "Fine. But if anyone finds out about any of this, I'm going to tell them I was against it. And I'm not sure this was an accident," he added, looking crossly at Kai. "I don't know what happened, okay? But she's bleeding like she got hit or something and she looks like she's been in there longer than he's saying, I think." Kai was about to respond, but Amy held her hand up to him and he remained quiet. Logan paced a little more. "Fine, you handle it." And he went back up the bank and started putting his clothes back on.

"Help me with her," Amy told Kai.

"What are we doing, Amy? We can't put her back in there."

"That's exactly what we're going to do."

"But what if nobody finds her. We can't just leave her in there."

"Look," she whispered angrily to him. "Do you want to go to jail? Maybe for the rest of your life?"

"Why would I go to jail?" he asked. "It was an acci . . ."

"An accident," she cut him off. "And are you willing to bet the rest of your life that you can convince a bunch of strangers that it was just an accident? You see how Logan is reacting," she told him. "He knows you and even he thinks maybe you did something to her."

"But I didn't," he said angrily. "I mean, yeah, we were kissing, and she got angry . . ."

"Shhh!" she told him, watching to make sure Logan was still out of earshot. "I don't want to know, okay? You can tell me later. We can talk about all of it later, but not here and not now. I'm just telling you, based on what you're telling me happened, this doesn't look good, okay? I believe you that she accidentally slipped and fell, but it doesn't look good. And even if we can convince everyone that's what happened, I don't know if you still won't get in huge trouble for giving her the alcohol, okay? We need to do this so nobody asks about all that stuff. And then hope to God Logan keeps his mouth shut. And you need to keep your mouth shut!" she warned him, pointing her index finger closely at his eyes. "I'm trying to help you. I'm trying to save you. You don't seem to understand what could happen to you, Kai. So just shut up and do what I tell you."

"But . . . what if nobody finds her? I can't just leave her here. Neither can you. You're her friend."

"And you're my brother," she countered. "I know when you tell me it was an accident that it was an accident, but I'm your sister who loves you. Others aren't going to just believe you, okay? Someone will find her. It may be a while, like next time the water is low or something, but they will find her and then nobody will doubt that it was an accident. Nobody will be accusing you of something you didn't do, do you understand?" He still looked doubtful. "She's dead, Kai," Amy added. "She's already dead. You just do what I'm telling you, alright?"

"Okay," he said. "I'm sorry. You really believe me, right? That it as an accident? I didn't even touch her. She just took a step back and . . ."

"Yes, I believe you, okay? But shut up about it before Logan comes back over here. Just grab her arms and come on," she told him. Together, they began carrying her up the bank, but Amy slipped. They tried again, and again she started slipping. "Dammit!" she cursed.

They heard loud footsteps approach above them. "Hurry up."

"I'm trying!" said Amy.

"Move," Logan told her as he came back down the embankment. "Help your brother." And he grabbed Emily's arms as Amy and Kai took hold of her legs and all three of them got her up to the top of the levee. "That's it," he told them when they reached the top. "I'm not doing nothing else."

"Thank you," Amy said, breathing heavily from her efforts.

"Yeah, whatever," he told her. "I better not get in any trouble for any of this."

"You won't," she assured him. Then she and Kai opened Emily's car door and began positioning her in the seat.

"Don't push it," Logan said.

"What?" Asked Amy.

"Her car. Don't push it. Use her keys. Turn it on, put it in reverse, and turn the wheel a little to the left. The idle will send it backward and it'll just go off on its own like it would if she had been trying to back out but went off the side."

"Oh," said Amy. She looked behind the car at the angle that would take it off the levee. "Yeah, okay, that makes sense." She took Emily's car keys out of her pocket. Then she started up the car. Logan stood back and watched. "Help me buckle her seat belt," Amy told Kai.

"Are you sure about this?" he asked.

"Just do it," she told him. He obeyed. Then Amy picked up her shirt which was still lying on the ground and she wiped the seat belt buckle and the end of the key. She looked at the window and then rolled it down a little.

"Why'd you do that?" Logan asked from a little distance away.

"So it'll fill up," she said.

He shook his head. "It will."

Amy looked at Emily's pale visage. She fought back the tears. Now was not the time. "I'm so sorry," she whispered to her. Then she looked at Kai. His eyes were cast downward, and he looked like a child there, skinny and wet. "It's going to be okay," she told him. "It was an accident," she told him, this time less accusatory. He said nothing. He was staring at the watch on Emily's wrist. "What?" Amy asked.

"Her watch . . ."

"Leave it."

"No, I mean . . . it's her sunflower. She loved sunflowers. They were her favorite."

"It's going to be okay," she told him again, but likely as much to herself as to her younger brother. Then she used her shirt to put the gear into reverse. The car slowly rolled backward. She walked with it at first and used her shirt to turn the steering wheel to the left. The car tracked and began to edge its way to the left. "Look out," she told Kai. Then she closed the door.

Logan walked far away from the car which was now creeping slowly backward. It slowly veered off the side, but then the front wheels turned further on the slope and it quickly raced down the embankment and into the water. The three of them walked to the spot where they could look down and watched the car floating on the surface.

"It's not sinking," Amy said with concern.

"It will," Logan assured her. And slowly, the car began to sink, trunk first as the car tilted upwards as the rear sank. The lights stayed on, rising in illumination of the three upon the levee as though a final accusation.

. . . In that moment, a shiver ran through me. I felt it run through the garden as well which was still there, just outside my dream, listening. Somewhere beyond it, beyond vision, the shimmer flickered, and a secret revealed itself in my mind in a dream within the dream . . .

"Are you sure?" Kai asked Amy again. He looked like he wanted to rush down to the car.

"Yes," she told him. "This is the only way people will know for sure it was an accident."

Logan looked at Kai with the speculation of guilt upon his expression. But he said nothing more as the three watched the car slowly sink. The last thing they saw was the headlights disappearing beneath the glassy surface of the water before flickering and then disappearing, leaving no sign of what now lay within the basin.

"We were never here," Amy said to the other two without looking at them.

"I damn sure wasn't," Logan replied. Then he stared hard at Kai. "You hear me? No matter what happens from here . . . I was never here." Kai nodded. "Say it," Logan demanded.

"Logan . . .," Amy started, but she quieted on seeing his anger.

"Say it," Logan told Kai again.

"You were never here," Kai agreed quietly.

"None of us were, Kai," said Amy. "Right?" He only nodded feebly. "You have to do better than that. This is serious. I know this was an accident, but nobody can ever know you were out here or either of us. Do you understand?" Again, he nodded. But he was hurt by the tone of his sister's statement. When she said she believed him, it rang hollow in his ears. He heard the echo of doubt. That was more poison in the wound. And now Amy was the one getting mad at his non-responsiveness. "Say it."

He looked up at her. "None of us were ever here," he said, angry and hurt. "This never happened."

"Right," she told him. "Now we just need to make sure it looks that way." The three of them finished dressing. Amy put the champagne bottle in the trunk of her car. She made Kai find the cork, the metal twine, and every scrap of foil from when they opened the bottle. She tried to smush down the divots on the embankment from where they had walked and carried Emily back up. She pushed the grass back up as best she could see by the light of her phone. She was glad there was some grass on the two tire trails along the levee such that no tire tracks were clearly visible.

"Okay, I think that's enough," said Logan. "We need to get out of here. We've been out here way too long. Someone could see us."

"Who's going to come out here?" Amy asked.

"They might see our lights," he said. "We've been out here way too long, Amy. Let's get out of here."

"Let me just look again. We need to check everything. There can't be any indication anyone was here. We need to dry off anyway before you go home, right?" After one last look around, they got in the car and she carefully began backing down the levee. "I can't hardly see a thing," she remarked. It was dangerous trying to reverse so far down a narrow stretch like it was. It wasn't hard at all to imagine someone accidentally reversing off to one side and a terrible accident ensuing. It made perfect sense, actually, for the police when they wrote up the final report.

Chapter 27

Purpose

"It happened so fast," Kai said. "She just slipped. But nobody believes me. Not Logan . . . not even my own sister. She thinks I did something to Emily. She won't say it, but I know she does." His face was welling up, red and pained, guilt and hurt burning him up like a fever.

"I believe you, Kai," I told him. And I squeezed his hand a little tighter.

"Why? Why would you believe me when they don't? Not even Amy."

"Because," I told him, "I've stared into the eyes of a murderer, Kai. The man who did this to me . . .," I used my good hand to push back my bangs and show him the crevice upon my brow . . ., "he was a murderer. When I looked into his eyes, do you know what I saw?" Kai just shook his head. I let my bangs fall back over my scar. "Nothing. I didn't see anything at all in that man's eyes. He didn't care about what he had just done when he shot my mom. Just like he didn't care about shooting me. He was drunk and angry, but it was more than that. He just didn't care . . . he had not an ounce of care in him. Mom . . . me . . . we weren't people to him. We were things. Mom was a thing he wanted and when he couldn't have it, he broke it so nobody else could have it. I was just a thing that saw my mom reject him, so he tried to break me, too. You're nothing like that man, Kai. I believe you because I know a murderer when I see one, and I'm not looking at one. And I know the truth when I hear it. What you just told me . . . I believe you're telling the truth."

He reached out with his other hand and placed it upon mine as well. "I am," he said. "I swear to God, I am."

"I know," I said again.

He let a few tears fall before wiping them away. "Thank you. I don't know why you're being so nice to me but thank you."

"I think you could do with a little kindness, Kai. And the last thing you should do is what you were going to do today."

He nodded a little. "I just don't know what to do, you know? How do I live with this? I can't sleep. I can't eat. I'm scared to get out of bed every morning. All I do is just keep thinking about everything over and over again like a broken record player. It won't stop. I just want it to stop."

I understood how he felt. It had been the same for me and Mom's death. I kept thinking about all the things I didn't do but could have the night she died. For years after, it would just play over and over again in my thoughts. "You're the record player, Kai. You're doing this to yourself. You got it in your head that you're responsible for Emily's death, but she just took a bad step. I mean, you get that right?"

"She was trying to get away from me."

"She wasn't running away from you. She was just taking a few steps back. Do you think she would have done that if she had known she was about to fall off?"

"Well, no," he said.

"She accidentally walked back too far. We've all done it. We've all tripped a hundred times or more backing up and not looking where we're going. It happens. Usually, we might just trip and fall on our butt or whatever. She didn't know the bank was right there or how steep it was. That's not your fault. And that's not her fault, either."

"I hope you're right," he said quietly. "I want to believe you. But I keep thinking about all the things I could have done that would have stopped it. What if I hadn't wanted to go to the levee, especially at night? It was so stupid. I had this idea of how it would go with the fireworks and champagne. So stupid."

"You were trying to be romantic with a girl you really liked. It's not so stupid, okay."

"Yeah, but what if I hadn't brought the champagne? What if I hadn't tried to kiss her? What if I'd given her space when she backed away like she wanted?"

"That's a bad case of the what-ifs," I said.

"What do you mean?"

"What if the levee had been wider? What if it hadn't been so dark? What if Emily hadn't drunk quite so much? What if she had walked to the other side of the levee instead?" I asked.

"It wasn't her fault," Kai objected.

"Exactly," I said. "It wasn't. And it wasn't yours, either. I know all about what-ifs, Kai."

He shrugged, "I understand what you're saying, but it still feels like my fault. I don't know."

"I do. I have a bullet right here in my brain that says I know. I'll tell you something . . . something I never told anyone before. When my mom answered the door that night, I think both she and I thought what happened might happen. But we opened the door anyway. Know why?" He shook his head. "Because we didn't know. A bunch of things could have happened, but only one of them did. How were we supposed to know which possibility was going to happen? That's just how life is. All sorts of things might happen, but only one does. And then after it does, we beat ourselves up saying we should have known that was the one thing that would happen, but most of the time there was just no way to know it."

He thought upon my words. I hoped I was helping a bit but wasn't really sure. We'd been talking now for a little while. Sooner or later Pops or Jackson were going to come check on us. They would probably think this scene awfully strange . . . me holding Kai's hand, clearly deep in conversation.

I stayed quiet as he contemplated. And after a long minute he said, "But we left her. I left her. How could we do that?"

. . . Three silhouettes against the blackness . . .

Did I understand enough? I felt I did. "That wasn't the right thing to do," I said quietly. And he looked at me knowingly. "But," I added, "you can't go back and change it. It sounds like that was Amy's idea and I think she really was just trying to protect you. It doesn't make it right, but I can sort of understand it." I looked at his gaunt face and pained eyes. "Emily would forgive you for that."

His face fell downward. "Do you really think so?"

"I do," I told him.

He looked back at me. "I just don't know how to move on from this . . . how to get up every day and try to live a normal life again. What should I do?" he asked.

The question caught me a bit off guard. *I wish I knew what to say,* I thought.

A man needs a purpose, came a thought. *Needs focus.*

What? I wondered. Where did that thought come from? Was that me? It seemed more like an errant thought out of left field.

Lincoln knew. He said adhere to your purposes and you will soon feel as well as you ever did. On the contrary, if you falter and give up, you will lose the power of keeping any resolution, and will regret it all your life.

Holy crap, I thought, *am I seriously having an Eddie moment right now?* Apparently so. What strange timing. But I wasn't sure what kind of advice to give Kai on this horrible situation, so maybe some of Eddie's crazy insights might not be such a bad idea right about now. The man did have sparks of brilliance in that wild mind of his.

"What is your purpose?" I asked Kai.

"My purpose?" he asked.

"Yeah, I mean in life. What is it you want to accomplish?"

"I don't know," he said. "I used to want to be successful, I guess. But now, I just want to not feel horrible every second of the day. I'm so tired, Ruth. And so sad all the time. All I can think about is how sorry I am and how I wish this whole nightmare would just end. At her funeral, I couldn't even look. I just played a game on my phone because I couldn't look at her casket or her parents or anyone. I couldn't look anyone in the eye." He paused and then continued, "That was the day I decided . . . well, you know . . . that I just couldn't take it anymore. I'd been thinking bad thoughts that day, but when they were burying her . . . I just couldn't take it anymore."

I thought about the shimmer and how it had appeared at the service. It had appeared in between Miranda and Kai, but he was so easy to miss, standing there as though just part of the background, looking as though he wasn't even paying attention and was just playing that game on his phone. I didn't even think of him at the time. He had so many things rushing through his mind at that time, so much pain, regret, and hurt, but none of us noticed a thing. We barely noticed him at all.

Then the shimmer had followed me home. I think it knew. It knew then what he was already planning on doing. It tried to tell me in my dreams. And then it led me to the park that day. Emily never blamed Kai. And she didn't want him to blame himself. They'd been friends. She had just been caught off guard by his declaration of love and advances. She didn't know how to react, so she retreated . . . just literally too far. *What a messed-up situation,* I thought. And now she was gone. Well, mostly. Something was still here. Something was still trying to stop things from getting any worse than they already were. "What do you think Emily's purpose was?" I asked.

"Art," he said almost immediately. "She only wanted to make beautiful things."

"And together you did, right?" I asked.

He shrugged uncertainly, "Mainly her."

"But you liked making those things with her, didn't you?"

He nodded. "Yes. It was the best thing I ever did." He looked at the watch on his wrist. "They're so beautiful, you know? The things she made. She was so beautiful."

"Find your purpose," I told him. "Maybe it's these," I said, tapping his watch, "or maybe it's something else or lots of something elses. But that's what I think you should do, Kai. Find a purpose. Make something. Don't let Emily's creativity pass with her. Keep it alive, for her and for yourself."

Another one of Eddie's memories planted itself in my thoughts. And this time I spoke it aloud, "Happiness lies in the joy of achievement and the thrill of creative effort," I said.

He actually smiled a little. "Who said that?"

"Franklin Roosevelt, I think."

Mm-hmm. Purpose, Eddie's memories agreed in my thoughts. *I had purpose. I kept the cemetery nice looking so folks could come visit their loved ones in a nice place. And I studied great men, the Presidents, so I could better myself. Mm-hmm. Didn't get past the eighth grade, no I didn't. But I learned me some books. Hundreds of 'em. I had purpose.*

"If you're asking me how to go on living after all this has happened, Kai, the only thing I can think of is to find your purpose. It's not enough to just live this life, you have to find something to live for. You're not done. You haven't even started yet. What happened to Emily . . . it's horrible and sad beyond words. But it was an accident. She wouldn't want her death to destroy your life, too."

He looked at me strangely for a long moment before saying, "Wow, Ruth. Who are you?"

I pat his hand. "I'm just me. I'm the girl from *The Incident,* the girl who got shot and everyone talks about at school. I read my books, help my Pops out in the cemetery . . . I'm just the Groundskeeper's daughter, I guess. But it's a pretty good gig," I added with a little smile.

After a slight pause, he asked, "Do you know what your purpose is?"

I thought on it a moment. "Ultimately, no. But I have time to figure it out. And so do you. But for now, yeah, I think know what my purpose is at least for now. It's to be here with you. You didn't kill Emily, Kai."

He took a deep breath. "My own sister thinks I did."

"She doesn't know what happened out there," I told him. "But you do. And Emily does." I looked at him intently. "It's not perfect, I know. But you can live with that. You'll be okay. Just give it time. Don't let the darkness fool you into thinking the sun won't ever rise again. It will. Just have faith."

We finally unclasped hands and he took a deep breath. Then he asked, "Are you going to tell anyone . . . you know, about everything I just said and what happened?"

I gave it a good think. As sad as it was to say, I knew what Kai had told me was the truth because I was able to daydream it, but Amy had been right that night. A lot of people wouldn't believe that what had happened to Emily was an accident. They would think Kai did something to her. And while I wasn't sure exactly what the right thing to do in a situation such as this was, my heart told me that people had accepted that Emily Tolliver had died from an accident and that, much like the sordid truth I had learned about my beloved garden and this town's beginnings after Lilith's death over a century ago, the full story of that account might not serve any greater good in its revelation. It would only cause people to speculate Kai had done something I knew he hadn't done. And, more importantly, I didn't think that was what Emily had wanted when she set me upon this path. "No," I told him. "I believe what you told me, Kai. But not everyone would. It was wrong for y'all not to call for help that night after you found Emily, but the past is past and hindsight is always 20/20. I truly don't think Emily would blame you for what happened and she wouldn't want others to do so, either. I think maybe we should just keep this between us, if that's alright with you."

He nodded and looked at me in a way that said a hundred things more than the simple words he spoke next. "Thank you, Ruth."

And in the background of my thoughts, I felt the flowers hum approval.

Epilogue

Sunflower

"I think that was the strangest first date I've ever had," Jackson told me on the other end of the phone. He had just dropped Kai off at home.

"Sorry," I told him.

"No, don't be. Not at all. You said you could tell Kai needed a friend and seems like you were right. I think it was nice of you to check on him and see if he was okay like you did. What made you think he wasn't, though?"

"I could just tell by his face when we saw him in the park that something was wrong."

"Well, I feel kind of bad. I didn't even notice. Can you tell me what y'all talked about?"

"Sorry," I told him. "I promised him it would stay between us. But you know how it goes . . . life was just getting him down. I hope he feels better."

"I'm pretty sure he does. He told me on the ride to his place that he never really talked with you before today, but that he thinks you're amazing. He said he's never met someone like you before. Whatever you told him, it seems to have had a big impression."

"That's good," I said. I hoped I had done some good.

"Oh," added Jackson, "tell your dad thanks again for me. My a/c is working great now."

"I will. I'm sure he didn't mind helping."

"Well, now that I have a/c working again, any chance you might want to go out again?"

"Sure," I told him. "I'd like that."

We made some plans to meet up later in the week. We would probably hang out with Lexi, Patrick, and Deja. I didn't know what we would do, but that was alright. Just the idea of doing it with my friends was good enough for me.

After hanging up the phone, I closed my eyes and listened to the garden. It was dusk now. I looked to the place where Lilith was buried all those years ago and saw the faintest shimmer. The flowers hummed. Where the shimmer was, something began to move. I saw something rising . . . the shimmer disappeared, but where it had been something new now stood. Something yellow.

For her, came a thought from the garden.

"Oh, that's so sweet," I told the garden. "Should I take it to her?" The flowers hummed approval.

I picked the sunflower and opened up the tiny gate, then headed out to the cemetery. Darkness was falling, but there was still time to get out there and back before true blackness reined.

When I reached Emily's grave, I was not surprised to see the shimmer appear. It was no longer as strong as it had been, and it wasn't flickering wildly anymore. "Hey," I said. "From the garden." I placed the flower down at her grave.

I thought I felt a thought, but it was faint. But it felt like . . . *thank you.*

"You're welcome." I wasn't sure if the thanks was for the flower or something else, though. "I hope that was kind of what you wanted me to tell him," I said. "I didn't know if you wanted me to tell him the rest . . . you know, about what happened in the end. But I didn't figure you did. It would have just crushed him, and he was already having such a horrible time dealing with everything."

Maybe I misunderstood her, I worried. Maybe that was exactly what she had wanted me to tell him. Maybe she had felt wronged, cheated, and wanted a reckoning. But then I felt something emanating from the shimmer . . . *agreement.*

"Oh, thank goodness," I said. "I wasn't sure. Plus, it would have been really hard to try to explain how I knew about it anyway, you know?"

I still saw it . . . the dream within the dream. Emily's eyes opening in those last moments as the water rushed up above her head. Amy's CPR, crude as it had been, had worked. As the car sank Emily's eyes had opened. She had tried to move, but her body's aches and the seatbelt made it impossible. She had hit her head really hard on that concrete culvert. She saw them, though, the three silhouettes standing upon the levee.

"They should have called for help," I told her. "I'm so sorry." I shook my head. "They killed you. I know they didn't mean to do it, but they killed you." I took a deep breath. "I know we didn't always get along and all . . ."

I felt a change in the air, a new emotion permeating the dusk. *Remorse.*

"No, it's okay," I tried to explain. "I mean, I know you didn't really mean what you said and all. That was years ago. We should have talked about it. But my feelings were hurt. And I haven't really tried talking to people except Deja and Lexi, but I'm going to work on that."

I felt *approval,* maybe even *support*

"Anyway, I wish I would have talked with you and worked it out. That's all, I guess," I told her.

Agreement.

I looked down at the flower by the headstone. "So, you knew what he was going to do, huh? I wonder how you did. But you knew and wanted me to stop him?"

Agreement again.

"I'm glad you got me involved, actually," I told her. "I told myself I would never get involved in something as bizarre and strange as all this. But I'm really glad you did. Kai's a good guy. He would never have hurt you on purpose, I don't think. I wouldn't want him to hurt himself, either. It was just an accident, after all. Amy should have known better, but I guess what's done is done." I looked at the shimmer, which was nearly faded away. "So, is this it? You seem different, like you're almost gone from here." The shimmer flickered a bit, but also faded a bit more. "I guess you're going, then, huh? Do you know where? I'd sure like to know."

Uncertainty. She didn't know.

"Well, say hi to my mom for me, will you? Tell her I love her. And tell her Pops still loves her, too, if you don't mind."

Affirmation.

"It's strange, isn't it?" I asked. "Who would have ever thought you and I would be standing here like this? What a strange day this was. Good strange, though. I'm sorry about what happened, but I think we did some good today."

As the shimmer began to slowly evaporate like steam in the air, a quote popped in my head, *yesterday is history, tomorrow is a mystery, but today is a gift. That is why it's called the present.*

I laughed. "I know that one! That's from Eleanor Roosevelt, right?!" I thought a second, "Hey, you haven't been hanging around with a weird dead guy named Eddie, have you?"

The shimmer flickered one last time. And maybe it was just my imagination, but I thought I heard a laugh.

And then the shimmer that was Emily Tolliver was gone.

The End.

Note from the Author

Thank you for reading. I hope you enjoyed the story. If you did enjoy the read, I would greatly appreciate a comment or review. They are so very helpful to Indie authors such as myself. Thank you again and have a great day!

Other Books by this Author

The Ghosts of Varner Creek
Border Crossings

CPSIA information can be obtained
at www.ICGtesting.com
Printed in the USA
LVHW051732291221
707358LV00011B/1204